I0601546

Dust Devil
L.E. Luttrell

First Published in Great Britain in 2025

Copyright © L.E. Luttrell 2025
The moral right of L.E. Luttrell to be identified as the author
of this work has been asserted in accordance with the
Copyright, Designs and Patents Act 1988.

All rights reserved. No part of this publication may be
reproduced, stored in a retrieval system, or transmitted in any
form or by any means, electronic, mechanical, photocopying,
recording or otherwise, without the prior permission of the
copyright owner and the publisher of this book.

All the characters in this book are fictitious and any
resemblance to actual persons, living or dead, is purely coincidental.

A CIP catalogue record for this book is available from the
British Library.

ISBN 978-1-0685868-3-5
ebook – 978-1-0685868-4-2

Typeset in Great Britain by Designed Memories
Published by Woolloomooloo
Printed in Great Britain

Cover photograph: Outback scene, Australia - licenced by
Shutterstock

This book is dedicated to Cath & Brian, loyal supporters
of my work

Also by **L.E.Luttrell**

India Hargreaves Series
DRAWING DANGER
THE BREAKDOWN
SMALL SACRIFICES
THE PHOTOGRAPH

Frank Bailey and Rachel Sharp Series
A CONVENIENT ACCIDENT
THE REVENGE TRAIL
DUST DEVIL

THE WAVE

Part One

1

May 2009

'Do you, Jeremiah, take Dinah to be your lawfully wedded wife?'

Jeremiah looked nervously at his bride to be. 'I do,' he said after a pause.

'And do you Dinah, take Jeremiah to be your lawfully wedded husband?'

'I do,' Dinah said without hesitation.

'I now pronounce you man and wife. You may kiss the bride.'

Although there had been a long run up to the vows, the ceremony was quite simple. Relieved that it was over Jeremiah leaned over and kissed his bride.

The crowd surrounding the couple cheered and clapped. Many of the men came up to pat Jeremiah on his back. Dinah was whisked off by the women towards the dining hall where a great feast had been laid out. Jeremiah allowed himself to be tugged along behind them. He felt sick to his stomach and was nervous about the celebrations he had to face. He could do with a strong whisky to help him get through it. But there would only be wine or beer on offer. He couldn't afford to drink too much of either. Not if he was going to be capable of carrying out the plan. He swallowed back the bile that had risen in his throat, pasted a smile on his face and turned to his companions. He could do this.

2

Paragliding Camp Site, Manilla N.S.W.
February 2009

'Sorry to disappoint you boys – I know you've only just arrived, but I have to tell you we won't be launching any flights tomorrow. There's heavy storms and strong winds predicted.'

Harry Meredith looked at his friend Felix McMurray, whose face was, he was sure, mirroring his own; a combined exhausted and extremely pissed off look.

'What about Sunday morning?' Harry asked. He and Felix had just picked up the key to their cabin after a 6-hour drive from Brisbane. They were due to return to Brisbane Sunday afternoon. They'd be pretty damned annoyed if they couldn't get a flight in before heading back.

Mike Holland, manager of the Manila Paragliding club, grimaced. 'They're predicting more of the same on Sunday. We'll have to just wait and see.'

'We checked the weather yesterday and they said it would be fine here,' Felix moaned.

Holland shrugged. 'You know what the weather's like

– it can change from one hour to the next.'

'So it looks like we've driven all this way for nothing,' Felix said, pouting.

'As far as flights are concerned. Yes. But the town has plenty to offer and there's a gathering at the club house tonight. I believe there's a couple of women who have also come down from the Oz Park Club, as well as others from clubs around the country. Some have even travelled here from other countries. We'll have a band playing and there'll be lots of fun.'

Felix shrugged. 'Do you serve alcohol?'

'Yes, there's a bar there.'

'Okay, what time does the party start?' Harry asked.

'I don't know that I'd call it a party, but meals will be served from about seven. The music starts at nine.'

'Right,' Harry said nodding. 'We ought to get our stuff into the cabin first.'

'Is the bar open now?' Felix asked checking his watch, 'it's six pm.'

'Yes, it should be. It opens at six.'

'Come on then Harry, I'm gasping for a beer.'

Nodding to Mike Holland, the two young men turned and went in search of their cabin.

Once they were out of earshot of the manager, Felix let forth a string of expletives. 'Just our bloody luck,' he added.

'Sunday might be okay,' Harry said, attempting to remain optimistic. He wasn't happy about the idea of a wasted journey either.

'Hey, what if we stayed on until Monday, to see if the

weather improves. We could maybe get a flight in then. I've got all of next week off. Your old man wouldn't mind you having another day off, would he? Now that he's back at work?'

After completing a four-year honours degree course at the Queensland University of Technology to become a surveyor, Harry had been in the process of applying for jobs when his father had had a heart attack last October. He'd taken over running the family tool hire business until his father recovered. Months later he was still there, although his father had returned part-time.

'I don't know mate. Let's wait and see. Now let's go and get that beer you're craving.'

The 'gathering' turned into a party. Scores of pilots, both young and old, from across the world had gathered for the weekend event. Since the World Championships, held at Mt. Borah in Manilla in 2007, the place had become famous for paragliding and hang-gliding.

A couple of beautiful female pilots from South America invited Harry and Felix back to their cabin. Felix's partner for the night seemed fascinated with his red hair, freckles and green eyes, which was in stark contrast to her dark hair, olive skin and brown eyes.

It was close to 5 am when they finally staggered back to their cabin, still inebriated from the tequila they'd been downing in the girls' cabin.

'Hey look at the sky,' Felix said. 'Not a bloody cloud in sight. I reckon they got the forecast wrong – as usual. How about we go for a flight now?'

'Nah, I need a shower and some sleep. I'm shattered.'

'Ah come on mate. What are you afraid of? We could get a flight in now while the weather's good.'

Harry stopped and pondered the sky. It certainly looked as though it was going to be a beautiful morning.

'We won't be able to drive up to the launching site. The track gates will be locked.'

'We can carry our gear. Come on. Don't be a spoil sport. We've come all this way.'

'I'm still quite pissed to be honest mate. And so are you. I'm not sure we'd be safe.'

Felix giggled. 'Yeah, you're right. But by the time we lug our gear up that mountain, it's a dead cert we'll be sober.'

'Ok, but I need a quick shower first.'

Fifty minutes later Harry and Felix were about to launch when they heard distant shouting from behind them. Harry glanced around and saw Mike Holland entering the launching site.

'Ignore him,' Felix shouted.

'He might have a weather update,' Harry said.

'Does it look like rain? No,' Felix said, answering his own question. 'And the wind conditions seem perfect. Come on, ignore the bastard.'

Harry hesitated. They were doing a tandem flight this morning and he was lead pilot. Felix was right though. The conditions looked perfect. There was something holding him back though. A little nagging doubt in his head. He felt sober now, so what was the problem? Oh, what the hell he thought. He had been looking forward to this experience. There was nothing he loved more than gliding like a bird thousands of feet above the ground. Without further hesitation he called, 'okay let's go'.

The winds took them westward soaring over the sparsely populated countryside. Behind him Felix was whooping and hollering with glee. Harry was concentrating and absorbing the landscape below him. It was so different here compared to their normal launching site at Mt. Tambourine up on the Gold Coast, which had lush green vegetation. Here the landscape was much drier. Horses were galloping across open ground below him, which was a patchwork of greens and browns. More horses were drinking from a small creek. Far into the distance he could see what might be a homestead. Ahead of them was a river and what looked like a lake. He'd studied the area before their trip and guessed it must be Lake Keepit and the Naomi River, which apparently, due to the drought the area had been experiencing, was much drier than normal. He guessed that was why the open ground surrounding the lake appeared very dry.

He turned to steer them south when out of the corner of his eye he saw a large brownish swirl. What the fuck …?

'We're flying into a dust devil,' Felix shouted. 'A bloody enormous one! Get us out of here!'

Before Harry could take evasive action, they were caught up in it. He'd read about these dust devils, which resembled mini dust storms acting more like a tornado. But he'd never seen or experienced one at close quarters and wasn't sure what would happen.

It didn't take long for him to find out. Harry lost all control; they were flung further up into the air, swirled around and around, turned upside down and then plunged earthward at a frightening speed. Although he couldn't see anything, he believed they would surely hit the ground any moment but they were swept up again and caught in the dust's rotation. Harry was struggling to breathe and he didn't dare open his mouth to say anything to Felix, who after initially screeching from the first upward thrust, had gone ominously quiet.

After what seemed like hours they were once again plunging downwards. The dust devil spat them out and Harry realised too late, that they were about to collide with the top of some trees and were heading towards a hill. 'Brace for impact, brace for impact,' he shouted.

3

Newcastle, NSW
Sunday

Beth Bailey was stacking the dishwasher with plates from their evening meal when her mobile phone rang. It tended to be family members who called her on the mobile. She walked over to where the phone was charging on the counter and looked at it. It was Matt, her son. Strange, was her first thought, as they'd had a long chat yesterday afternoon on the land line. Perhaps he had forgotten to mention something in their conversation. She picked the phone up and pressed to accept the call.

'Hi Matt,' she said. 'Is everything alright darling?'

'I'm not sure mum.'

'What do you mean?' Beth was instinctively alert. Had something happened to one of Matt's children? Charlie who was three and the twins Ella and Evie, who were almost one?

'It's Harry.' It took Beth a moment to register the name. Harry was Matt's younger half-brother.

'What's happened?' Beth asked.

'*He's missing. Dad received a call from the Oz Park Club this afternoon. Harry travelled to Manilla on Friday afternoon with his friend Felix to take part in a paragliding event there this weekend. The event was cancelled due to bad weather.*'

'So, he's disappeared in the Philippines?' Beth wondered why Matt was ringing her about this. Unless Steve, Matt and Harry's father had had another heart attack with the worry.

'*What?*'

'You said he gone to Manila, in the Philippines.'

'*No, sorry mum, there's a town called Manilla in New South Wales. Slightly different spelling. The one in New South Wales has a double 'll'.*'

'Oh. I've never heard of it. Where is this Manilla?'

'*It's not far from Tamworth.*'

'Okay. So, when you say Harry's missing and the event there was cancelled, what's happened?'

'*Harry and his friend took off of a tandem flight on Saturday morning. Nothing's been heard from them since.*'

Beth thought back to Saturday morning. Apart from it being a little windy, the weather was fine. Rain had been predicted, but it hadn't appeared until late that night. She knew next to nothing about paragliding, but surely the weather couldn't have been an issue.

'It was a little windy on Saturday morning. Perhaps they were blown way off their planned course and just haven't made it back yet.'

'*That's what the Club Manager initially thought. But they've heard absolutely nothing. They drove down in Felix's car. The car is still at the cabin. All their luggage is there. They were due to check out this morning, but they haven't returned.*'

'Could they have had a bad landing somewhere and been injured?'

'*That's one possibility. Although Harry is an experienced pilot. Dad wanted to drive down there tonight, but I don't think he's up to that yet. He's still a bit fragile. I'm going to take him down in the morning if we've heard nothing further.*'

'Okay.'

'*Dad was wondering if Frank could become involved.*'

'How do you mean? Frank's based in Newcastle. If Manilla is near Tamworth, it's a completely different Area Command.'

'*I thought that would be the case, but perhaps he could contact someone up there. The paragliding club manager told dad he'd been onto the local police and they had noted the details, but they've done nothing about launching an air search and rescue operation. Dad thought Frank might have some sway in persuading them to undertake one.*'

'Right. Okay I'll have a word with Frank when he comes back. He's just popped over to his sister's, with a card and present. It's his niece's birthday on Tuesday.'

'*Thanks mum, I'd appreciate it. Could you – or Frank, get back to me on this?*'

'We will. Is Steve okay? Is he particularly worried?'

'*Yeah. He is. We're all a little worried.*'

'Right, well, we'll see what we can do.'

Beth and Matt spoke for another few seconds before saying their goodbyes.

She could imagine Steve working himself up into a state over young Harry's disappearance. He would be 60 on in another two weeks and had already had one heart attack. Matt assured her that Steve's workaholic lifestyle led to the attack, rather than from any inherited heart condition, but to ease her mind, Matt had gone for a medical check-up – where thankfully, nothing was found. She'd been worried that there might be something in Steve's family medical history. Steve's father had apparently died when Steve was still quite young after a road traffic accident, so it was never known if he had any heart disease. She hoped the stress over this issue wouldn't lead to Steve having another attack.

'I can understand Steve's concern,' Frank said, when Beth filled him in on the details. 'Harry and his friend should have either returned or been in touch with someone by now. It's been what, about thirty-seven hours since they took off. I'll make some calls to Tamworth and see if they have any searches planned.'

'Thanks Frank,' Beth said, relieved that he was willing to do something. She'd received a text message from Matt about 20 minutes ago to say there was still no word.

'They're planning a helicopter search first thing tomorrow,' Frank said after returning from the study. 'Apparently word only came through from the Manilla police station a couple of hours ago. Too late to do anything today.'

'Okay, I'll phone Matt and let him know. Do you think I should take some time off and drive up there to meet up with Matt and Steve tomorrow? I've been thinking about it and I can't help but worry that Steve might work himself up into a terrible state over this. If it was Matt who was missing, I'd be pretty distressed. With Steve's condition …
'

'Hmm. If you think being there might help them, then yes. Isn't Steve's wife travelling with them?'

'No, they've got a seven-year-old daughter remember.'

Frank shrugged with one of his 'I haven't got a clue' looks. Beth knew it was hard for him to keep track of all the extended family connections. Steve's eldest daughter, Eliza, was now also the mother of a one-year-old. Apart from Matt, Steve's family was nothing to do with her and Frank, but Matt kept them abreast of matters. Jodie, Steve's current wife, was Matt's stepmother. And all Steve's children were his half-siblings. Eliza's daughter (whose name Beth couldn't recall) was Matt's half-niece.

'I'll make a decision tomorrow after the search helicopter has done a first sweep. Matt and Steve should arrive early in the afternoon. I just hope Matt makes sure he takes plenty of breaks on the journey. It's a long drive.'

4

Monday

Beth went into the office as normal in the morning, but warned them that she might need to take some time off, after explaining the circumstances. She'd qualified as a solicitor in the UK, but since marrying Frank and living in Australia, she'd joined a firm of lawyers (as they were referred to in Australia) and worked largely on conveyancing – her speciality. It wasn't a particularly exciting job, but it brought in the money. The firm were understanding and agreed Beth's paralegal could deal with matters if she had to take time off. She'd packed a small bag this morning, and if she did head off this afternoon, she could collect it on her way out of Newcastle.

Frank phoned her shortly after midday. *'There's been no sighting of the men from this morning's search,'* he told her.

'Right, well I think I might head up there if you don't mind. If nothing else, it will be a chance for me to see Matt. I'll call you tonight.'

'Okay, drive safely.'

At Area Command Headquarters in Newcastle Frank had just hung up from his call with Beth when the phone on his desk rang.

After hearing what the person on the line had to say, he terminated the call and went in search of DI Rachel Sharp. He found her in her office hanging her jacket over the back of her chair. Rachel had been promoted to Detective Inspector rank a couple of months ago, just before she discovered she was expecting her first child.

'Afternoon Rachel, I've just popped in to tell you, Lee Wells has gone walkabout.'

It took a moment for the name to register and then her eyes widened in surprise. 'You mean he's escaped from prison?'

'In a manner of speaking. He was out on a day release yesterday and didn't return. He was supposed to be staying with his sister, but when he failed to return and the police went around to their house in Wallsend, they found the sister and her husband out for the count.'

'They were drunk?'

'No. They claim they sat down to watch a footie match and the next thing they knew the police were slapping them around after gaining access through the rear of the property. Slapping them gently, I might add.'

'I should hope so.'

'Apparently they had to throw some water over the husband as they couldn't rouse him. He said he had only had one beer and the wife drank a cup of tea. So they claimed. By all accounts Lee served the refreshments.'

'Sounds like he drugged them.'

'Yes. They were tested and traces of Rohypnol showed

up in their systems. No alcohol in the wife's blood. Very little in the husband's.'

'Mm. It would be difficult to smuggle a drug like that out of the prison. They do a thorough search, from what I understand. He must have got his hands on it from someone on the outside. How long did he have to go on his sentence? He got four years, didn't he? Is he up for parole already?'

'Yes, he's served a little over two and a half years and been a good boy. He's due for parole soon and this is second time he's been let out on day release.'

'If he's due for parole, why would he want to take off? It makes no sense.'

'I agree. He must have had some news that prompted him to take this action. We'll need to question the Harpers.'

'That's the sister's married name?'

'Yes, Edward – commonly known as Ted, and Sarah Harper. I'd like you to do it, seeing as it was your case.'

'And yours, sir. Don't you want to be involved in questioning them?'

Rachel paused after her question, half expecting Frank to tell her off for saying 'sir'. The word still slipped out automatically on a regular basis, long after he'd insisted she call him Frank. From her earliest days of working with him, DI Bailey, as he was then, always called Rachel and other team members by their first name. Only in more formal environments would he address them by their rank. It was at her wedding to Andy (where apart from one other uniformed officer she'd trained with, Frank was the only colleague she'd invited) that he'd said "call me Frank." She found it almost impossible to do until attending *his* wedding to Beth some years later where she accepted he was Frank Bailey – not DCI Bailey. At work, calling him Frank smacked of an intimacy or 'mateship' than men fell into easily with their bosses, but female officers (and there were so few of them) struggled with. In her early days in uniform, she'd soon realised that it was one rule for men and another for the women. As soon as women spoke to male colleagues on first name terms they were gossiped about (by the *men*) and imaginary affairs alluded to. She'd finally given way to Frank after he'd raised it with her many times and she accepted that maybe she was being too stuffy and formal. Today her 'sir' seemed to pass him by. Clearly his mind was on more important things.

'I *would* be curious to see what they have to say.'

'Well why don't we both interview them?' Rachel would welcome the opportunity; it was a while since they'd done an interview together whereas, when they first worked together, it was commonplace. She thought they made a great team. Since his promotion to DCI, he tended to delegate interviews to his team members. If he did take part in them, he would do it with someone of a lower rank.

'It seems like a waste of … oh to hell with it. Yes, we can both do it. I'll set it up.'

5

Rachel discovered that Frank had already requisitioned the case file on Lee Wells and popped into his office to see if he'd had time to look through it. Although she knew the case well enough, it was always good to re-visit it.

Frank's office was empty, but she could see the file on his desk. She picked it up and, taking a seat, starting reading through it.

Lee Wells was arrested after two young women had disappeared over a period of four weeks. Both were in their early twenties, but were described as vulnerable by family members, due to having moderate learning difficulties. Wells worked at the drop-in centre which the young women attended. It was an adult learning centre where people could mix socially with others, carry out craft activities, or develop their basic skills (and give their families some respite).

The women's families had reported them missing and had been very concerned for their safety.

Staff at the centre had been questioned by the missing person's team. Wells had denied knowledge of the women's whereabouts. It wasn't until a witness came forward, who had previously been a neighbour of Wells, that the police had been able to take action and Frank's team were called in. The former neighbour had recently moved north to Kempsey, but after spotting an image of Katherine Dickon on a TV news program he came forward with information. He was sure Katherine was the same woman he'd seen entering Wells' house many weeks prior. A search warrant was issued and there they found the missing women.

A good-looking man in his early forties, Wells had persuaded the women that he was in love with them and wanted them to find God. Both had willingly gone with him to his house. He took Katherine Dickon first, followed by Martha Richardson.

It became obvious after questioning that Wells was using them as domestic servants and to warm his bed. They found Katherine gagged and tied up in her bedroom, which Wells claimed was for her own safety as she had accidentally started a couple of fires in the kitchen. She had bruises on her wrists where she'd been tied, but was otherwise unharmed physically. The same could not be said for her mental state and she had been very distressed when she was freed. The house was full of religious images and symbols. Long robes were found folded in the living room which, according to Martha, they wore for prayer services every night.

It was due to the state they'd found Katherine in that they were able to press charges against Wells – even though Katherine didn't want to. Martha didn't have a bad word to say about him either. Eventually he was charged with imprisoning someone against their will and causing bodily harm. With the defence arguing such a strong case for Katherine's willingness to be with him, Wells received a light sentence of four years.

A couple of months after his arrest, it was discovered that Martha was pregnant, carrying Wells' child.

Reading all these notes, Rachel thought the obvious place to start looking for Wells was with Martha. Rachel knew Martha had been placed in sheltered accommodation after leaving Wells' house as she hadn't wanted to return to her family. She was unsure whether Martha had been allowed to keep the baby. Perhaps Frank would know. She flicked through the file to find the name of Martha's social worker. A couple of years down the road, there was no guarantee that the same person would still be attached to her. Social workers often only worked with clients for a short time before moving on. Rachel supposed it was because it was a stressful job, but from her experience, those who were in need of social worker support needed continuity and someone they could learn to trust. If the social worker was constantly changing, how could a decent, trusting relationship be established?

Rachel made a note of the social worker's name and number and returned to her office with the file. She was informed when she made contact with the service that the worker in question, Lane Wilson, was still working in the department and yes, she was still attached to Martha. But she wasn't in the office and they were reluctant to give Rachel the woman's mobile number. Rachel left her name and number, requesting that Lane Wilson call her back.

What had never been understood was why Wells was working at the drop-in centre. He'd refused to answer any questions or give any reasons. They'd learned that he had obtained a Batchelor of Science Degree with a major in Human Biology at Macquarie University in Sydney. Employment records showed that he'd worked at the prestigious CSIRO (Commonwealth Scientific and Industrial Research Organisation) in Canberra for some years in Health before moving to Farming and Food Productions. Outside work he became a lay preacher in a group which had since disbanded. Rachel had learned from the police in Canberra that Wells was known to them. There had been a couple of sexual assault allegations made against both Wells and one of the group's previous leaders – but were withdrawn before formal charges were made.

On his application form to the charity which ran the drop-in centre, Wells had failed to specify that he had a degree. He'd stated that he worked as a lab assistant at CSIRO and had been a voluntary worker in the community – downplaying both his previous roles.

Enquiries at CSIRO had revealed no cause for concern at any point in his employment and Wells had left the company with good references. So why had he taken such a low paid job back in Newcastle?

Rachel sighed and closed the folder. Perhaps Wells' sister might be able to provide them with some information to fill the gaps. She hadn't been interviewed when Wells was charged as she'd lived in Western Australia at the time and had not returned to Newcastle for his trial.

'I saw you were re-acquainting yourself with Wells' file,' Frank said startling Rachel momentarily after popping his head into her office. 'I spotted you reading it in my office as I was about to head off to the canteen.'

'Yes. I hope you didn't mind me sitting in there reading it – or removing it. I saw that you had the file. Have you skimmed through it?'

'Of course I didn't mind and yes, I looked at it. The Harper couple will be here at two pm, which gives you about thirty minutes to grab some lunch, if you haven't done so already. There's a good chicken curry on special in the canteen today. I don't normally eat hot meals at lunchtime, but I thought I'd grab the opportunity as Beth is away and there won't be a hot meal tonight – unless I cook it. Now I won't have to bother.'

Rachels stomach churned at the thought of curry. Since she'd discovered she was pregnant, she hadn't been able to eat the spicy food she normally loved.

'Has Beth gone to visit family in Sydney then?'

Rachel knew Beth's father and two brothers lived in Sydney. Although by all accounts, her father was due to retire soon and was moving into an annex they planned to build on Frank and Beth's property in Newcastle.

'Not Sydney,' Frank said shaking his head. 'She's meeting her son Matt up in Manilla this afternoon. Beth's … I'm not sure what you'd call him, her sort of step-son, Harry, is missing after a paragliding flight.'

'Oh?'

'Yes, he apparently flew off on a tandem flight on Saturday morning and the two young men haven't been seen since.'

'They've had an accident?'

'No doubt. Look, you don't need to hear all this at the moment, if you want some food, you'd better scoot up to the canteen,' Frank said looking at his watch.

'I brought a packed lunch with me. I'll just go and make myself a drink to go with it,' Rachel said, standing. The smells in the canteen often bothered her these days. Although she'd passed through the morning sickness phase, strong food smells often made her feel nauseous.

6

Beth made good time heading out of Newcastle. She'd made herself a sandwich for the road, and much as she knew Frank would disapprove, she ate it while she was driving, taking careful bites and placing it on her lap, never taking her eyes off the road.

When she and Frank went on long journeys, he always insisted that they stop and take a break when they wanted to eat. She had no intentions of stopping, unless her bladder forced her to re-consider. She'd calculated that with no hold-ups she might make it to Manilla in just over four hours.

She couldn't help but think back to her relationship with Steve and wonder if they had stayed together would this incident have occurred. It was a stupid thought really, she had no way of knowing that and of course it was likely young Harry would still have taken up paragliding.

Beth and Steve had been engaged back in 1975 when she'd been involved in a serious accident that changed the course of her life. In her head Beth split her life into 'before the accident', and 'after the accident'. Injuries she'd sustained in the crash left her with few memories of her life 'before the accident.' For 25 years she'd lived, largely in the UK, unaware that she'd left behind a loving family and fiancé. Steve had left her with a little parting gift though; her son Matt. In England, she'd married Richard Carey, her old boss who, with his brother and sister, ran a family law firm. From that marriage, she'd had her daughter Ali, who now lived in Sydney with her husband Stefan and baby son Paul.

Richard died of cancer when Ali was seven in 1988 and Beth had remained alone until being reconciled with Steve in 2000. At first all was well, but the relationship was doomed from the start. Too much time had passed. Besides, Beth lived in Bristol, England, while Steve lived in Brisbane, Australia. With neither of them willing to budge on moving, the long-distance affair stood little chance of surviving. Steve married his current wife in 2002. From everything Matt told her, Steve seemed happy and settled.

Beth had met Frank in June 2000 when he'd turned up in Bristol to question her about her about the 1975 car accident. There had been an instant mutual attraction between them, but being reconciled with Steve had prevented anything developing between them. It wasn't until 2003 when they met in Australia again, that she and Frank started seeing each other, culminating in their marriage in 2004. Matt was already living in Australia and once Ali finished her degree, she was more than happy to move there also.

She hadn't seen Steve since Matt's wedding back in December 2003. Matt had shown her photographs he'd taken of Steve, his wife Jodie and their daughter, but it was different to seeing someone in the flesh. By all accounts he'd put on a bit of weight since his heart attack. Matt had recently been encouraging him to take daily walks in order to shed some of the excess, arguing that if he remained overweight, it made him more vulnerable to having another heart attack. According to Matt, Steve now completed a 2 kilometre walk first thing every morning.

She wished Frank would do something similar. Since she'd known him, he'd always been a little overweight and the only exercise he had most weeks was doing yard work at weekends – if he managed to be at home. They enjoyed walking exploring different places in the region – but the opportunity to do so was infrequent.

One of her favourite old rock songs came on the radio; Beth turned it up sang along with it.

'I need you to pull over at the next rest stop,' Steve told Matt.

'Yes okay,' Matt replied. This would be the fourth time they'd had to stop for his father to relieve his bladder. Matt supposed that's what happened to people when they aged. It also helped Matt to revive at the stops, where he would get out and pace up and down for a few minutes, before taking a few sips from his water bottle. Being the sole driver, he needed the breaks.

His father had dozed off a couple of times on the trip, much to Matt's relief. Conversation had been fraught with Steve suggesting various scenarios of what could have happened to the missing 'boys' as he called them. Being in their twenties, neither of them were boys, although he supposed his father found it difficult to think of Harry as a 'man'. But each option his father had suggested, resulted in injuries that could prove fatal and caused Steve more unease.

'There's no point in thinking like that,' Matt had said.

'I can't help it. It's got to be bad news, otherwise we would have heard from them, wouldn't we?'

'They might be staying somewhere that has no phone contact. There's a lot of open country out that way. Some places are pretty remote and probably wouldn't have a mobile signal.'

'But they'd have a land line or some form of radio contact.'

'The *boys* might be holed up in outbuildings in a place where the owners are away. They wouldn't have any transport, would they? Then they'd have no way of contacting anyone.'

The conversation had gone round and round in circles like this, until Matt had run out of possible optimistic options and kept quiet. He had to agree with his father, that it wasn't looking good. He just hoped by the time they arrived, there'd be some good news.

7

Harry felt someone running a damp cloth over him as he came around. Where was he? What had happened?

He opened his eyes to see a woman with long, straight, pale pinkish red hair moving a cloth over his stomach. Her hair was tickling him. He tried to sit up but the pain in his side was too great.

'What … where am I?' he croaked.

'You were in an accident,' the woman said turning to face him. She was young, a girl really, and like Felix, her face was covered in freckles. Unlike him, her freckles were tiny and not so noticeable. She had large pale blue eyes and he guessed she was still in her teens.

Harry attempted to move again, but found it too painful and difficult. He lifted his head to see that his right leg was elevated and the lower half was encased in plaster. His right arm also seemed to be wrapped in plaster.

'What—'

'You've broken your right leg and arm,' she told him. 'And you have injuries to your side. Try not to move.'

'But I need to … I need to pee,' he said feeling embarrassed.

'No problem,' she said reaching behind her for a large shallow bowl. 'You can go in here.'

'How am I supposed to do that?' he asked.

'That's what I've been using with you,' she said.

She removed the sheet which had been covering him and gently moved his left leg to drape it over the side of his makeshift bed before saying, 'just let it go. I'll catch it.'

Harry had never experienced anything like this before in his life and felt excruciatingly uncomfortable at what he was about to do – and at the thought that this young woman had been dealing with such intimate matters. Try as he might he couldn't hold out any longer and felt such relief as he peed into the dish.

'You're very dehydrated,' she said examining the contents of the bowl. 'I think you need some water. She picked up a jug of water and an enamel mug, poured some in and helped him lift his head a little to take sips.

'Thank you,' he said when he'd had enough.

'Where am I?' he asked looking around him. He seemed to be in some sort of very large wire enclosure inside a barn.

'You're on our farm,' she said shrugging.

'Where's my friend Felix?'

'He left.'

'What do you mean he left?'

'He's being dropped into a town called Manilla. He said he had his car and your belongings there.'

Harry was relieved to hear this. That meant Felix would be bringing back help for him.

'Is it still Saturday?'

'No, it's Monday.'

'Monday? That means I've been here two days!'

'Yes, you were too poorly to move.'

'Felix didn't have any injuries from our crash?'

'A few cuts and bruises, but otherwise he was okay.'

'Why didn't you take me to a hospital?'

'There are no hospitals around here. Jacob is a doctor, so he has been treating your wounds. They're not that serious.'

'Jacob? Who's Jacob?'

'He jointly owns the farm and is one of our Elders.'

'Elders? What kind of place is this?' Harry asked. 'I need to call my father. And Felix.' He struggled to sit up, feeling a searing pain shoot down his right side.

'You shouldn't be moving, Jacob said. You have injuries down your right side.'

Feeling defeated, Harry collapsed back onto his bed. He seemed to be lying on a flimsy mattress that was on top of bales of hay. The enclosure he was in didn't seem right. Why was he here rather than in a proper bed somewhere?

'Why are we out here in a barn? And is this some sort of cage?' he asked the girl.

'We do sometimes use it to hold animals, like, when one of our cows or goats are giving birth.'

'I don't understand. Why am I in here then? Why not in your house?'

'Jacob said it wasn't safe for you to be in the infirmary, which is why you're out here. I'm sorry, it was the best we could do.'

'Who are you anyway? What's your name?'

'Dee', she replied.

'Dee?'

'Yes,' she said nodding.

'How old are you, Dee?'

'I'm twenty.'

'Really? You look younger.' He was relieved at least to hear it wasn't a young teenage girl who had been looking after him. That wouldn't have been right.

'Are you a trained nurse or something?'

'Sort of. Jacob and my mother have trained me to take care of people and deal with minor injuries they might have.'

'Such as?'

'We've had broken limbs, cuts, fevers – you know that kind of thing.'

'So where is this farm?'

'Pretty much in the middle of nowhere.'

'Where's the nearest town or city? And how far are we from Manilla?' Harry had no idea where he was. The last thing he remembered seeing was Lake Keepit, before the dust devil hit them. They could have been blown miles from that spot and he didn't know what other towns were in the area.

'I don't know. I never leave Babylon.'

'Babylon?'

'That's the name of our property. It's a working farm.'

'What do you mean you never leave here? Are you being held here against your will?'

Dee threw back her head and laughed, unnerving Harry a little. What was so funny? Did she have mental health problems?

'How long have you lived here?' he asked her once she'd calmed down.

'We moved here when I was about seven.'

'Where did you go to school then?'

'I didn't, once we moved here. I was taught on the farm.'

'What about shopping? Don't you go to the shops with your mother?'

'No. Never. Some of the men drive to some distant town for supplies. We don't need a lot as we grow much of our own food.'

'So what town do they go to?'

Dee shook her head. Either she didn't know or wasn't willing to tell him. It sounded like this was some crazy place he and Felix had landed in.

'Now I've got a tablet to give you for pain relief. I think you need to take it and then get some more rest.' Dee reached into the pocket of her apron and pulled out a little white tablet.

'No, I want to make a phone call. Where's my mobile phone?'

'There's no signal for mobile phones here and Jacob said you weren't to move because of your injuries. It could cause further damage. You don't want that, do you? The more you rest now, the sooner you will heal. Come on you need to take the tablet.'

Reluctantly, Harry allowed Dee to place the tablet on his tongue. She held up his head enabling him to take a few more sips of water.

'That's good mister, now you need to rest.'

'My name is Harry. Call me Harry.'

'No, I can't. It's not allowed,' Dee said. 'We need to wait and see what Jacob says.'

'What do you mean "what Jacob says"?' Harry burst

out laughing which caused him to wince in pain. 'What the bloody hell are you going on about? My name is Harry. Harry Meredith.' He suddenly felt overwhelmed with tiredness and battled to keep his eyes open.

'Names you had from the *outside* don't always count in here.'

'But that's my name. I'm not moving in with your *family*, or whatever these people are to you. I'm going home,' he whispered. What he was hearing was madness. Absolute madness. Were they all like this or was it just this girl? He needed to get out this place as soon as possible.

'This is your home now,' he heard Dee say before he slipped into oblivion.

8

Rachel watched Sarah Harper enter the room and take a seat opposite Frank and herself. The constable who had escorted her shut the door and left them to it. Sarah had declined the presence of a lawyer. Frank had requested that she be brought to them, rather than have her waiting in an interview room. He wanted to see if she showed any signs of still being under the influence of the drug she'd been given the previous afternoon. Her face looked pasty, and around her eyes she looked as though she had a hangover. Otherwise, she looked fine and walked steadily.

Rachel knew from the information in front of her that Sarah Harper was 49 years old. Older than her brother by three years, she had been married to Edward Harper for 25 years. The couple had two sons, one aged 24 who had remained living in Perth when the family returned to Newcastle two years ago and a second son aged 22 who was currently living in Sydney.

Rachel could see that Sarah dyed her hair a deep brown as silvery-grey growth was showing at the roots. Her hair was short, with a fringe and framing her face in a bob style. She was wearing a light brown and white striped sleeveless cotton dress with sandals and, judging by the deep tan on her arms and legs, looked as though she spent quite a bit of time in the sun, but had the sense to protect her face; the part of the body where Australians most commonly developed skin cancer.

The Harper couple were both originally from Newcastle, but according to their notes, Edward Harper (known as Ted by the family), an engineer, had obtained work in Perth, where they remained for ten years until their fairly recent return.

Sarah and Lee's mother was still alive and lived in Newcastle. At the time of his trial Rachel remembered Wells' father had been there also. Had the couple divorced?

'Good afternoon Sarah,' Frank said greeting the woman. 'I'm Detective Chief Inspector Bailey, and this is Detective Inspector Sharp.'

Sarah nodded greetings at them.

'How are you feeling?' Frank asked her.

'Although I apparently slept for many hours, I'm feeling exhausted. I can't believe Lee slipped us some drug. How the hell was he able to leave the prison carrying drugs.?'

'We don't believe he did.'

'Then how did he get his hands on it? It didn't come from our house; I can assure you.'

'We thought you might be able to provide us with some clues on that,' Frank said.

'I don't see how. We were with Lee the whole time.'

'The whole time?' Rachel interjected.

'Well yes, either at Mum's or at our house.'

'He didn't leave your sight at any time?' Rachel asked.

Sarah shook her head, then paused for a few beats.

'He said he needed some fresh air after we returned from Mum's. He went out into the back yard for a bit, but he didn't leave our property if that's what you're thinking. Otherwise, we were with him the whole time. We picked him up Saturday morning and we were supposed to drop him back Saturday at 7pm – only you know what happened. This'll kill mum. It destroyed Dad when Lee was convicted. He found it difficult to cope afterwards. He went into a deep depression, took a sabbatical, went off travelling soon after and … well he died in a stupid car accident. That's why we moved back to Newcastle – to support mum.'

Rachel nodded in empathy. She'd come across similar cases of depression occurring with family members who couldn't believe a parent, sibling or offspring had committed a serious crime.

'Did Lee make any phone calls while he was with you?' Frank asked.

'None that I'm aware of. As far as I know he didn't have a phone. Your lot checked *our* mobiles and he hadn't used them. I imagine they're also checking our land line?'

Frank nodded to confirm this would be the case. 'We'll also be checking your mother's land line. How long were you at your mother's? Can you walk me through your movements from the moment you picked Lee up?'

Sarah took them through their day up until the point where they all sat down to watch an English football match Ted had recorded.

'That was about two thirty or thereabouts,' Sarah said. 'The next thing we knew your lot were shaking Ted and me many hours later.'

'It is possible that someone gained access to your backyard while you were at your mother's place and that that person hid the drug Lee used on you, seeing as he went out into the yard shortly after you returned home. Can you think of any obvious places where it might have been hidden?'

Sarah looked blank. 'I don't know. I guess if it was a small droplets bottle, like one of your constables said, it could have been hidden anywhere amongst my plants – or in the peg bag. I don't know,' she repeated shaking her head.

Edward Harper confirmed virtually everything that Sarah had. The only discrepancies in their stories had been the estimated times of arrival and departure between the two houses. Sarah was out by twenty minutes.

'I don't think there's anything to be learned from them,' Frank concluded after organising for the couple to be taken home.

'What about Wells' mother? Should we pay a visit to her?'

'It doesn't sound as though there'd be much she could add to what the Harper's have told us. We'll check her phone records. I think our priority is to look at any prison visitors Wells has had. Also, we need a list of everyone who has been released over the past few months and any phone calls Wells made in recent weeks and months.'

'Yes, okay,' Rachel said. 'I'll organise a visit to the prison.'

'Take Ryan Pullman with you.'

Rachel nodded. DC Pullman was the best of the bunch

currently on duty at the station. Ayesha Patel would have been her first choice, but Ayesha was away on holiday. She was the only other female detective in the department, and Rachel really missed her. Rachel wished *she* was holidaying somewhere. There'd be no holidays for her and Andy for a while after having the baby. They'd only managed to have four days away over Christmas.

She sighed, stood with difficulty (her bump seemed to be growing by the day – she was convinced she was expecting triplets) and went in search of Ryan Pullman.

9

'Can we go straight to the police station?' Steve asked when they approached the outskirts of Manilla. 'It's at 64 Manilla Street, which must be the main drag of the town.'

'It may be, but given that we don't know the town, and we'll need to find our motel, I think we need to call into the tourist information office first while they're still open. It won't take long and they'll give us a map,' Matt said. He could see the sign up ahead and turned off the highway, pulling into their car park.

'They'll have toilet facilities; do you need to go again?' Matt asked.

'I may as well,' Steve said releasing his seat belt. 'I doubt the police station will offer those facilities.'

There was a small queue at the counter, but Matt spotted a Manilla town guide and opened it to find a map covering everything he needed, including the paragliding club information, which was some way out of town.

He'd booked a family room for them at the Manilla Motel. Ideally Matt would have preferred his own room, but given the delicate state his father was in, he thought it best that they shared. He'd passed the motel details onto his mother, who was due to meet up with them later.

When he'd looked at booking accommodation, Matt had seen that the motel looked to be in a potentially quiet back street. Often motels were on the highway with constant passing traffic. There had been three lovely old hotels which offered accommodation, but they *had* been on the main street of the town and from his experience, they could be noisy with local customers, restaurants and possibly even live music. Some of those old hotels didn't offer en suite bathrooms either – which is what his father needed.

Matt browsed through items for sale while waiting for Steve, wondering if people really bought the Manilla key rings. Books he could understand – if you were interested in the history of an area, but key rings? He reasoned they must sell, otherwise they wouldn't have them for sale.

When Steve appeared, he waved his map and they returned to the car.

'The police station is not far down the main street. The Highway diverts off, skirting the town, but we carry on straight,' Matt told him. 'We could walk it, but let's see if there's somewhere to park outside.'

A few minutes later they pulled up outside the police station. Matt knew it wasn't a 24hr station, and he just hoped someone was on duty. If they closed for lunch they should have been back by now. It was 2.30pm.

The door was open and they walked in to find a young female constable behind the counter.

'Good afternoon, my name is Steve Meredith, the father of Harry Meredith, one of the paragliders who has gone missing.'

'Ah right,' the constable said. 'If you'd like to take a seat, I'll get our sergeant to come out and talk to you.'

They'd only been waiting five minutes when the sergeant appeared.

'Mr Meredith? I'm Sergeant Booth,' he said reaching out to shake Steve's hand.

Matt judged the sergeant to be in his mid-50s, which could be advantageous. He would have experience, and unless he was a lazy bugger, that experience could prove invaluable. He'd been concerned though to hear that a report hadn't been sent through to Tamworth until Sunday afternoon. Was it standard practice to wait so long, or was it down to laziness?'

'This is my son Matt,' Steve said pointing to him.

The sergeant nodded at Matt.

'Can you give us an update on what you've done so far, anything you've found and what you intend to do to help find my son.'

'I think it might be best if we make ourselves more comfortable in a meeting room,' the sergeant said. 'It will afford us greater privacy. If you'd like to follow me.'

Once they had settled into what was clearly an *interview* room, not a meeting room, the sergeant filled them in on the air search and rescue operation they'd done so far. He had a map spread out in front of him and Matt could see it was a vast area the helicopter had to cover.

'The boys were spotted by the wife of a horse stud farm owner out at Rushes Creek. She was hanging out the washing early on Saturday morning and saw them approaching from the direction of Manilla. She said the glider was heading towards Lake Keepit. As soon as I heard that I put a call through to the owner of the Holiday Park at the Lake. She hadn't seen or heard anything about it, but offered to go around asking their campers and guests – they rent out cabins there in addition to having spots for camper vans and tents. She phoned me back about an hour later to say that a camper van owner had seen them heading in their direction. The camper then went into the van to make a cup of tea, intending to come out and watch them, but was delayed by a phone call and when she stepped outside the van again there was no sign of them.'

'They couldn't have landed in the lake, could they?' Matt asked.

'No, I asked that question. Although it was still quite early in the morning, there were people on, or around, the lake.'

'How far away is Lake Keepit?' Steve asked.

'It's about 35ks from Manilla. There's more I haven't told you yet from the stud farm. The husband heard a disturbance with the horses in the home paddock not long after his wife had seen the glider. He went out and saw a dust devil not too far away. He waited some time to see if it was heading his way and when it didn't, he returned indoors.'

'A dust devil?' Steve asked looking puzzled.

'Yes, it's like a mini dust storm. More like a dust tornado, where the dust is rotating from an intense uplift of air like you see in tornadoes.'

'You think they were caught up in that?'

'They could have been. Apparently, it was a huge bastard – pardon my language. And it can change direction in the blink of an eye. It didn't arrive at the stud farm, but swirled off and was spotted in Somerton and then the next report we have of it is north of Curlewis – that's south of Gunnedah here,' he said pointing to the map. 'Then it seemed to peter out over near Goolhi – which was the last sighting. They don't normally last that long, but given that it was so large, it seemed to break apart and a smaller section of it carried on towards Goolhi.'

'How did you learn about the route of the dust devil?' Matt asked.

'We had the radio stations in Gunnedah and Tamworth put out an appeal for anyone who spotted the boys to get in touch. Some people phoned in about the dust devil. I also made phone calls to other clubs and camping places around the lake. No one else seems to have seen the glider, but a few people spotted the dust storm, or I should say dust devil.'

'If Harry and Felix were caught up in that dust devil thing, what might have happened to them?' Steve asked.

The sergeant grimaced and shook his head. 'Well, that's the question. They would have struggled to have any form of control. They could have crashed, or they could have been swept off in a different direction. Paragliders have been known to travel many hundreds of kilometres with a strong wind behind them.'

'So what areas have you searched?' Matt asked.

'They've covered the area around Rushes Creek, Lake Keepit and beyond,' Booth said indicating the areas on the map. 'There was no sign of them in those areas.'

'But they've got to be out there somewhere. What about a ground search? Are there any dense bushland areas they could have landed in where they wouldn't be spotted from a helicopter?' Steve asked.

'There's small pockets of it, but nothing major until you get to Pilliga State Forest which is much further inland over near the Newell Highway. It's highly unlikely they travelled, or were blown that far.'

'How many times has the helicopter been up looking?'

'It was out for several hours this morning. They're up there again now as we speak.'

'And how long will you continue looking?'

'I couldn't tell you that and it's not down to me. Area Command in Tamworth will be making those decisions. Now where in town will you be staying if I need to get in touch with you?'

'The Manilla Motel,' Matt said. 'We'll give you our mobile numbers, but we'd also like a number from you where we can get hold of you direct. And a number for someone who might be in charge of the search in Tamworth.'

'Yes, no problem. I can give you my number, but I'll have to find out who is dealing with it in Tamworth. I can get back to you on that.'

Matt nodded.

'I'd like to know why nothing was done about looking for my son until this morning. They were reported missing on Saturday afternoon.'

'I wasn't on duty on Saturday. And it was a bit premature to be listing them as missing on Saturday afternoon and take any action. They could have been making their way back to Manilla.'

'How would they be making their way back to Manilla, if they had no transport?' Steve asked.

'A local could have picked them up. We've had similar situations before.'

Steve grunted. 'Maybe a local did pick them up and for some reason hasn't allowed them to make contact with anyone.'

'I think that's highly unlikely. You'll find that most people around the area are friendly and helpful.'

'*Most* people? So *some* aren't friendly and helpful?

'Well like anywhere, you will find some cantankerous characters, and out here you might find the odd person who would be hostile and suspicious of strangers. But I can't believe anyone would be holding two men somewhere. No, it's more likely they were caught up in the dust storm, carried off course and are stranded – possibly with injuries that have prevented them from seeking help.'

'Harry or Felix would have had their mobile phones with them,' Matt said jumping in. He didn't want Steve to dwell on the idea of the boys lying injured somewhere. 'We've tried to reach them without success. Has anything been done by you to do a search on the phones? Isn't there some kind of technology the police have to trace the whereabouts of mobile phones?'

'I believe Police Area Command in Tamworth are dealing with that,' Sergeant Booth said. 'Now unless there's anything else, I suggest you check into your motel and I will make contact with you later this afternoon to let you know how the search went.'

The sergeant stood, making it clear the conversation

was being terminated.

'One more thing,' Steve said. 'Where's the nearest air field where we would hire a plane to take us over the area.'

'Tamworth regional airport, but I don't think—'

'I intend to do everything I can to help find my son,' Steve said. 'Come on Matt, we need to make enquiries about that.'

10

After returning from Cessnock prison, Rachel went straight to Frank's office. He had his door open and she could see he was on the phone, but he waved her in, gesturing for her to sit down.

'Did you find out anything that may be of interest to us?' he asked her, once he'd completed his call.

'I think so. When Wells was first being held in prison, pending his trial, his father paid him one visit. Since then, the only visitors Wells has had are his mother or his sister.'

'Okay, so nothing there.'

'Recent releases who were part of Wells' circle include a Nick Pollard and a Wade Collins. They were both released in December, shortly before Christmas. Pollard first. Then Collins a week later.'

'Did you say Wade Collins?'

'Yes.'

'I remember that name. I've come across him before. He's from up Tamworth way – which fits the name of course.'

Rachel wasn't sure what Frank mean by that comment. Perhaps he was alluding to Tamworth being famous for

Country and Western music.

'Years ago, I saw him performing at one of the venues during the Country and Western festival,' he said.

'You went up there for that?' Rachel asked surprised. She wouldn't have taken Frank for a country and western fan. The odd time he'd played music when they'd been on journeys in a car together, he'd played rock music.

'A friend asked me to go with him one year. I thought I'd give it go. Some of the music was okay, but it's not really my scene.'

Rachel nodded.

'When I was up at Tamworth a few years back I read in the local paper that Wade Collins had been convicted of fraud. The name stuck – you don't come across many men by the name of Wade. So, Wells, Collins, and Pollard hung out together?'

'Yes, they were chummy. Wells shared a cell with Collins at one point. Pollard was Wells' cell mate before he was released in December.'

'And Nick Pollard? His name also rings a bell. What was he in there for?'

'DI Lowry nabbed him for some burglaries when he was with the drug squad. Pollard broke into a few pharmacies to steal drugs.'

'Ah that's right. Now that would fit with this current little caper pulled by Wells. Perhaps our man Pollard had a stash of drugs somewhere. He's local, isn't he?'

'Yes, he is, and as well as sharing a cell, Wells used to eat his meals with Pollard and Collins according to information I was given.'

'Okay. And phone calls?'

'The only official calls Wells made were to his mother and sister. Of course, he might have had access to a mobile phone which he used to make contact with other people.'

'Yes, he might. They always seem to be able to get their hands on them somehow. Well, I think we need to be visiting our two released prisoners then, don't you?'

'Yes. Do you want to do that with me – or should I take DC Pullman?'

'I'll leave you to call on Pollard with Ryan – bring Pollard in if he won't co-operate. If Collins has returned to Tamworth, I think we need to go up and see him. I'd like to go. There's another matter I might need to follow up there.'

'The missing paraglider?'

'Yes.'

'Okay. I'll head off to see if I can get hold of Pollard now. Will you still be here when I get back?' Rachel asked noting that it was almost 5pm. That meant it was likely she'd be in for another late night.

'Yes, I'll wait for you. I'll check whether I can pick up a current address for Collins. With Beth away I have no inclination to rush home.'

Beth had just finished checking into the Manilla Motel, when she spotted Steve and Matt outside reception. She'd sent Matt a message saying she'd arrived. She thanked the proprietor, picked up her key and walked out to join them.

'Hello darling,' she said, giving Matt a kiss.

'Hi mum, thanks for coming.'

Turning to Steve she said, 'Hello Steve. I'm so sorry to hear that Harry is missing.'

Beth did her best not to show her shock at Steve's appearance. He *was* quite overweight, as Matt had mentioned. His hair was completely grey now and he had a haunted look about his face. As though he had already accepted that Harry was dead. Much like he did with her all those years ago.

Steve nodded at her and she could tell he was fighting off tears.

'Have you heard anything new?'

'The air rescue team has just returned to base. They found nothing from their searches today. Dad and I have hired a small plane to take up out over the area where the boys were last seen. We're flying out of Tamworth in the morning.'

'So someone saw them?'

'Yes, the police did a radio appeal, and the owners of a horse stud farm called it in. The same people spotted a dust devil in the area.'

Matt must have picked up on her puzzled expression, because he quickly explained what a dust devil was. It wasn't sounding too good.

'Would you like another pair of eyes in the plane tomorrow? If there's room?' Beth wasn't too keen on flying in small aircrafts. She'd only done it a couple of times with Frank, but they were usually short trips, unlike the tedium of long-haul flights she'd experienced travelling back and forth to England.

'That would be helpful, thank you,' Steve said. 'The plane I've hired can accommodate six people.'

'We've bought a couple of large-scale maps of the region,' Matt said. 'As we go across each area in the plane, we can mark it off.'

'Okay. So, what are your plans now?'

'We thought we'd go up to the paragliding club and see if we can speak to the manager. Harry and Felix still have all their things in the cabin. Felix's car is also there. Dad thinks we should pay for the cabin for another few days in case Harry and Felix make their way back there. Presumably they will have the key on them.'

'What about Felix's family? Are they coming down to

Manilla?'

'No, his mother is stuck at home with a couple of teenage kids. Felix's father is dead and his stepfather walked out on the mother and Felix's half siblings years ago. She's leaving it up to us to liaise with everyone.'

Beth nodded. It was going to prove complex if they had to make arrangements to return Felix's car to Brisbane. But then that was jumping the gun. The car would be needed if the boys were found safe and well.

'I'll leave you to get on with visiting the paragliding club then. I'll settle into my room. Give me a knock when you come back.'

'I will,' Matt said, squeezing her arm.

11

Nick Pollard tried to slam his flat door shut after Rachel produced her ID, but anticipating his actions, she'd wedged her foot inside the opening.

'Now come on Nick, we only want a friendly word. Otherwise, we'll have to take you down to the station.' She didn't say that they might be doing that anyway.

Pollard had the pale face of someone who hadn't seen the sun in a long time. Although they were given exercise time outdoors, when many prisoners were released, they carried that same pasty look. Pollard also looked like someone who had once been (and might still be) a drug addict. He was wafer thin and undernourished. Rachel didn't think he carried an ounce of fat on his body. His hair was long at the top but short at the sides and back, and hung in greasy strands, looking as though it needed a good wash.

With some reluctance Nick stepped back and allowed them to follow him into the lounge. The place was disgusting; Rachel also considered it a potential health hazard. It stank of a mixture of body odour, rotting food, cigarettes and beer. Open cartons and containers of take-away food were strewn around the room, with mouldy scraps of pizza and other unidentifiable blobs apparent along with empty beer cans. There was an overflowing ash tray sitting on a coffee table. The TV, on a stand in the corner of the room, was blaring out. With her olfactory senses enhanced due to her pregnancy, the smell in Pollard's place immediately made Rachel feel nauseous.

'Turn that off Nick,' she said pointing at the TV.

With a sulky look on his face, Pollard picked up the remote and complied.

'I see you take real pride in your home,' Rachel said sarcastically, walking over to open a window. She couldn't stand the smell for another minute.

'Hey, what did you do that for?' Pollard shouted at her when she managed to prise open the window.

'You might be able to stand the smell Nick, but I'm afraid we can't. So we either have the window open or we take you down to the station to answer our questions.' She could see Ryan was holding a hand under his nose.

'How I live is my business. What do you want?'

'Lee Wells?'

'What about him?'

'We think you might have done a small favour for him.'

'I dunno know what you're talking about,' Pollard said. But Rachel noticed his eyes started darting around the room nervously. Was he hiding some drugs here?

'Rohypnol. We think you provided him with a vial of Rohypnol to help him escape. Was that left over from a stash you hid before you were convicted?'

'I dunno know what you're talking about,' Pollard repeated.

Pollard hadn't shown any surprise at the news that Wells had escaped. Although to be fair to him, it had featured on this morning's news.

'You do know he's escaped, don't you?'

'Yeah. I saw it on the news. Nuthin' to do with me. I dunno why he wanted to take off when he was due for parole soon.'

It was an interesting way of phrasing things – as though Pollard knew Wells had planned an escape.

'You knew he was planning to escape then?'

'What? No!'

'So, he didn't talk about escaping when you had your cosy chats in Cessnock?'

'No. We didn't talk about things like that. We were both gettin' out soon.'

'But on parole, he'd have to check in regularly with his parole officer, wouldn't he? If he walked away then he wouldn't have to deal with such tedious things. What were his plans, Nick?'

'I dunno. Really, I don't.'

'But you did supply him with the Rohypnol?'

'No, I didn't,' he said shaking his head, but with guilt written all over his face.

'If we were to search your flat, we wouldn't find any drugs here?'

'You'd need a search warrant and no, you wouldn't.'

'Ah, so is that because you'd get rid of them before the warrant arrived or you've hidden them somewhere else? What if I was to tell you I'm carrying a warrant on me?'

Pollard showed no concern at her final statement. Either because he believed she was bluffing or he really didn't have any drugs on the premises.

'There's nuthin' here. Search all you want.'

'So you're giving us permission to search your home, are you?'

'You said you had a warrant. If you haven't, then piss off.'

He waited a few seconds before saying, 'So you haven't got a warrant. Then if there nuthin' else, I'm busy.'

'There is something else Nick. Wade Collins.'

'What about him?'

'I was told that Wade and Lee were quite chummy.' Pollard shrugged.

'What can you tell me about them?'

'Nuthin.'

'Do you know what Wade's plans were when he got out?'

'Not really. I do know he was plannin' to take up music again though.'

'Did Lee talk about meeting up with Wade.'

'Not to me. I know nuthin' about them.'

'Well, we won't trouble you any more at the moment Nick, but we might be back soon,' Rachel said, giving a nod to Ryan to indicate they were leaving.

Once they were back in the car, Ryan turned to Rachel and said, 'I don't know how people can live like that.'

'I've seen worse. I'm surprised you haven't. If you think that was bad, wait until the come across a place covered in cat, dog and human—'

'I get the picture, no need to spell it out for me. Pollard told you how he lived was his business. I just don't understand how people can think that not showering – and it was clear he hadn't for some time, and living in an environment like that is okay.'

'Self-loathing and low self-worth are contributory factors I would imagine,' she said.

'We should have taken him in for questioning, not stayed there. I feel like all my clothes are contaminated now.'

'I know what you mean,' she said, starting the car. She couldn't wait to get home, strip off all her clothes and jump in the shower.

12

Frank was still at the station when Rachel returned. She'd told Ryan he could head home, knowing how uncomfortable he'd felt after leaving Pollard's place.

Worried that she might smell, Rachel stood at the door of Frank's office and filled him in.

'Come in and sit down Rachel, I have some more news for you.'

'I'm afraid I might smell, sir. Pollard's place wasn't very pleasant.'

'Oh, don't worry about that. We have greater things to worry about. I had some social worker put through to me; she'd been trying to reach you.'

'Lane Wilson?' Rachel asked, edging into the office and taking a seat.

'Yes, that's right.'

'I left my mobile number for her to contact me.'

'It seems whoever took the message wrote the number down incorrectly, so she tried reaching you through conventional – and more reliable channels: on the land line. The upshot of her call was to tell me that Martha Richardson and her child have disappeared.'

'So, she was allowed to keep the baby?'

'Yes, she had a little girl she called Rebecca. They've been in an independent living flat with an on-site warden. Martha's free to come and go as she pleases. Apparently, she left the flat Saturday afternoon to go for a walk – or so she told a neighbour who passed her in the hallway. Nobody realised that she hadn't returned until Martha's mother called in to see her this morning. After receiving no answer at the flat, the warden let her in. There was no sign of Martha or the child who turned two a couple of months ago. Some items belonging to Rebecca and other things are missing from the flat. Such as Rebecca's special drinking mug, bowl etc. Martha's mother noticed them missing because she'd bought them as a present for Rebecca. Mrs Richardson is sure clothing items – for both the child and mother are missing also. She collects Martha's dirty washing every Monday and returns clean washing from the previous week. So she is aware of most of the clothing items her daughter and granddaughter own.'

'Was the neighbour questioned? Was Martha seen with a bag?' Rachel asked.

'The social worker and warden knocked on doors near Martha's flat. The neighbour who Martha spoke to didn't see a bag – but she said Martha had Rebecca in a stroller – one of those ones that has a shelf underneath for holding shopping. She said that was full of stuff.'

'Okay – so what – you think she's gone off with Wells somewhere?'

'It seems the most likely scenario. The timing fits. I've sent a team of uniforms to do a door to door around the area to see if anyone saw Martha and the child,' Frank said.

'Right. Unless Wells kidnapped Martha, no crime has been committed – other than the fact that he's broken his visit conditions and will be unlikely to be released on parole. I wonder what prompted him to take action *now*. Why not wait until he's released?'

'Interesting question. I haven't told you the second part yet. Wells was featured on a news broadcast at lunch time which went out across all NSW networks. A local in Tamworth called in to say he had seen a man, who looked like Wells, standing with his 'family' at a bus stop on the outskirts of Tamworth on Saturday night. A woman and a young child were with him. The local man was also waiting at the bus stop and when the bus arrived, the 'family' didn't get on it, telling the local guy that they were waiting to be collected.'

'Did the bus stop have CCTV?'

'I don't know. I've asked the DC who phoned me to check it out. If it was Wells with Martha and Rebecca and they were picked up by someone, hopefully it was all captured on camera.'

'Okay. So, are we heading up to Tamworth tomorrow?'

'I think it warrants a trip up there, yes. I have a current address for Collins. He has moved back to Tamworth and it's possible he was the one who picked up Wells and Martha. You okay with heading up there tomorrow?

'Yes, that's fine. Will we be staying over up there or returning to Newcastle later in the day?' The idea of returning to Newcastle after a long day, held little appeal for Rachel. She tired very quickly these days with her pregnancy. She was relieved to hear Frank say they should stay up there for at least one night.

'You're still in your rental, aren't you?'

'Yes, we haven't found anything we want to buy yet. Andy and I looked at properties up in Cardiff last weekend, but we didn't like them and it was too far out for me.'

'Beth and I don't mind being out in the sticks a bit. It's very peaceful. But I imagine it might be awkward for when you become a mother. You'd want to be handy for everything, especially after being in your current place where you're almost in the city.'

'Yes, but houses like our rental are too small. Parking is an issue as well. I want a large sprawling house with off road parking – preferably with a double garage.'

'Yes, it seems to be what all young families want these days. I'll pick you up at seven if that's okay. Now why don't you head off home?'

'I will if you don't mind. I'm dying to get these clothes off after being at Pollard's. I'll type up my report from our visit to him from home.'

'No need to do that tonight. Leave it and have a night off.'

'Ok, thanks I'll do that,' she said.

Rachel stood and moved swiftly out of Frank's office, heading for the lifts. She'd texted Andy earlier saying she'd be a bit late, so she hoped he'd prepared a meal for them. Otherwise, they'd be digging through the freezer.

'Dinner's almost ready Rach,' Andy called up the stairs to her from the kitchen.

'I'll be down in a couple of minutes,' she called back.

Good old Andy had started on the meal by the time

she'd walked home. She'd just stepped out of the shower and was rubbing a towel over her wet hair as he called up to her. It was a relief to discard her dirty clothes which certainly had an unpleasant whiff about them. She'd stuffed them into a carrier bag and intended to take them down to wash separately after they'd eaten. The front loader machine was in the kitchen where they'd be eating at the table and the noise of it was really annoying. Normally she wouldn't dream of washing just one small bundle of clothes, but when she visited homes like Pollard's it simply had to be done. She'd made the mistake of putting clothes into a normal wash load in the past and contaminated all her other clothes with the odour.

She was looking forward to relaxing with Andy for an hour or two before heading off to bed. She'd take her laptop away with her and type up the Pollard report tomorrow night when she was in Tamworth.

Frank stood looking at the contents of the fridge, undecided what he wanted to eat. He didn't need a big meal after his lunch time curry. There was some cold cooked beef left over from the joint they'd had on Sunday night. A beef sandwich and a glass of whisky sounded just the ticket.

The house was quiet without Beth. Not that she was noisy. But normally they chatted for a bit when he came in, or over their meal. After clearing up, they might sit down and watch something on TV together, or go off to do their own things. Beth liked to read in bed. Frank was okay with it, but he preferred to sit in the lounge sipping his evening whisky and read there.

Beth had sent him a message to say she'd arrived safely

in Manilla and would be in touch later. Glancing up at the kitchen clock he noticed it was almost 9.30. They'd probably be out eating a meal right now.

A few minutes later he retreated to the lounge, with his sandwich and whisky. He switched on the reading lamp and looked around. Now where was his book? He spotted it on the dining table. Had he put it there last night? Or had Beth left it out for him – knowing he often misplaced it?

He was about to walk over to pick it up when he heard the distant sound of his mobile ringing. Had he left it in the kitchen?

13

Beth was about to terminate her call when Frank answered. She knew she wouldn't be able to leave a message for him. Frank claimed he didn't understand how voicemail worked or how to access messages. The truth was he hated using mobile phones. So she'd disabled voice messages for him and if she couldn't reach him, she sent a text message. He did know how they worked. She'd tried their landline earlier without success and decided Frank must still out working.

'Hello Darling. Sorry to take so long to answer. You know me, I couldn't find where I'd put the bloody thing,' he said.

She could just envision it. Frank moving from room to room, lifting items to see if his phone was hiding underneath. Or moving files about in his office to locate the phone. She'd often had to call his phone from her mobile or the land line when they were at home to help him locate it. He hated using mobile phones and seemed to have an unconscious habit of losing it or forgetting to charge it.

'Are you home now?'

'Yes. So, tell me what's happened so far.'

Beth filled Frank in on what Matt had been told by Sergeant Booth. Unlike her, he knew what she was talking about when she mentioned the dust devil.

'That means they could have been blown way off their planned course.'

'That's what the sergeant at the local police station told them. Steve and Matt met up with the Paragliding Club manager this afternoon and booked the cabin for several more nights. Felix and Harry had been due to check out on Sunday morning and already owed a few days rental on it. The manager hadn't been too happy about them taking off like that. Apparently, he tried to stop them.'

'Right. But the weather was fine, wasn't it? It sounds like this dust devil might have caused the problem.'

'It wasn't only to do with the weather – the manager thought the boys were drunk. They'd been partying much of Friday night. But Steve insists that Harry wouldn't have considered taking a flight if he was drunk. He would lose his hard-earned licence if he did.'

'How is Steve?'

'Fragile, I'd say. He's not looking too well. I can understand why Matt insisted on driving him down here. I don't think he would have been up to doing the drive himself.'

'That's not so good. He wants to avoid getting too stressed over all this.'

'I know. He's hired a plane out of Tamworth tomorrow. I'm going to join them. We're going to see if we can spot anything, searching areas that haven't been covered.'

'I'm going to be up in Tamworth tomorrow. There's been a sighting there on a prisoner who's gone walkabout from

Cessnock. One of his old prison chums lives up there. We're going to interview him.'

'How long will you be in Tamworth? You're staying over I assume?'

'Yes, driving up with Rachel in the morning. I can't guarantee what time I'll be free, but we could meet up later in the day if you want. You could stay with me.'

'Okay, that sounds like a plan. It's not too far from here. Even if we come back to Manilla after the flight – I can drive over to join you later.'

'Right. Well I'll send you a message in the afternoon sometime. I'm going to love you and leave you now. There's a beef sandwich and a whisky waiting for my attention. And before you ask – I had a meal in the canteen at lunch time.'

'Okay, good to hear. Speak to you tomorrow. Bye Frank.'

'Bye.'

Beth heard a knock at the door as she was disconnecting the call. Matt had said he'd pop in for a cup of tea with her once Steve was settled. The motel provided tea and instant coffee, but she'd brought her own supplies and a cafetière with her.

'Come in, I haven't put the kettle on yet,' she told Matt after opening the door.

'Did you bring any Chai with you?'

'Yes. Is that what you'd like?'

'Yes, thanks mum.'

In the recessed kitchenette area Beth made herself a camomile tea, which she often had before going to bed, believing it helped her to drop off. She carried both teas back towards the main part of the room. Matt had plonked himself down on the single chair in the room. She perched on the bed.

'Has Steve settled?' she asked Matt.

'I made him pop a pill. I know it's not a good habit to get into, but he has them on prescription and needs to take them sometimes. He hasn't slept for a few nights, so I insisted he take one tonight.'

'Ah, that's why he looked so haggard.'

'Yeah. I'm worried about him mum. He's not good. It was bad enough that Harry was taking a day off for this trip leaving everything to dad on Saturday. Now with this happening, I'm worried it will push him over the edge. I think he went back to work too soon. He only goes in for half a day, a couple of times a week, but I just don't think he's up to it.'

'How often do you normally see him?'

'Usually once a week with the family, but since his heart attack I've been dropping in to see him every couple of days.'

'What does Jodie think?'

'She thinks he should do whatever makes him happy – and he is happy to be back at work – but you know what he's like – he doesn't take things easy.'

Beth didn't *really* know what Steve was like. He'd done flying visits to her in Sydney when they'd first got together again in 2000. She'd spent a short amount of time with him in Brisbane and he'd been over to visit her in the UK. But both times he'd taken time off work. He *had* seemed restless, as though at a loss of what to do with himself and so had packed the days and nights full of activities when she'd been in Brisbane. And expected much of the same in the UK. What she did know about him was that he liked to think he was in control of things. Having a serious heart attack, followed by a triple by-pass operation that left him unable to work for a time would have been difficult for him.

Now with Harry's disappearance, he had little control over what was happening. Beth suspected the hiring of the aeroplane tomorrow would give him some sense of control. She hoped the search would bring them success.

Matt stayed with her for about an hour, talking about his family until she pleaded tiredness. Much as she treasured any time spent with him these days, she was struggling to keep her eyes open.

'I promise I'll make a pot of decent coffee in the morning for us all,' she said as Matt left her.

14

Harry woke to hear sounds of groaning coming from the other side of the barn. Was that Felix? But hadn't the girl told him Felix had left? Had she lied?

'Is that you Felix?' he called out. 'Can you hear me?'

There was no reply – simply more groans.

He needed to get out of the cage and get across to see who was groaning. But how? Lifting his head, he saw that his right leg was hooked up in some sort of sling and was at least 20cm off the bed. If he could lift his leg out of the sling, he might have a hope of being able to stand. His attempts proved useless, but he found he was able to lift the leg a little. Maybe he could shift his leg backwards instead. Looking over his shoulder he could see there was plenty of space behind him to manoeuvre back. Lifting his right leg, he managed to wriggle back a little. Not enough to pull free of the sling. After several further attempts his heel was caught. The problem was his right arm, encased in plaster, was so awkward he couldn't use it to grip the bed. *Come on, one more lift and you can do it*, he told himself. After a grunting effort he managed it; his right leg dropping heavily onto the bed.

Using his left hand to grip the mattress, he swung his legs out, bent and lowered his left leg to the ground and tried to propel himself into an upright position, ignoring the pain shooting down his right side. He failed and fell back onto the bed. The bloody plaster on his leg was making it so difficult for him to get upright. He made another attempt this time putting more pressure on his left hand and, with an almighty push managed to get upright. Not sure if he should put weight on his injured leg, he hopped towards the cage entrance with his plastered leg suspended behind him and fell against it as he lost his balance. He gripped the cage with his left arm to prevent himself from collapsing.

He could see his cage door was bolted from the outside, and his attempts to squeeze his hands through the opening were unsuccessful. He'd need something long and thin to manage it. Something like a screwdriver – which he didn't have. *Fuck*.

'Felix?' he called out again, squinting into the semi-darkness that the other cage was enveloped in. There was a lantern in his own cage but it was behind him now. If only he could reach it. Hopping around clinging to the sides, he made his way back until he could reach the lantern, then gradually edged forward again. His supporting leg was aching from the strain of supporting all his weight. He made it back to the entrance and held the lantern up.

The other enclosure where the man lay groaning was a good three metres from his. He could see the top half of a man, down to his waist. He was unrecognisable and he couldn't tell if it was Felix. There was some sort of covering over the man's head so Harry couldn't tell if he had Felix's red hair. His face was one swollen mess and looked as though it was covered in blood. What the hell had happened to him?

Just as he was about to have another go at releasing the sliding bolt, Dee came bustling in saying: 'I told you, you shouldn't be out of bed. You'll cause yourself more harm.'

She stood outside his cage as she spoke to him.

'There's someone with bad injuries over there in another cage. Is it my friend?' Harry asked. 'And why have you bolted my door?'

'It's to stop animals wandering in. We have animals roaming around the barn area and they're nosey little things. If they smell the hay, they could wander in here.'

'Right.' That seemed a feasible explanation. The bales of hay were inside the cages.

'Who is that over in the other cage?'

'It's one of our men. He fell off a roof today badly injuring himself.'

'Why is he in here then?'

'Because it was the best place to put him.'

'I don't believe you. Let me out so I can see him.'

'I can't.'

'What do you mean you can't? And did you just happen to be passing or did you see me struggling to get up?' He wondered if she'd been standing near the barn entrance watching him.

Her eyes darted up behind him at the beams near the roof. Harry turned around to see what she was looking at. He could make out what looked like security cameras.

'Are those cameras?' he asked.

'Yes, we had them installed so we'd know when the

cows were beginning to calf. Then no one has to sit out here the whole time with them.'

'Right. So you, or someone else, saw me struggling to stand.'

She nodded.

'If you had been here and helped me, I wouldn't have had to go through all that.'

'I told you Jacob said you were to remain lying down. It's for your own good.'

'I'd like to meet Jacob. Can you ask him to come and see me?'

'He's away at the moment. He came to see you last night but you were sleeping. He checked everything and seemed happy with your progress. The wounds on your side are healing and there's no obvious damage on your spine.'

'Okay, but I'm up now, so why can't you help me across to see the man who is lying there. It's my friend Felix, isn't it?'

'No, it's John. And I'm not looking after him. Ethan said I was to only to look after you.'

'Ethan? Who's Ethan?'

'One of our men.'

'I don't bloody care what Ethan said. I want to see this 'John'. He's been moaning and is obviously in pain. I haven't seen you go in there to him. He needs help.'

'Someone else is looking after John. As I told you, I've been assigned to you.'

'Well that makes no sense and I've not seen anyone else come into this barn. You're here now. Why can't we look at him?'

'I'm not allowed to.'

'No allowed to? Why for Christ's sake. This is bullshit. I want to talk to this Ethan guy then.'

'He's busy checking on the edit for next week's show. Because Jacob had to go away, he left Ethan and some of the others to deal with the recording.'

'What show? Recording what?'

'Part of the way we make an income is through broadcasts Jacob does every week on something called YouTube.'

'What kind of broadcasts?'

'Just broadcasts,' she said shrugging.

'Oh *come on*, what sort of answer is that? What are the broadcasts about?'

'God, I think. I've never seen one, so I don't know. Now can you move back towards the bed so I can come in and help you settle again.'

'I don't want to settle again. I want to see the man you call John.'

'I'm afraid I can't allow you to do that.'

'Why not? And don't spin me some bullshit about someone else being in charge of his care.'

'I'm just following orders,' she said in a quiet voice, hardly moving her lips.

She stepped back until she was in the darkness a little, but not before he saw tears running down her face. Was she afraid? If so, who was she afraid of? Jacob? Ethan?

'If you don't want me to help you, then you'll have to move back onto the bed yourself,' she said, wiping her nose. 'I'll come back later with a hot drink and some more painkillers. You be careful now.' With that she turned and left the barn.

Frustrated, Harry called out a few more times, but all that greeted him in return was silence. The groans had ceased.

15

Tuesday

Steve, Matt and Beth flew out of Tamworth at 8am the following morning. They had hired the plane for two hours and hoped to cover land to the south of the stud farm. The air search-and-rescue helicopter had already covered much of it, but Steve didn't trust them to have been thorough. Sergeant Booth had phoned them last night to confirm the helicopter would be out again this morning and intended to follow the dust devil trail heading between Carol and Goolhi this morning so they wouldn't be overlapping in their searches.

Beth didn't hold out much hope of them getting a result, but adopted an optimistic attitude for Steve and Matt's sake. Matt was sitting to her right, with one of the maps stretched between them. Steve was in front of Matt, armed with his binoculars, while she and Matt were relying on their eyesight.

As the plane banked over Rushes Creek Beth could see the homestead, stable block, outbuildings and vast paddocks of the stud farm. It was south of this area that the dust devil had first been seen.

In the distance she could see low hills and as they got closer, a mixture of cattle and sheep grazing. They passed over a number of small creeks, whose water volume looked quite depleted, dropping to almost non-existent in some patches. The motel owner had told them the area had been experiencing a severe drought. The anticipated and desperately needed rainfall expected over the weekend hadn't materialised.

'I think I can see something,' Beth shouted in excitement. 'There's a clump of trees near the base of a hill and I'm sure I spotted something red amongst them.'

Steve had told her Harry's paraglider was red and white.

'Make a note of the co-ordinates Matt,' Steve shouted. He moved forward and asked the pilot to turn the plane around and fly over the area again, taking the plane as low as possible. The plane flew on for a bit before turning and flying back. Before it turned Beth could see a cluster of buildings in the distance and what looked like fields with crops. There were people working in them.

'Is the name of the property listed on the map?' Beth asked Matt.

'No, but I'm sure we'll be able to find out.'

'You're right Beth,' Steve called out to her. 'There's definitely something there. It looks as though it was covered with black sheeting that has blown off, exposing the red you saw. I can see glints of metal as well, but I can't make out what it is.'

'I've taken a couple of shots of it,' Matt said.

'There was a pretty strong wind last night so if

something was covering the glider, it's blown loose and exposing some of it now. I think that's a property we need to ask the police to visit. You got the co-ordinates didn't you Matt?' Steve asked.

'Yes, don't worry. And I've marked it on the map.'

'Where to now?' the pilot asked.

'Could you turn again and head further south. On the way back though I wouldn't mind flying over all the buildings attached to that property,'

'Right you are.'

Dee watched as the plane circled over towards the far boundaries of the property. She'd seen and heard the helicopter which caused John's fall yesterday and knew they were out searching for signs of a crash. They were wasting their time as the damaged glider had been hidden under sheeting. Some of the men were due to drive out there and bring it back later today, once they were sure there would be no more aerial searches. Moses was angry that it hadn't been done on Sunday.

She wondered if her patient had calmed down. She was on her way back to him with some vegetable stew, laced with a little something to knock him out. She hadn't looked too closely at John, because he wasn't her patient, but the quick glances she'd taken confirmed what the man who said his name was Harry had described. John was unrecognisable and he did look like he'd been beaten up. She couldn't understand why they had put John out in the barn instead of in their sick bay. Had John really received those injuries in his accident, or had they lied to her? She wasn't sure, but she knew she'd say nothing and just keep her head down. It was the only way to survive.

16

Frank and Rachel arrived at Tamworth Police Area Command shortly after noon. They were kept waiting in reception for a time before a young indigenous detective, who introduced himself as DC Jacko, came to escort them to Detective Superintendent Susan Rawlings' office.

Rawlings stepped out of her office just as Frank and Rachel arrived. 'Detective Jacko, why don't you take Detective Sharp with you, make some refreshments and fill her in, while I update DCI Bailey.'

Jacko nodded and led Rachel off through the squad room towards where Frank knew the kitchen was located. He had been about to protest that he would prefer to have Rachel in on his meeting with Rawlings but decided against it.

'Come in, come in,' Rawlings said. Frank had met the Detective Superintendent on a couple of occasions in the past during joint actions with the Sydney homicide squad. Rawlings had been a DI like him back then. He knew that she had risen through the ranks while stationed in Sydney, but then applied for the DCI posting back in Tamworth, her home city. She was now a Detective Superintendent.

Rawlings was several years younger than Frank and had once been married, but had no children. Word among male officers was that she preferred women. Frank never took any notice of gossip like that, and believed that her sexual preferences were her own business. She always dressed in smart trouser suits and kept her prematurely silver-grey hair very short at the back with a longer sweeping front and a side parting. Frank wasn't sure how her hair always looked immaculate. When his hair encountered a strong wind, it stood on end and looked like he'd had an electric shock. He guessed she put spray on it. He'd love to touch it to check out his hypothesis – but of course that wasn't appropriate. Today Rawlings was wearing dark blue trousers with a matching short sleeve jacket, over an impeccable white crew neck top. White shirts were another thing he struggled with – they always ended up with stains from the coffee or food he'd consumed during the day. He'd taken to wearing black, navy blue or maroon shirts more often as a result.

'How's everything Frank? I must say I was surprised to hear you were travelling up here today for your absconder Wells.'

'I had a dual purpose in coming. I worked on the Wells case some years back. And you might have heard that there's a search on for the two paragliders who went missing last weekend?'

'Yes, I had heard. I don't know a lot about it. It's not something my division is covering.'

'My wife, Beth, has a connection to one of the missing men.'

'Oh?' Rawlings said, her eyebrows lifting in a comical

puzzled expression. He resisted the urge to smile.

'Beth's son Matt, is a half-brother to one of the men.'

'Right,' Rawlings nodded. 'So, you thought you'd check that out while you're up here?'

'Yes, if that's possible. It would be good to know if any progress has been made. But first, what can you tell me about Wells?'

'We picked up shots of Wells and a woman with a young child. It's possible they were collected by a white ute at about 9pm on Saturday night. That's if it is Wells. The footage is not very clear, but he fits the description. And the young woman fits the description you sent through to us,' DC Jacko told Rachel, once they settled at his desk with their drinks.

'When you say it's possible they were collected by a white ute, what does that mean?'

'The ute didn't pull into the bus stop, but it looked like it slowed as it passed it and the three individuals waiting at the stop moved off towards where it might have pulled over.'

'I see. And was it possible to obtain the registration plate of the vehicle?'

'No, but at the next set of traffic lights, we managed to pick up the rego of a couple of white utes that went through soon after. We couldn't be sure which one was the one near the bus stop, but you can see a couple of people seated in the front of them. I visited the owners at their addresses this morning and have eliminated them.'

'Right. What about this Wade Collins? Have you been able to locate him?'

'He was playing at a club in Quirindi on Saturday night, and at another club in Tamworth last night. I managed to get hold of his booking agent to pick up the details. Collins wasn't answering at his home this morning, so I haven't managed to see him yet. I thought we could try him again this afternoon.'

'Okay.' Rachel noticed he said "we". Did he mean the two of them? 'Let's wait and see what my DCI suggests first.'

'This is Senior Sergeant Perry Richards,' Rawlings said, introducing Frank to the uniformed officer who had entered her office. 'He's co-ordinating the search for the missing gliders.'

'Has there been any news?' Frank asked him.

'Our searches haven't produced any results, but we've just received a call from the brother of one of the missing boys, a Matt Meredith,' Richards said.

'They're half-brothers,' Frank told him. 'What did Matt have to report?'

'They went out in a small plane this morning and spotted what could be the missing glider in a clump of trees on a remote property. I called Sergeant Booth in Manilla asking him to make contact with the owners. But he said he doesn't have a phone number for them. He's told me that some kind of hippy, religious group run a commune out there. We have heard of them through some of our local social workers.'

Frank's ears pricked up at this news. Could there be any connection to Wells who had once been part of a strange religious group.

'Are any members of the group known to the police in Manilla?'

'We know a little about them through locals chatting in the hotel bars. Farmers who have bought livestock from them. I looked them up. There was a complaint made against one of the members some years ago but it was dropped. The police have never had any cause to visit the property, even though they've taken in some troubled young people.'

'When you say troubled young people, do you mean ex-prisoners?' Frank asked him.

'There might have been a few, but in the main, the troubled young people they take in are those with a previous history of drug or alcohol abuse. Apparently one of the people who runs it is a doctor and they have trained nurses out there. Some of the social workers we've had contact with over the years have referred people to them. I don't know much about them myself, but from what I've heard they manage to get young people off the drugs and alcohol and start living a clean healthy life. Some of them stay on and become part of the community.'

'Do you know who owns the property?'

'Yes. It's a charity called The Mark Foundation and the property is called Babylon. I contacted an ex-social worker I know this morning and she told me one of the leader's has a YouTube religious broadcast each week. That's one of the ways they raise money.'

From what Frank recalled of the group Wells once belonged to in Canberra, it was called the Wisdom Foundation. Could there be any connection?

'How did your ex-social worker make contact with

them?'

'By email.'

'Not phone?'

'No, she doesn't have a phone contact for them. They used to have a land line but apparently, they had it disconnected some years ago. I couldn't find a listing for them. Contact has been by email for the past seven years. She told me that as far as she knows, there hasn't been any referrals to the Foundation for some years now. Barbara retired last year though, so she isn't completely up to date.'

'And what about Sergeant Booth? He doesn't have a number for them?'

'Not as far as I know, but he was going to make contact with some other local property owners he knows to see if they have a number.'

'So what happens next?' Frank asked. 'Will Booth make a trip to the property?'

'I doubt it. He'll want to speak to them first. What we'll do is take the helicopter out over the same area where the sighting occurred tomorrow morning and see if we can spot anything. Now if there's anything else, I need to get on.'

'Thanks Perry,' Rawlings said nodding at him.

Frank waited until the door closed behind Richards. 'Thanks for getting him up here. Our absconder Wells belonged to a religious group called the Wisdom Foundation in Canberra before he moved back to Newcastle. It's possible he's connected to this group. We need to be looking into the Mark Foundation and see if we can find out the names of any people linked to it.'

'I'll get Jacko onto it. He's the only one I can spare for

the moment – we have a lot of cases on the go. You were lucky to get any accommodation – most of the motels are still pretty full. Many people stay on once the festival is over.'

'Does the music festival always bring a lot of cases for you? I haven't heard of anything too serious this year. All reports on it were very positive.'

'Yes, correct. We've had no murders if that's what you mean. Just a couple of stabbings – unrelated to the festival. Uniforms deal with festival incidents which are usually drink driving related or road traffic accidents. Now would you like to go and have some lunch, Frank? There's a great restaurant down the road.'

'I don't think I could eat a heavy meal, but I wouldn't mind something light. I'm meeting up with my wife Beth later – she's up here in Manilla. And before we go anywhere, I need to check on what DI Sharp and your DC Jacko have planned.'

'How long have you been a DC?' Rachel asked Jacko on their way to Wade Collins' house. Jacko was driving very fast, as though he was in a police car chase. She was gripping the hand rest on the door and every time he approached an intersection, she automatically stamped her foot on an imaginary brake. She thought if she could get him talking, he might slow down a little.

'A bit under a year. I made senior constable in uniform, then took a step back to gain a detective constable position. It seems that's what blokes like me have to do to get into the detective squad, although I've seen women constables step sideways without any problem.'

Rachel wasn't sure if he was referring to his indigenous origins or because he was a male. She'd also made a sideways move to a DC position, but she had known others who'd gone from being a senior constable to being a detective constable and they *were* all men.

'Hmm. Yes, I've seen it in our Command area. Perhaps there's an unwritten policy about promotions for women because there's so few of us. I was about to go for a senior constable promotion when I heard that a detective constable position was coming up. Maybe if I had, the same would have happened to me. How long have you been in the force?'

'Just over six years. I mucked about for a few years trying to decide what I wanted to do when I left school. Doing odd jobs labouring or working in warehouses. It wasn't for me.'

'You didn't want to go to Uni?'

'I thought about possibly doing a criminology degree or something in forensics, but decided against it. I could've picked up one of those grants they give to my mob, but I was keen to earn my own money and pay my way in life.'

Rachel knew when he said 'my mob' this time he did mean indigenous people. Study grants and heavily subsidised courses were available for Aboriginal and Torres Strait islanders.

'Did you go to university?' Jacko asked her.

'My parents wanted me to. I started a course in law, but dropped out to join the police. I met my husband at uni so it had some usefulness.'

'This your first one?'

It took Rachel a moment to work out what he meant. He

was referring to her pregnancy of course. So he'd noticed her bump.

'Yes. Do you have any children?'

'No. My sister has two little nippers, the second one was born just a few months ago. I can honestly say crying babies don't hold any appeal for me. I'm not in any rush.'

Rachel wasn't looking forward to the crying baby part either. With any luck she'd have a docile one.

'So you're local then. You grew up in Tamworth?'

'No. I'm from down south, just outside Sydney. My sister wanted to come up here to stay with an aunt after our mother died. I was already eighteen at the time, but my sister was only sixteen. I'd like to go back down south when I get the chance.'

'Couldn't you get a transfer down to Sydney? They're always recruiting there.'

'I don't want to be in Sydney. I'd rather go to my old stomping ground. In the Hawkesbury Area Command. Vacancies don't come up that often.'

'Hmm. Well, I hope you get to do that some time. I can understand you not wanting to work in Sydney. I wouldn't want to either. Newcastle is lively enough for me. Now any chance you could slow down. No offense, but the way you're driving is making me feel a bit sick. We're not in any urgent hurry and could you also turn the air-conditioning blower up a bit? It's still stifling in here.'

17

Wade Collins was at home this time. When he opened the door Rachel immediately noticed his healthy-looking glow – a world removed from Nick Pollard's pastiness. He'd been released a week after Pollard, but to look at him, you would never guess Collins had recently been incarcerated.

'How can I help you fine members of the law?' Collins asked with a generous smile. 'You are from the police, aren't you? Either that or you're from that Mormon lot – although I've never seen them send a woman before.' His eyes flickered up and down Rachel and she noticed he hadn't once looked directly at Jacko.

'We are police,' Jacko confirmed showing his ID with Rachel following suit. 'We'd like to ask you a few questions.'

'You'd better come in then, but don't expect any tea or coffee. I'm out of milk and I haven't been shopping so my kitchen supplies are depleted. I've not long come home and I've been very busy with work.'

'Yes, I've called around here a couple of times,' Jacko said. 'Can I ask where you've been Mr. Collins?'

'You can,' Collins said flippantly, walked over to sit down and waved them to seats in his open plan living room.

They waited for Collins to speak but he remained silent. Rachel rolled her eyes and looked at Jacko to see if he'd got it. They had a bit of a clown on their hands.

'Detective Jacko asked you a question Mr. Collins. We'd appreciate you answering it, or we might have to take you down to the station.'

'And I've answered his question. He can ask all he likes. It doesn't mean I am about to tell you where I was.'

'Why is that Mr. Collins?' Rachel asked.

'Call me Wade please. I was with a *gorgeous* woman last night and I am not about to give you her name and address so that you can confirm that. Her husband, whom she recently separated from, might get to hear of it and cause her problems. What crime am I supposed to have committed? I can assure you the only crime I've committed in the past few days had been inflicting my singing on audiences in clubs – but come to think of it they seemed to appreciate me, so I don't think you can count that.'

Rachel ignored his comments. 'We're looking into the disappearance of a young woman and child, plus looking for one of your friends from Cessnock; Lee Wells. We believe he might be with the missing woman and child. He was seen in Tamworth on Saturday night. Has he made contact with you?' Rachel asked.

'Lee Wells?' Collins looked surprised. 'I didn't think he'd been released yet.'

'He hasn't. He didn't return from his leave last weekend. Don't tell me you haven't seen the news.'

Collins shook his head. 'I haven't seen any news on the TV. I've been rather busy. I've heard snippets on the radio driving from one place to another.'

He frowned and looked confused. Rachel thought he was either a good actor or he genuinely was clueless.

'Why would Lee do that? He's due to get out in another month anyway.'

'We thought you might be able to help us with that,' Jacko interjected.

'I haven't seen or heard from him since I've been out.'

'Does he have contact details for you?' Jacko asked.

'No. I didn't acquire a mobile phone until I returned home. But anyone could soon find out how to reach me at venues. I've been pretty booked up since coming out. Of course, the music festival helped enormously. I was able to fill slots when other performers let venue organisers down. I've been surprised at the welcome back I've had.'

'Why would Wells come to Tamworth? We know you spent time with him in prison. Did he ever talk about the area?' Rachel asked.

'I've no idea why he'd come here. Perhaps he had some mates up this way, but if so, he didn't mention that fact to me. I know he has some friends who live out in the sticks in some place where they're pretty self-sufficient – growing their own food and all that. I also know he wanted to meet up with his ex and his daughter whom he'd never seen. He thought that perhaps her parents had prevented her from making any contact.'

'I'm sure the young woman's parents did their best to prevent contact,' Rachel said. 'If she hadn't been in touch, how would he know where to find her?'

'I guess he had mates on the outside who helped him. I don't know.'

Rachel pulled out a photograph of Martha and her daughter Rebecca to show Collins. 'Have you seen this woman or child anywhere in or around Tamworth?'

Collins glanced at the photo and shook his head. 'I recognise her. Martha, isn't it? Lee showed me a picture of her when we were inside and talked about her all the time. But I've never met her, or seen her in the flesh.'

'So you're saying you've not heard from Wells?' Jacko asked.

'Not a squeak. Now if that's all you wanted to know, I would appreciate you leaving. I need to shower and then get some rest before tonight's gig. I'm quite worn out.'

'Thanks for your time,' Rachel said standing. Jacko stood and nodded at Collins. They left without saying another word.

Wade Collins checked out the window to make sure the police had driven off before he went into his bedroom and pulled out his second mobile. He pressed the number of the only contact he had in it. It answered after several rings.

'A couple of detectives have just been here. I'm afraid you'll have to tell your man to stay away for a bit. They might be watching my place. They're looking for Lee Wells – apparently, he was seen up this way. Did you know he's done a bunk?'

He listened to denials, protests and swearing, letting the man vent his anger.

'I know. I know, but I can't take the risk. And don't

make contact with me. You need to leave it for another few days at least.' He disconnected the call, opened the back of the phone and removed the sim card. He then went into the kitchen and wrapped the sim card in cling film before returning to the living room where he hid it in the soil of a cactus plant that stood on the sideboard.

He wiped the phone before replacing it in his bedroom.

The question now was, should he move the bag that was sitting is his garage?

'Did you believe him?' Jacko asked Rachel as they drove away from Collins' house.

'Which part? The fact that he was with a woman last night? Or that he hadn't seen or heard from Wells?'

'Any of it.'

'I think he's a smooth character who thinks he can charm the pants off everyone. I suspect the woman part was correct. He reeked of sex. Not sure about anything else.'

'Yes, I saw him give you the once over when we first arrived and then when he noticed your bump he seemed to lose interest.'

'Would it be possible to get some eyes on him?'

'I don't know. It's a bit of a crazy time up here at the moment. There're still huge crowds around from the festival which finished just over a week ago. Uniforms are stretched and I know I'm the only one the Super assigned to help you from our squad. The team are flat out at the moment. I can ask when we return to base.'

'Collins claims he hasn't heard from Wells,' Rachel

explained to Frank. 'What he did say though was that he knows Wells had some mates who live on a rural property and grow their own food.'

Frank thought about it for a moment. 'There's a religious group not that far from Manilla who would fit the bill for that and might well tie in with Wells. Beth and the others had a possible sighting of the downed glider on their land. There's going to be another aerial search over the property tomorrow morning.'

'Shouldn't we drive over and see them in person?' Rachel asked. 'The possible sighting of the glider would give us probable cause to go there.'

'Are you talking about the two guys and their missing glider?' Jacko asked.

Rachel looked at Frank who nodded.

'Yes. DCI Bailey has a connection to them,' she said turning to Jacko. 'One of the missing men is his wife's stepson.'

'A sort-of stepson. The young man's father was once my wife's partner and they share a child.'

'Right,' Jacko said nodding. 'All the more reason why we should approach this group. Hasn't anyone been in touch with them?'

'I've been told that contact is difficult. I would rather we went in person anyway.'

'So you want to go out there?' Rachel asked Frank.

'Yes. I would prefer to head over there now, but I think we'll have to wait until tomorrow and arrive at the same time that the aerial search is being carried out. That's if Detective Superintendent Rawlings will still give us a warrant. If the aerial searchers spot anything they can radio it down to us.'

'I wouldn't mind coming with you,' Jacko said. 'I'll run it by the super.'

'Okay. I'll also have another word with her. I know she was going to ask you to dig up some information on the group. After that I think we need to check into our motels,' Frank said looking at Rachel.

'Are you meeting up with Beth later?'

'Yes, she'll be joining me tonight. We could all go out for a meal somewhere. Would you like to join us DC Jacko?'

'Thanks, but I'm expected at my sister's place later on. I have a few more things to follow up on here first anyway and it sounds like the Super is going to be passing more tasks my way.'

'Speaking of Beth, that's her now,' Frank said after looking at his vibrating phone. 'Excuse me,' he said stepping away from Rachel and Jacko.

A few minutes later he re-joined them. 'There's been an interesting development. Steve Meredith, the father of one of the missing gliders has received a call from the manager of the gliding club. The car the two young men drove down in has been collected.'

'From the glider club?'

'Well from outside the cabin they were renting. Someone has cleared out the cabin. Both the car and the boys' belongings are gone. Whoever collected the car must have had a key to the cabin. They've left the key inside.'

'When did this happen?'

'They're not sure. Everything was still there yesterday afternoon. They think it must have happened last night.'

'So they've made their way back to the club? Has

anyone heard from them?'

'No, they've tried both Harry and Felix's phones, but there's no response.'

'Could the two men have made their way back to the cabin, collected their things and taken off back to Brisbane?' Rachel asked.

'It's possible. But they would have known that they owed money on the cabin as they were due to check out Sunday morning. They wouldn't know that Harry's father had paid for the extra nights. He thinks it's highly unlikely that either Felix or Harry would take off without attempting to sort the bill. It's all sounding highly suspicious.'

'How does that affect the aerial search planned for tomorrow then?' Jacko asked.

'I don't know, but we need to find out.'

'Okay, I'll see if I can pick up any information on that. Do you still want to visit this property?'

'Definitely,' Frank said. 'Let's get tomorrow's plans sorted and arrange a time to meet here if it's all still going ahead. Detective Superintendent Rawlings agreed to a search warrant earlier. Let's hope that's still the case.'

18

Wednesday

The group set off in a convoy of four vehicles from Tamworth the following morning, including three four-wheel drives. Rawlings, in agreement with the Area Commander, had given them a handful of uniformed officers to travel with them to the property where there had been the potential sighting of the glider. They could then drive to the co-ordinates they'd been given and examine the area from the ground. The aerial search had been cancelled due to mist and rain forecasts. Documents had been provided granting them the necessary permissions for the search.

Frank left Beth asleep in the Tamworth Motel; she was due to return to Manilla join up with Matt and Steve later that morning. Steve had asked Frank if he could join them this morning, but he'd refused, explaining that only police personnel could enter the property.

Jacko was leading the convoy, with Frank and Rachel in the second vehicle. The predicted rain had arrived; an unpleasant drizzle shrouded in a fine mist. They'd hoped that the rain would bring a drop in temperature. It was already 30° at eight in the morning so it had brought little respite. It wasn't until they were several hours out of Tamworth that the mist began to lift.

'Sounds like Detective Jacko had a late night at the station,' Frank said. 'That rego plate he picked up must have taken him hours to find. It's like looking for a needle in a haystack when it comes to white utes.'

'I know. He had someone working on it yesterday, but said he took over last night.'

Jacko had identified a ute which was registered to the Foundation whose property they were about to visit. He'd picked it up entering Tamworth earlier on the same day that Wells had been sighted. It clearly showed it with the driver as the only occupant. He spotted it leaving some hours later but from the rear so it was impossible to tell if there had been any passengers. Jacko had also passed Frank details of the Foundation where he learned that the Foundation head was a man called Doctor Jacob Phillips.

'According to Jacko, the doctor seems completely clean – no record of any kind,' Rachel said.

'Hmm. Good to know, I guess. Jacko seems a decent and efficient detective. We could do with more like him on our team,' Frank said.

'He's hoping to transfer down to the Hawkesbury region at some point in the future. That's where he's from,' Rachel told him.

'I see. That's a shame. I was considering having a word with him.'

A high wire fence branched off in both directions from

the Babylon gates which were barricaded and padlocked from the inside as Jacko and Frank discovered when they examined it. Through the fence they could see the land disappearing into the distance with no sign of buildings.

'Clearly they don't welcome visitors,' Jacko said. 'We're being watched as well,' he added, nodding to the cameras mounted on the gates.

Frank walked over to press the intercom buzzer mounted on the side of the gates. No-one answered so he pressed it again.

'*Hello, can I help you?*' a male voice finally responded.

'Police here. We have a warrant to search part of your property. And I would like a word with the Head of your Foundation, a Doctor Jacob Phillips. Can you have someone come and unlock these gates?'

'*What do you mean you have a search warrant?*' the man asked. '*What are you looking for?*'

'We are looking for what might have been the crash site of a glider that went missing a few days ago,' Frank said.

'*We haven't seen anything like that here,*' the man said.

'Am I speaking to Doctor Phillips?'

'*No, he's not available at the moment.*'

'When will he be available?'

'*Doctor Phillips in currently away in Sydney.*'

'I see, well, nevertheless, you are required to let us onto the property to search the area where it was spotted,' Frank insisted.

'*Alright. Someone will be with you shortly.*'

It was a further ten minutes before a four-wheel drive came racing down the dirt track. It pulled to a stop just short of the gate and a large man, with a light brownish red hair and beard stepped out of the vehicle. He reminded Frank of a large grizzly bear. There was a second man sitting in the front passenger seat, but Frank could make out no discernible features.

'Let's see your warrant,' the man said.

Frank pushed it through a gap in the gate and the man walked back to his vehicle and passed it in through the passenger window. A pale arm eventually passed the warrant back to the driver, murmuring something. Frank noticed that the arm didn't look like it belonged to a young man. It reminded him of his father's arms when he was close to death. Loose crepey skin and in the quick glimpse he'd had of it, Frank thought he'd seen liver spots on the hand. So there was an older man who was deferred to for decisions. The bear like man walked back towards the gate with keys and unlocked the padlock.

'Tell the driver of the last vehicle to shut and bolt the gates behind him,' the man said.

'Are you an employee of the Foundation?' Frank asked.

'No, I'm a resident. We don't have employees here.'

'I see. Well, I would like to speak to whoever you have in your passenger seat when we reach the homestead as he seems to be making the decisions here.'

'You're not going to the homestead area. Your warrant is to search within a particular radius. When we reach a fork in the drive, you'll turn to the right and will be escorted to that part of the property.'

'I wish to speak to whoever runs this place,' Frank persisted. 'I have other enquiries to make. For example, a white ford ute registered to this property was seen in

Tamworth on Sunday. We'd like to know the purpose of the visit there.'

'We only go to Tamworth to either deliver produce or purchase general goods. If you saw one of our vehicles there, that would be why.'

'I'd still like to talk to someone in charge. I have further questions.'

'Your warrant states—,'

'I know what the warrant states, but that is not our only purpose for being here,' Frank said, frustration mounting.

'You will not be permitted to venture onto any other part of the property.'

'I don't think it's an unreasonable request to speak to—'

'He has no wish to speak to you. You can go about your business, but nothing else. This is private property and you have no right to be on any part other than what is stated in the warrant. We are under no obligation to speak to you.'

Frank gritted his teeth, and clenched his fists, fighting to suppress a growl of anger. Rawlings had only allowed him a search warrant for a small part of the land. He really would have liked to search the whole property, but her argument had been they had no justification to do so. Frank was at liberty to question Foundation leaders or residents, and to search the designated area but that was all he could do. Now it looked like there would be no questioning, which made him highly suspicious. What did the group have to hide? Were they harbouring Lee Wells, Martha and the child Rebecca?

With some reluctance Frank and Jacko returned to their

vehicles. Once the four-wheel drive had done a U-turn, they followed it down to a fork in the road where two other vehicles were waiting for them. The driver of one of the vehicles waved his arm to the right and set off down a rougher track. Frank pulled over to the side, where he and Rachel climbed out of his car. If the ground was going to continue like this, his car wasn't up to it. They jumped in with Jacko and continued to follow the escort vehicles.

They passed large fenced-off areas where cattle and sheep were grazing. Over in the distance to their left, Frank could see a range of buildings and what looked like people working in fields. They were too far away to make out whether they were male or female.

Under a cluster of trees, Frank noticed the black sheeting that had been spotted from the light aircraft. With help, he pulled it back to reveal what looked like animal feed. There was no sign of anything red, blue or metal that had been seen from the plane.

The ground was damp, but not soggy; there had been insufficient rain to turn the earth into a quagmire. Frank could see traces of tyre tracks and footprints showing in the earth surrounding the clump of trees.

If he were to question any of the men from the escort vehicles who were standing off at a distance, he was sure they would tell him that they recently brought cattle feed to store in the area. He knew that some farmers were having to hand feed their cattle in parts of the upper Hunter area due to the drought. There was no sign of cattle in the immediate area, but he was sure they would say it had been set up in case it was needed. He called Rachel over and asked her to question the men anyway.

'Show them the images of Lee and Martha and Rebecca to see if they show any sign of recognition,' he added.

While other members of the search party were focusing on the ground, Jacko spent his time wandering among the trees looking up. He reasoned that if the glider had come down in the area, it could have clipped the trees, leaving some tell-tale signs. The trees were of a young eucalyptus variety and he was easily able shake the branches on a few of them. He climbed up into one of the taller ones and shook it. A few leaves and something small and red dropped to the ground. He jumped down and examined the red scrap, making sure to keep his back to the escort group. It looked like some kind of man-made fabric that could have come from the glider. It only measured approximately two centimetres square, but would be enough for forensics to make an analysis. He pulled out an evidence bag and, donning a glove, placed the scrap into his bag.

'I found something,' Jacko told DCI Bailey in a quiet voice after walking over to join him. 'I won't show you here in front of these blokes,' he said nodding his head towards the escort group. 'It's a fragment of red fabric that might have come from the glider. I reckon it could have clipped these trees and crashed into the hill there.'

'Good work,' the DCI said. 'Okay, listen up everyone, I think we should move the search over to that hill. Look for any indication of something impacting on the ground or signs of blood – although this morning's rain might have washed away any of that.'

The small team moved towards the hill and as they did so Rachel re-joined Frank.

'Did you get anything useful from them?' he asked her.

'I swear I noticed a flicker of recognition in one of the men when I showed them the photo of Wells and Martha. It could simply be that he saw something on the news though. They all claimed they didn't know them and hadn't seen them. And, as you thought, they claimed this area is often used for cattle. They brought the feed up here a few days ago as they're planning to move a small herd into this area later in the week.'

Frank nodded. It all sounded perfectly feasible. Apart from the fragment Jacko had found, he doubted they would find anything else. And he knew it could be argued that with the dust storm, the fragment could have blown in from another area.

He decided to drag out the search for as long as he could to see how the residents reacted. His team had more ground to cover yet and it could take some time.

19

Rachel checked the mobile signal strength as they drove back towards Babylon's gates. 'The signal's gone again. There was none where we started searching, although I was able to pick up a single bar at the brow of the hill. Then nothing again until on the drive back, closer to the buildings. So they can pick up intermittent mobile signals here. Jacko said he also spotted satellite dishes on the top of a building he could see in the distance.'

'He must have bloody good eyesight then; I didn't notice that. And he was driving.'

'He did have a pair of binoculars with him for the search, but he said he spotted it on the drive down.'

'Hmm. I don't know what you think, but I don't think the search was a complete waste of time today. Although they came up with excuses for the feed load and the fragment Jacko found will be argued away, I think this Foundation group is highly suspect. Why wouldn't they let us go to the homestead to talk to anyone for example?'

'Yes, that seems suspicious. Although before we set off this morning Jacko told me that the group are paranoid about outsiders coming in and making judgements on them. He spoke to the ex-social worker who had referred young people to the group. Apparently, the Foundation have been here about thirteen years and some while back there was a spot of trouble with a teenage girl. A seventeen-year-old whose parents agreed she should go there.'

'Oh? Senior Sergeant Richards made reference to a complaint. Is it the same one I wonder?'

Frank slowed as he approached the gate and waved at the bear-like man who was back on gate duty as they passed through.

'I don't think it ever came to anything,' Rachel said, picking up the conversation again. 'The teenage girl was a drug addict who had been referred to the group and she managed to get off the property and make it back to Tamworth somehow. She went to the social worker's office and initially made a claim for sexual assault plus said that the group had held her there against her will. She later dropped the sexual assault charges. When the social worker looked into it, it would seem that the girl didn't like being weaned off her drugs; they had kept her locked in a house with support during the first few weeks of being there. The girl believed she was there on a voluntary basis and thought they should let her go when she demanded it.'

'Right. Perhaps it would be worthwhile interviewing the girl then to find out more.'

'That's what Jacko thought, but when he looked into it, he learned that the girl in question died the following year. Of a drug overdose.'

'Hmm. It's sad when young people destroy their lives with addictions like that. I wonder if the social worker knows *anyone* who has left the group voluntarily, rather than escaped.'

'I think Jacko asked that question. She said she knew of a few, but didn't have any current contacts for them. She said she'd look into it and get back to him.'

Frank made contact with Beth and updated her on their visit to the Babylon property.

'*If it was the damaged glider that we spotted from the plane, they've obviously removed it now,*' Beth said, sounding deflated.

'Looks like it. They deny all knowledge of it though.'

'*Why would they do that? Surely if they came across anyone who had been injured or god forbid, any dead bodies, they'd call for an ambulance and the police.*'

'You'd think so and the head of the Foundation is a medical doctor apparently. So he'd know exactly how bad things were if the boys crashed there.'

'*I don't understand why they'd cover it up then – unless they were doing something dodgy on the property itself like growing cannabis.*'

'I've been assured that they're not. The police in the region carry out random checks with night searches, looking for signs of cannabis farms. Nothing has ever been picked up there.'

'*How do they make any income then to be able to buy products or equipment? Surely they need an income.*'

'They sell cattle and lamb. They have a largely vegetarian diet and they grow most of their own food. They do have a couple of creeks running through the property and although levels are low, they manage to irrigate their crops without any problem. The foundation leader also makes religious broadcasts on YouTube which raises money.'

'*How do they make money on that?*'

'Subscribers and advertisers apparently.'

'*Right. Well Steve will be disappointed to hear this news.*'

'How long do you think he and Matt will stay in Manilla?'

'*I'm not sure. Steve swears he's staying here until he has some answers. But if time drags on, I don't think that will be feasible. Felix and Harry haven't arrived back in Brisbane and Felix's family have heard nothing from him. We still can't reach Harry either. Matt can't stay off work indefinitely and there's Steve's business to consider. I know Jody is checking in with the manager each day, but still.*'

'Are you going to head back to Newcastle tomorrow?'

'*I might as well. Apart from emotional support, there's little I can do to help. What about you?*'

'We might stay on for another day or two. We're hoping to meet up with some ex-foundation residents. I'll let you know.'

20

Harry was roused by the sound of the wire gate being opened. He opened his eyes to see Dee approaching him with what looked like food. He was hungry, but loathed the thought of eating which would then necessitate a need to use the 'potty'. He'd experienced some embarrassing moments with his nurse. She didn't seem to be fazed by any of it though. Presumably she'd seen it all before while nursing other patients.

When she'd come with her usual bowl of soup at lunch time, he'd been unable to resist finishing it all. Whoever did the cooking in this place was bloody good. It was all vegetarian food though and he was craving a steak.

'Good evening,' Dee said. 'I hope you had a good nap. I've brought you some food.'

'Some steak I hope,' he said with a stupid grin on his face.

'You know we don't eat things like that – except on special occasions. I've brought you some lentil loaf, broccoli and some potato wedges. I need to prop you up so you can eat it while it's still hot.'

The mattress Harry was sleeping on seemed to be made

of foam. When Dee propped him up, she hefted a bale of hay onto the head end of his 'bed'. The mattress then folded flexibly so that he could sit upright, leaning against the bale.

'I'm not sure I want anything to eat,' Harry protested as Dee organised the bed.

'Not that again. You need the food to build your strength. Once your leg and arm heal, you'll be able to move around easily. If you don't eat anything, you will be too weak.'

She placed the tray with his food and a fork on his lap. It did smell good. Perhaps he'd just have a few bites. It wasn't a large plate of food and Dee was right; he would need to be strong when he left this place. He wasn't sure if he would be able to leave with their consent or whether it would be in the form of an escape. He hadn't quite worked out what his position was; was he a prisoner or a patient? What he did know was that it his situation wasn't normal.

In his new position he saw a rucksack he recognised down on the floor. He hadn't noticed it when he'd been lying down.

'That's my rucksack,' Harry said.

'Yes, your friend passed it to our men to bring back to you when they dropped him off.'

'I'd like to see it. Can you pass it up to me?'

'You should eat first or your food will go cold.'

'I want to see my rucksack first.' Perhaps Felix had written him a note.

Dee removed the tray of food and passed the rucksack to him. Harry unclipped it and rummaged through it. His clothes, including his and Felix's dirty washing seemed to be in there. He couldn't find any trace of a note. Why would Felix pack their dirty washing in his bag? Did he scoop the clothes up in a hurry? Felix could be a bit of a slob but he wouldn't make the mistake of putting his dirty things in with mine, he thought. Something wasn't right.

'Happy? Now you need to eat,' Dee said, removing the bag and placing a tray of food back in front of him.

'Why hasn't your Doctor Jacob come to see me, and what's happened to the man you called John? I know he's not here anymore,' Harry asked when he finished eating. 'Has he been taken to hospital?'

'Doctor Jacob *has* been to see you. You've been asleep each time he's called in to check on your injuries. He came to see you last night when he returned. John didn't make it. His head injuries were too bad.'

'Are you telling me he died?'

Dee nodded.

Harry started retching, bringing up some of the food he'd just eaten. Dee managed to place the tray on his chest to catch it just in time.

'I'm sorry. Maybe I shouldn't have told you.' Using a damp cloth, she wiped his mouth. 'Drink some water,' she said, pouring some into a mug from a jug she'd placed behind her.

After a few sips, Harry leaned back against his head rest. Involuntary tears sprang from his eyes. He wasn't sure why. He never knew the guy. But he still wasn't convinced that the man he'd seen was called John. He had an awful suspicion that it was Felix. Felix wouldn't leave like they said he had without speaking to him first. Unless they forced him to go. That would be more like it. Dee continued dabbing the cloth on his face.

'There's no point in asking me the exact details of John's death, because I can't tell you,' she said. 'Doctor Jacob had to sort all that out and issue a death certificate. I did ask, and all I was told was that he had severe head injuries.'

'Where is he? Where have they put the body?'

'I think it's in the walk-in fridge.'

'Has his family been contacted?'

'Whose family?'

'John's family, for fuck's sake. Who else would I be talking about?'

'His family lived with him here. He was married with a few children.'

'What about his family before he came here?'

'I don't know. I don't have anything to do with those things.'

'Well can you send someone to talk to me who can make contact with family members? You should have been in touch with my family to let them know I'm here. They would have collected me by now. I bet that was a helicopter searching for me yesterday. I heard it, off in the distance. And a plane. I know they'd be looking for us.'

Dee shrugged.

'Doctor Jacob said God had chosen for you to join us here. He had a vision of you in his dreams.'

'Bullshit. It was a dust devil brought me here.'

'Created by God.'

'Created by bloody nature. Not God. I don't believe in any of that God or Jesus bollocks. You lot are giving me the shits.'

Dee looked down at the bed, as if expecting to see that

he'd soiled himself. The stupid cow thought he meant literally. Had she never heard of the expression before?

'I mean I'm pissed off – angry with you. God has nothing to do with me being here and I want you to contact my family. My contacts were all in my mobile phone.'

'It smashed when you crashed,' Dee said. 'So we don't have any information.'

'Righto, well I can give you my father's land line number. I know that off by heart.'

'There's no point in giving me anything. We don't have a phone I could use. Your friend will have been in touch with your family. You need to stop making a fuss. It will only cause you more problems.'

'Oh for fuck's sake. It's like I've landed in my worst bloody nightmare.'

'I'll let you rest then,' Dee said, removing the bale which had formed his head rest and lowering him back onto the bed. 'I'll leave this water here for you in case you want it and pop back later to see if there's anything you need.'

With that Dee left him, taking the lamp with her.

'Argh,' he screamed into the darkness.

Dee waited until the officials were busy talking to some of the elders. Checking no-one was around she opened the walk-in fridge door and stepped inside. The first thing that hit her was the smell. Despite the low temperature in the fridge, her nose picked up the stench of a rotting corpse. She'd dealt with enough dead animals to recognise the smell. She edged towards the shape laid out on a table and lifted the sheet, instantly recognising John. So they hadn't lied to her, it had been John she'd seen. She could see marks of injuries to his face, but nothing like she'd glimpsed in the semi-darkness of the barn. Had the shadows exaggerated John's injuries? Or had they cleaned him up for the pathologist? She dropped the sheet covering back over the body and turned away.

If all went well, John was due to be buried the day after tomorrow. She knew John's wife and children were distraught, she'd had to persuade Miriam to take a tranquiliser last night to calm her. Miriam had seen John immediately after his fall, but they'd kept her and the children away from him since. Dee still couldn't understand why John had been put in the barn and she wasn't convinced it was to ensure that Miriam and the children didn't see him.

She placed the vials of medicine she had in her pocket on a shelf and as she turned, she was startled by Ethan, standing at the door watching her. Had he seen her looking at John?

'What are you doing here Dee?' he asked her.

'Just putting medicines back on the shelf. They have to be kept refrigerated.'

'I thought you kept those in the fridge in the sick bay?'

'We do normally, but the pathologist and coroner were in there and I didn't want them to see me putting medicines in the fridge in case they asked me questions about their use. I thought it best to put them in here instead.'

Ethan's face relaxed. He believed her. As she walked out of the fridge, she hoped he couldn't see her hands were shaking.

21

'There's been an interesting development,' Rawlings told Frank when he returned from the Foundation property.

'Oh?'

'The pathologist and coroner were called out to the same property you were at today to view the body of a man who had died in an accident there.'

'Died how?'

'Apparently he fell off a roof while doing repairs. Witnesses say he was startled by a helicopter appearing suddenly over a hill not far from where he was working – it would have been our helicopter, which caused him to lose his balance and fall.'

'Did the helicopter pilot or his spotters witness it happening?'

'I've checked. No. But they confirmed they did rise over a hill not far from some buildings. They must have been looking in a different direction. The doctor they have on site examined him, but said there was nothing he could do for him, even if they had driven him straight to the nearest hospital.'

'What does the pathologist think? And, are they going

to carry out a post-mortem examination? Are they sure he was one of their residents and not one of our missing gliders?'

'Photographs were taken of the man. The dead man was in his late forties, so he definitely wasn't one of the gliders. That has been confirmed. They've concluded there is no need for a post-mortem examination. The Foundation want to bury him on their property anyway. They have a small cemetery there which dates way back to the nineteenth century and they are permitted to inter people there once official documentation has been completed.'

'What about the man's family? Have they been contacted?'

'He had a wife and several children living at the Foundation with him. The wife wants her husband to be buried on the property. His birth family have been notified. The man has had little or no contact with them over the past twelve years since he's been with the Foundation. Originally from Canberra, his real name was Roger Wilkinson, but was commonly known as John at the foundation. It seems they all adopt names from the bible.'

'You say he was from Canberra?'

'Yes.'

'Lee Wells lived in Canberra for some years and was part of a religious group called the 'Wisdom Foundation. I wonder if this Wilkinson bloke and Wells had any connection.'

'I couldn't tell you.'

'Is it possible to have a copy of the photographs that were taken? I'd like to make sure that it's not one of our gliders.'

'Okay I can organise that, but I can assure you the man was too old to be one of them.'

Frank felt his shoulders relaxing on hearing this news.

'Would it be possible to have contact details for the family in Canberra? I'd like to follow up with them and see if the family have ever come into contact with Lee Wells or whether Wilkinson had any connection to the Wisdom Foundation.'

'Sure Frank. I'll organise that for you. Now I'm afraid I have some bad news. Because the gliders' car and belongings were collected from the club in Manilla, a decision has been made to call off any further aerial searches.'

'But as far as I'm aware, there were no witnesses to confirm that it was one of the gliders who collected the car and belongings.'

'I know. Most of the cabins were empty by Monday. There were two South American girls still on site and they reported the sound of a car driving away but didn't see anyone.'

'So it could have been anybody who gained access to the cabin. Including someone from the Foundation.'

'It could have been but the most likely scenario is that it was the boys themselves and they headed off back to Brisbane. Why would someone from the Foundation be involved?'

'Because they don't want us sniffing around their property – perhaps because Lee Wells is there.'

'Your supposition for that is based on a tenuous link with religion. There are religious groups like this all over the country. Most are pretty harmless and don't go in for kidnapping. That's what your suggesting isn't it? That they have the gliders somewhere on their property and are holding them against their will. All to cover up their link with Wells. It's pretty far-fetched Frank.'

'It does sound unrealistic, doesn't it? But if Harry and Felix collected the car and their belongings, why haven't they been in touch with anyone?'

'They're both young men. They could be taking a little adventurous detour before heading home.'

'Mm. I'm not convinced. Are you okay with us following up on former residents of the Foundation? Jacko has heard back from the ex-social worker. She has a couple of names and contact details for us.'

'Yes, go for it. But I can only spare Jacko for another day. Tomorrow will have to be his last day with you. We have two stabbing incidents still being investigated. Last night there was a shooting – sounds more like a domestic incident. A drunken husband shot his wife, claiming he thought it was an intruder. And we have a missing twelve-year-old girl who didn't return home last night.'

'Right. Well, we'd better jump to it then,' Frank said standing. 'I'll go and talk to DI Sharp and Jacko. Could you dig out that information on Roger Wilkinson's family in Canberra while I'm doing that?'

Frank filled Rachel and Jacko in on the news about Roger Wilkinson.

'That's a bit of a co-incidence, isn't it?' Rachel said when he'd finished.

'Hmm. That's what I thought. Strange that there was a Coroner and pathologist out at the property at the same time we were there. Can you two follow up on the names you have and while you're out, I'll make contact with Canberra police and the Wilkinson family. I'd also like to have a word with the Coroner and check out the photographs they took of Wilkinson.'

'You don't think it was one of the gliders, do you?' Rachel asked.

'I'm assured it's not. He was far too old to be one of them. I want to make sure though. We've only got you for another twenty-four hours Jacko.'

'Right you are. We'll get going now,' Jacko said collecting the contact details and nodding at Rachel.

The first name on the list was Joe Sutherland and the address they'd been given turned out to be his parents' home. They told Rachel Joe no longer lived with them. Mrs Sutherland gave her a new address which Jacko made a note of. After checking his street directory, Jacko drove to a small house on the outskirts of the city.

'Joe Sutherland?' Rachel asked when a young man who looked to be in his late twenties answered the door.

'Yeah, who's asking?'

Rachel introduced them, both she and Jacko showing their identification.

'We'd like to ask you a couple of questions relating to the Mark Foundation. We believe you spent a little over two years with them when you were younger?'

'That's right. You'd better come in then. But we have to talk quietly, Gilly's just got the baby to sleep.'

The young man ushered them into the living room where a television was on with the sound very low.

Sutherland turned it off and gestured for them to take a seat.

'I'll just ask Gilly to stay in the kitchen if you don't mind,' he said, popping through to where Rachel had spotted a woman with a tea towel and she could hear the sound of cutlery being put away.

Sutherland returned and shut the door leading to the kitchen.

'What exactly did you want to know? The Foundation were very good to me at a time when I had gone off the rails a bit.'

'When you say "gone off the rails a bit", what do you mean?' Rachel asked him.

'I was only sixteen and was drinking heavily. I kept doing stupid things. Wagging school, trying to steal beer anywhere I could. Mainly from my old man and from the homes of people we knew. Then I started on the whisky. I was lucky no-one pressed charges against me. A social worker was attached to us, much to my parent's horror. When things didn't improve the social worker suggested I be referred to the Foundation for a period of time. As my parents didn't have any money to pay for any fancy rehabilitation, I was sent there. Against my will I have to say. I didn't want to go, but I'm glad I did. If it wasn't for them, I suspect I'd be dead now or in prison. They soon straightened me out.'

'And how did they do that?' Jacko asked.

'They don't keep alcohol on the premises and residents are expected to work hard to contribute to the community. During the first week I was confined to my room until they found something I was willing to do. I didn't appreciate the loss of freedom so I smashed the room up a bit. They didn't blink an eye about it except to say I had to sleep on the mattress on the floor after I'd broken the bed. One of the blokes out there was a carpenter and he took me under his wing. They were building extra accommodation units and I worked six days a week while there. I was eventually allowed to re-build my bed – I hated sleeping just on the mattress. I can't stand spiders and had this fear of a spider coming into my room and walking over me while I was asleep.'

'You weren't punished in any other way?' Rachel asked.

'No. There were other things I didn't like. They don't eat much meat so I missed it, but I soon adjusted and began enjoying myself. I never did very well at school – I'm not academic, but once I started doing the carpentry work, I felt like I was achieving something. Apart from all the God stuff I really liked it there; if you play along with that, it's a pretty good life they have. I had to be called Joseph while I was there – even though that's not my name. It's just Joe. But they like everyone to have a name from the bible. The main reason I left was because there weren't any females of my age there. I wanted a girlfriend. There were a couple of young adolescent girls, but too young for me and touching them wasn't an option anyway.'

'So there's more males than females live on the property?' Rachel asked.

'Yeah. There was back then anyway. Otherwise, I might have stayed longer. But that was eight years ago. Things might have changed.'

'And there were no problems when you said you wanted to leave?' Jacko interjected.

'No. Why would there be? I was only supposed to be there until I straightened out anyway. As soon as I got out, I managed to get on a carpentry apprenticeship and went to TAFE. I'm now a fully qualified carpenter. I'd like to build a house for us and any more kids we have one day.'

Rachel nodded. It certainly sounded like the time this man had spent at the Foundation had turned his life around.

'During your stay there did you see anything that gave you cause for concern?' Jacko asked.

'No. Like what?'

'Anything at all.'

'No. Like I said, they really helped me.'

Jacko looked at her and asked if she had any more questions. When Rachel shook her head, he turned to Joe and said, 'Okay, well thanks for your time, Mr Sutherland.'

'Mr Sutherland is my father, I'm just Joe.'

Jacko nodded as they stood to leave. Andy was the same, Rachel mused. He hated being called Mr Sharp saying that's how his father was known. He insisted everyone call him Andrew or Andy Sharp. That reminded her, she'd have to call Andy to tell him she was staying on in Tamworth for another night.

22

Jacko joined Rachel and Frank for a meal that night, at a hotel he'd recommended.

'How was your steak?' Rachel asked Frank. She and Jacko had opted for a gourmet burger.

'Excellent, thank you. A good choice Detective Jacko. Your Super told me you don't like people using your first name. If you don't mind me asking why is that?'

'I don't like it. Simple as that.'

Frank nodded. Rachel knew Frank didn't particularly like his name either. He thought it too old-fashioned. He'd told her he was named after one of his uncles. 'But it's better than Francis, which was my Uncle Frank's real name,' he'd told her.

'So Joe Sutherland only had good things to say about the Foundation,' Frank said. He said it as a statement rather than a question. 'It will be interesting to see what your other two young men have to say. I wonder if they left due to a shortage of females.'

'Quite possibly. The next two were there immediately after Sutherland. Both for less than two years,' Jacko commented. 'The only female name the social worker gave me was Ruth Ratcliff, and by all accounts she stayed on at the Foundation. This was after the boys left. She was one of the last referrals made.'

'Her name would fit in. There's a Ruth in the Bible. Isn't one of the Old Testament books called Ruth?' Rachel asked.

'I couldn't tell you,' Jacko said. 'I never went to any Scripture classes, apart from what they made us do in school.'

'I believe you might be right,' Frank said. 'There's definitely a Ruth in the Bible anyway. I attended Scripture classes at Sunday School when I was a child.'

'You were going to tell us what Roger Wilkinson's family had to say,' Rachel reminded him.

'Right. Yes. I spoke to one of his sisters. She was the only contact number Wilkinson's wife had for his family. He had three sisters and one brother. Roger was the youngest child. The father is dead and the mother had a stroke last year and lives in a Care Home. Roger apparently turned to religion after meeting a young woman called Miriam Palmer. She belonged to a group called – and wait for it – the Wisdom Foundation.'

'The group Lee Wells was attached to,' Rachel said.

'That's right. Apparently when the Foundation folded in Canberra, Roger and Miriam, who were married by then, moved to the Mark Foundation property which had started up the previous year. The family didn't hear from Roger very often. The last time he was in touch was when he wrote to inform them of the birth of a son. Three years ago. It was his fourth child. He had two daughters and two sons – the eldest being a girl of fourteen. The family doesn't even have the address of the property. They only have a P.O. box number at the Post Office in Manilla.'

'Now that you've established a link between Wells and the Mark Foundation, would that give you probable cause to obtain a warrant to search their property?' Rachel asked.

'Rawlings says not.'

'Why not?'

'The Wilkinson couple moved to the property twelve years ago with one young child. There's no clear connection to Wells other than they once attended his congregation in Canberra. Rawlings said they were obviously a couple with religious leanings who had sought out an alternative lifestyle for themselves. I tried to find the names of any other members of Wells' group in Canberra through Wilkinson's family without any luck. If the names of anyone associated with it were ever recorded those records were either destroyed or lost. When Wells was arrested pamphlets and religious sermons were found at his house which were linked to the Wisdom Foundation, but no names – other than his and his co-founder. You might recall we looked into the Foundation's tax records when we were investigating Wells and only his name and one other deceased person was registered with the charity. He folded it once his partner passed away. Wells was only in his early thirties then.'

'What's the bet that the leaders of the Mark Foundation are connected?'

'I'm inclined to think they are, but we don't have any evidence to prove it unfortunately. I'll keep digging, but I'm not optimistic. We've only got tomorrow to conclude questioning witnesses. Maybe you will learn something that can move things forward.'

Nick Pollard welcomed his visitor with enthusiasm late that night. He'd begun to think no one was coming – it was almost 2.45am. He was expecting a large pay-out for his efforts and a promised treat. He didn't notice when the man placed a hand under his nose to lessen the smell.

'Have you got it?' he asked the man.

'Yes, I have. Here's the treat you were promised,' he said passing a small wrapper to Nick. 'And here's your money,' he added. 'I'll just put it on the table here, shall I? I need to hit the road, so I won't hang about. I'm going to need our mobile back though.'

'Yes, yes, that's fine,' Nick said, unable to take his eyes off the wrapper. The sooner his visitor left the better. He dug out the mobile and passed it to the man.

Nick leant over and took a peep at the envelope which seemed to be full of 50-dollar notes. Happy days. That should fund him to expand his business.

As soon as the door closed on the man, Nick opened his little tin of equipment. A few minutes later he was ready and plunged the needle into his arm. It was the first hit he'd had since he'd been out and had been holding out until he had good stuff. He didn't want to chance buying the rubbish the local dealers sold.

He felt the warmth spread through his body and welcomed it like an old friend. He laid back on the couch and closed his eyes in ecstasy.

23

Thursday

Thursday morning Jacko and Rachel called at the address of a man named Luciano Spinetti; more commonly known as Luc. 'You reckon he's from an Italian background?' Jacko grinned at her as they pulled up outside the address they had.

'In my experience Italians are predominantly Catholics. I can't imagine them allowing their son to be sent to some other type of religious organisation,' Rachel said as they stepped out of the car. 'I would have thought they'd try to organise something through their own church.'

'Yes, I thought it strange too.'

A woman with blonde hair answered their knock. Rachel didn't think she looked the least bit Italian.

'Good morning,' she said, holding up her identification. 'We're looking for a Luc Spinetti. Would that be your son?'

'Yes, but Luc's at work at the moment. What do you want him for?'

'We'd like to ask him some questions about the Mark Foundation, where we understand he spent some time when he was still in his teens.'

'That's right. His social worker recommended them to us. He spent about fifteen months with them.'

'Did you ever visit him while he was out at their property?'

'No, it wasn't allowed. They collected him and delivered him back when he was ready to leave. I couldn't believe the change in him. My husband was reluctant to let him go there, but we were at our wit's end. He'd become addicted to heroin and was stealing from us all the time, desperate to raise money for his bloody fix. I had to stop working for a bit to ensure we still had any furniture left in the house. I don't know if you've ever lived with an addict like that, but it was a bloody nightmare.'

'Luc still lives at home with you?'

'He does at the moment. He was living with his girlfriend for a bit, but after they broke up, he asked if he could come back here for a while.'

'You say Luc is at work. What does he do and where could we find him?'

'He works at the local radio station – on the technical side of things, editing and I don't know what. Don't ask me exactly what it entails – I'm a bit of a technophobe; I can just about operate the remote control on the telly. When he returned from the Foundation, he went to TAFE and did some courses to develop skills he'd learned there. It was the best decision we ever made for him, sending him to that place.'

'Do you have a contact number for Luc?' Jacko asked. 'We'd really like to speak to him.'

'Hang on a minute, I'll get my address book. I refuse to

have one of those mobile phone things.'

A minute later Mrs Spinetti returned with a small hardcover notebook, which Rachel could see had an alphabetical index. Opening it to 'S' she passed it to Rachel who entered the number listed under 'Luc' into her mobile.

'Thank you very much for your time,' she said. 'We'll give Luc a call.'

'No worries,' the woman said, closing the door.

'Interesting,' Jacko said as they walked away. 'So they must have quite a bit of technical equipment out on the property. I'd be interested to know exactly what that includes.'

'Hmm.'

Rachel tapped in Luc's number as Jacko drove off. She wasn't sure if he was heading back to the station or towards the radio station in question. There was no answer so she left Luc a voice message, asking him to call back.

'Where are we heading?' she asked Jacko.

'To the next address on the list.'

'You've memorised it?'

'Yeah. I thought that would be easier.'

A few minutes later they pulled up outside a single storey fibro house that looked like a Housing Commission home. The area looked run down with every other property having piles of junk lying amongst weeds and knee-high grass in their front yard. The one they were visiting was a little better – the grass was at least cut – but there was a rusty old car sitting in the driveway.

The young man they were visiting was clearly not one of the Foundation's successes. Jacko had told her that he had completed a one-year stint in prison on an assault conviction and been released in November last year.

An unshaven, thin, grey-haired man who looked to be in his 60s responded to their knocks. He was propping himself up on a walking stick and looked quite fragile Rachel thought. His eyes were swollen and bloodshot.

'Mr O'Leary?' Rachel asked.

The man nodded. 'We're from the police and we're looking for Timothy,' she said, showing her identification. 'Is he home?'

'You mean you haven't heard?'

A woman with similarly swollen eyes appeared behind Mr O'Leary.

'Heard what?' Rachel asked him.

'Tim was killed in a motorbike accident last night. Whoever knocked him off the bike didn't stop.'

'I'm so sorry. We hadn't heard. Where did this happen?'

'On the Manilla Road. They think it happened about eleven; some uniformed officers came to tell us very late last night.'

The woman behind Mr O'Leary burst into tears and dropped her head on to her husband's shoulder.

'I thought when you showed me your ID you were the ones investigating it.'

'No, I'm very sorry,' Jacko said. 'The information about the accident hasn't filtered through to us. I'm sure you will be receiving a visit from someone soon though.'

'Why were you looking for Tim?' O'Leary asked.

'We wanted to ask him some questions about the time he spent with the Mark Foundation.'

'That bloody place. Worst thing we ever did sending

our boy there,' Mrs O'Leary said through her tears. 'They got him off the drugs right enough, but he changed for the worse. He became hard and was a closed book. We couldn't get him to talk about it, but we know he didn't have it easy out there. All we know is that he had to do hard labour six days a week. I saw him getting changed once after he came back and his back was covered in scars. They did that to him I reckon. I mentioned it to that bloody social worker but she didn't believe it and Tim wouldn't confirm anything, so there was nothing we could do about it.'

This information was in complete contrast to the stories they'd heard so far about the other two men. It sounded like Tim O'Leary had been whipped, Rachel thought. Punishment for something he'd done? Luc Spinetti's time at the Foundation overlapped O'Leary's. So it was important that they spoke to him as soon as possible. Just as she had that thought, her mobile rang. It was Luc.

'Excuse me, I have to take this call,' she said turning and walking back to the car. After explaining what they wanted to talk to him about, Luc agreed to meet them at midday when he would take an early lunch break. He named a café which she memorised the details of, thanked him and rang off. In case she forgot the details, she pulled a notebook out of her handbag and jotted the information down. Looking at her watch, Rachel could see that they had another two hours before they met Luc. They could use that time to visit the ex-social worker. Jacko had managed to extract himself from the sad couple who were closing the door. She quickly tapped out a message to Frank with the information about Timothy O'Leary, suggesting he should check it out.

'Well that was awkward,' he said joining her. 'Was that Luc Spinetti calling you back?'

'Yes, we're meeting him at midday. Do you have the ex-social worker's address? I thought we might just have time to pay her a visit.'

'I do, but I don't know that address in my head, except that I know it's out of town a bit. I'll have to check my notes in the car.'

Once they were back in the car Jacko looked through his notes and nodded to himself.

'Will we have time to call in to see her before meeting Luc?'

'I should think so. If she's the talkative type, we'll have an excuse to make a hasty retreat,' he said starting the car and doing a U-turn. 'Where are we meeting Luc?'

Rachel rattled off the address after referring to her notes.

'Great. They do fantastic pies there. We can have lunch at the same time,' Jacko said grinning.

'You're a pie man, are you? My husband Andy is too. He'd have one for lunch every day if he could. In fact, judging by the stomach he's beginning to develop, I suspect he does.'

'He needs to work out to keep it under control,' Jacko said patting his stomach.

'Yeah. Andy does little of that. We walk when the opportunity arises, but not often enough. What do you do to work out? Do you belong to a gym?'

Jacko was wearing a short sleeve shirt as he seemed to most days. She'd noticed that he was rather fit. He was a large man, but judging by the muscles she'd seen, it was obvious he worked out.

'I work out at home on my own equipment. I never know when I'm going to be able to get to a gym, so I invested in my own gear. It's my only vice, unless you count the pies, as I don't drink or smoke. I'm not fanatical about it, but I endeavour to do an hour's workout at least three times a week.'

'Hmm. Self-disciplined also,' she mumbled. 'Andy and I probably drink too much. We like a glass of wine or two with our meals and Andy always has a beer when he comes in from work. I'm sure that doesn't help. Not that I've been drinking since I became pregnant, and he's making an effort to cut down seeing as I'm not drinking.'

They drove in silence for a few minutes before Rachel said, 'I felt awful after seeing the O'Leary's. I made a judgement about the state of Mr O'Leary's appearance, believing him to be a drinker. But they were grieving for their son.'

'Yeah, they were. It doesn't necessarily mean that they're not drinkers though. He had the look of a drinker.'

'Maybe. I need to stop rushing to judgement about people though.'

'It's one of bad habits we acquire in this line of work. Bit of information that may or may not prove interesting. When you went to take the call from Luc, I asked the parents if they knew where Tim had been going last night. They said he received a phone call and then left. You know he served his time in Cessnock Prison. The same place where Lee Wells was incarcerated.'

'Mmm. Now that *might* be interesting. I wonder if they

were in the same wing. I'll check it out,' she said, pulling out her phone.

24

Beth knocked on Matt and Steve's door. It was already eleven and time she was on the road. They'd walked into town together earlier to have breakfast and at the time the men were undecided on what they planned to do for the rest of the day. On their way back they'd called in to see Sergeant Booth who was unable to give them any further information.

'I thought you were trying to reach the owners of that property called Babylon,' Steve had challenged him.

'I was. But no-one seems to have a number for them. Only email. I've sent them an email, but I've had no reply as yet. Area command went out there yesterday.'

'I know. I wanted to go as well. Can you give me the email address then,' Steve had asked. 'I'll contact them myself.'

'I'm afraid I can't do that. Not without agreement from Area Command at least. I'll speak to them and let you know.'

Steve had, understandably, been frustrated and angry at this response. Steve had also been disappointed when Frank had said they couldn't join them on their search yesterday.

As Frank suspected, the Superintendent didn't think the small piece of evidence found on the property, that might have come from the glider, warranted a detailed search of the property as it could have blown over into the tree.

Neither Steve nor Matt believed that the boys had collected the car and their belongings and thought somehow the Foundation were involved in the ominous silence from the boys' phones. Steve was becoming obsessed with wanting to get onto the property somehow and although Beth had relayed Frank's information that it was securely fenced with security cameras, nothing seemed to be deterring him from this mission.

Beth was worried that an attempt to break onto the property might prove dangerous. What if they had weapons? She'd asked Matt to dissuade Steve from attempting it.

Matt opened the door to her knock and told her to come in.

'I'm just about to set off,' she told them. 'What have you decided to do?'

'We're going to visit the horse stud farm and speak to them. You know the ones who spotted the glider,' Matt said. 'As far as we can determine, their property adjoins the Mark Foundation one.'

'I hope you're not planning an attempt to sneak onto the Foundation's property, are you?'

'No. But we can have a good look at the boundary of their land – if the horse stud owner is willing to take us out there. And we'll see what he has to say about his neighbours.'

With some time on his hand, Frank decided he should pay a visit to Wade Collins. He wasn't sure that the answers Collins had given Rachel and Jacko were the full story. It was too much of a co-incidence that Wells was sighted in Tamworth where Collins happened to live.

As he pulled up outside Colin's house his phone beeped. It was a message from Rachel. He opened it to see that Tim O'Leary, one of the young men they were due to visit this morning had died in a hit-and-run incident the previous night. He'd heard something on the local radio news about the death.

As Frank approached Collins' front door, he could see that there had been a forced entry of both the fly screen and the wooden front door. The main door was partially open and through the fly screen he could see Collins scratching his head.

'Mr Collins,' Frank called out, opening the fly screen door and taking a step inside.

Collins looked at him with a startled expression tinged with fear, if Frank wasn't mistaken. 'I'm Detective Chief Inspector Frank Bailey,' he said whipping out his ID. 'Two of my colleagues spoke to you a couple of days ago.' Frank could see that drawers had been pulled out and papers were lying strewn about the floor.

''When did this happen?' he asked Collins.

'I don't know. I arrived home about fifteen minutes ago to be greeted by this. I wasn't at home last night.'

'Has anything been taken?'

'From what I can see just some cash I had hidden in my

bedroom. The TV and my laptop are still here.'

'Have you reported it?'

'As I said, I'm not long home. And I don't think there's much point in reporting it. It's unlikely that I'll ever get the money back. We're not talking millions here. It was only about five hundred odd dollars.'

'Still, judging by the search that was made, the burglar might have left fingerprints. They might be in the system.'

Collins shrugged. 'I'll think about it.'

'You don't want to clean the place up if you're going to report it, you might lose valuable evidence.'

'What did you want to talk to me about? Lee Wells again?'

'Yes, Lee Wells.'

'I don't know anything more about Wells than what I told your colleagues.'

'Right. I'll come to that in a moment. Tell me, were you with your married woman again last night? Could her husband have found out about your affair and paid you a visit?' Frank said nodding at the mess on the floor.

'No. Definitely not. He's in the army. Based up in Townsville in Queensland – although this is their home town and they still have a unit here. Leonie… I mean the wife returned home for the festival and to see family and has no plans to return to Townsville. Her husband has no idea about our little affair and although they've separated, I don't want him finding out. Which is why I wasn't willing to pass on her name.'

'You haven't answered my question Mr. Collins. Were you with her again last night?'

'Yes. She came to my show and then we went back to

her place.'

Frank nodded. 'So back to Lee Wells. Did he ever mention the name of the property you discussed with my colleagues?'

Collins looked at him with a puzzled expression as though he had no idea what Frank was talking about.

'You told my colleagues that Lee Wells made reference to a rural property.'

'Ah,' he said nodding. 'No, he never mentioned the name. And I haven't a bloody clue where it is, so there's no point in asking me that again.'

'What specific things did Wells say when he talked about it?'

'He said something about them being self-sufficient – but I've already told your colleagues this. He also talked about religion – I think in connection to the group. He was a bit of a god-botherer – regularly going off on one about God – I tended to switch off when he started. Although to be honest, I'm not sure how genuine he was. He was always saying he'd say a prayer for us – that kind of thing. Words are cheap though, aren't they? I know he wanted to meet up with his woman and child when he was released.'

'How did he know about his daughter? As far as I am aware, neither Wells nor his family were told about the child.'

Collins shrugged again. 'I wouldn't know. Now if there's nothing else, I need to get hold of someone to come and sort out my door.'

'You shouldn't have that fixed if you're going to report the burglary.'

'I don't think I'll bother reporting it,' Collins said.

'It'll be more hassle than it's worth. I have another show tonight so I don't want to be going out leaving my house unsecured.'

'I can make a call for you and get someone down here fairly quickly,' Frank said. He was suspicious as to why Collins was reluctant to report the break-in; was there something he wanted to hide?

'Thanks all the same, but I would like to clean the place up, have a shower, get the door sorted and then get some sleep before I have to leave for tonight's performance. If you lot come that will delay everything. I can't afford to miss my show. I'm still in the process of building up regular bookings and re-establishing a following. I can't be seen as unreliable – for the venue owners or the fans.'

'Okay, I'll leave you to it then,' Frank said turning to leave. He heard Collins flick the manual lock on the fly screen and shutting the main door as he headed down the front path.

He was about to climb into his car when he noticed a man in a house opposite washing his car in the front driveway. Frank walked across to him, pulled out his identification and introduced himself. The man looked to be past working age – just the sort who would be home most days and nights.

'I wonder if you could tell me whether you saw anyone near the house opposite last night.'

'Umm. I did as it happens. I was out here having a puff while the dog relieved himself – the missus won't let me smoke in the house. Anyway, I saw what looked like a young man come out of the house carrying a black bag, jump on his motorcycle and drive away. I don't know the bloke to speak to who lives there – he's only been there a few months, but I know *who* he is and what he looks like, and it wasn't him. I assumed it was someone who was staying with him. Why? Has there been some trouble over there?'

'A break-in. You didn't see the man entering the house?'

'No, only leaving. I was watching something on the telly before that.'

'What time was this?'

'I'm not sure. Maybe around ten-thirtyish. I know my programme finished at ten and I'd started watching something else – but it was on one of the ad channels. Because their ads are so bloody long, I thought I'd have time for a ciggie and to let the dog out.'

'Can you describe the man for me at all?'

'Not in any detail. He looked young. He was quite a skinny runt. He had dark hair and was wearing black jeans – I think they were black – dark anyway and he was wearing a black leather jacket. I noticed the jacket because I remember thinking he must be dripping in that. It was a warm night. Oh, and he had dark boots with a small heel – you know a bit like those Cuban style boots.'

'What about the bag he was carrying? What size was it?'

'It wasn't large. A holdall – that type of thing. He put it into the storage area on the back of his bike, put on a black helmet and set off. He was taking his time and wasn't acting suspiciously. Do you think it was him who broke into the house?'

'I don't know, but you've been very helpful. Thank you. You didn't notice what type of bike it was did you?'

'Nah. Don't know much about bikes. I've never ridden one. Too dangerous.'

'Well thanks for your time,' Frank said and began to walk away. His phone beeped again. Another incoming message from Rachel.

Tim O'Leary did time in Cessnock until last October. He was in the same cell block as Lee Wells, Nick Pollard and Wade Collins. I think we need to follow it up with Collins.

He sent a message back telling her he was at Collins' house and would deal with it.

Collins opened the door with a scowl on his face. 'What is it now? I'm waiting for a call back about the door.'

'Tim O'Leary. He served his time in the same block as you at Cessnock. Were you familiar with him?'

'I came across him a few times. Bit of a madman. Why?'

'Your neighbour saw a young man leaving your house last night carrying a bag. He took off on a motor bike. I'm wondering if it could have been O'Leary. What did you have in your house that he might put in a bag?'

'I've told you, as far as I have seen from looking around, only some cash is missing. None of my bags are missing. And O'Leary wouldn't know where I live. Why would he come to my house?'

'I suspect it would be easy enough to find out where you live. Perhaps he thought you'd have a lot of money lying around. Or something else valuable?'

'I don't have any valuables, unless you count my laptop. And that was second hand like my TV. I didn't have a lot of money when I came out of prison. My mother lent me some money for the bond on this place and to set myself up. The money that was stolen was money I had put aside towards paying her back.'

'Have you seen O'Leary since you've been out? He came out just over a month before you.'

'No. He's not the type I would hang around with.'

'Well, he's dead. He was knocked off his bike last night out on the Manilla Road.'

Even though Collins was standing out of the sunlight and was behind the screen door, Frank could tell his face paled significantly and a worried expression crossed his face.

'What was in the bag Wade?'

It took a moment for Collins to collect himself and reply. 'I've no idea. If the person who broke in here was carrying a bag, it wasn't mine. Perhaps he brought it hoping to fill it with money. Some people seem to think that entertainers like me earn a fortune and that we're paid in cash. We don't and we aren't. Venue owners pay my agent and then he pays my earnings into my bank account. I never have much cash around. It's just that I've been taking bits out to build up a lump sum to pay back my mother.'

It all sounded quite plausible to Frank and Collins appeared to be telling the truth. But he could well be lying by omission. Frank wondered what he wasn't telling him. He thought his next stop should be the morgue.

25

The ex-social worker, Barbara Symanski's house was located on the outskirts of North Tamworth. It was an old weather board raised on stilts. Looking around Rachel could see that many of the other houses were similarly raised.

'Is this a flood plain area?' she asked Jacko after telling him Frank was at Collins' house and would follow up on O'Leary.

'Yes, a one in one hundred.'

'Does that mean it's likely to flood once in every one hundred years?'

'Yep.'

'When was the last time it was flooded?'

'I wouldn't have a clue. Not since I've been living in Tamworth.'

They climbed the ten steep wooden stairs up to the front veranda and knocked on the door. Rachel thought she wouldn't like to live here if she was elderly. Access could prove difficult.

Barbara Symanski looked to be in her 60s. Despite her grey hair, her face had a youthful look and judging by her large size, Rachel guessed she didn't spend a great deal of time racing up and down those entrance stairs. The house smelled of home baking which made Rachel's stomach rumble. At the motel this morning she'd only had half a slice of toast for breakfast and a few sips of tea.

'Mrs. Symanski? Good morning,' Jacko said. 'I'm Detective Jacko – we spoke on the phone a couple of times …'

'Oh yes. Come in, come in,' she said her face lighting up. 'But please call me Barbara.'

Jacko introduced Rachel, not bothering to explain she wasn't from the Tamworth station.

'Would you like a drink – tea, coffee or a soft drink? And you're in luck I've just finished baking a batch of double chocolate chip cookies.'

'A glass of water would be fine for us both thanks. We haven't got long – we have an appointment in town at midday.'

The disappointment on Barbara's face was apparent. Perhaps she was hoping they'd stay for an hour or two.

'But I hope you will have a cookie. You will be helping me if you did, otherwise I will eat them all myself.'

'Well, we can't allow that, can we,' Jacko said jovially. 'We'll certainly give you every assistance possible with the cookies.'

Beaming at Jacko, Barbara disappeared into the kitchen and returned a few minutes later with a tray she placed on a coffee table and proceeded to pour them each a glass of iced water. Using a pair of tongs, she placed two cookies each onto small plates for them.

'Enjoy,' she said, stuffing a cookie into her own mouth.

'Is your surname Polish?' Rachel asked to break the ice and get her chatting. Not that she thought talking would be a problem for this woman.

'Yes, my husband was the son of Polish immigrants who moved to Australia after the Second World War. I say was, because he sadly passed on thirty years back now. We never had children so I decided to follow a career path instead and didn't re-marry. I have plenty of nieces and nephews from my husband's family anyway.'

Rachel decided to let Jacko take the lead with any further questions and tucked into one of the biscuits. They were heavenly. No wonder Barbara was so large if she baked like this all the time.

Ignoring the goodies for the moment, Jacko launched straight into his questions.

'Can you tell me how you first came to hear of the Foundation? It was a point we didn't discuss in our calls.'

'Yes. We had a visitor from the Foundation addressing our Church congregation one week. This was many years ago now. Many members of our congregation come from poor backgrounds and have their share of problems. You would have passed the housing estate on your way here. The visitor, a Doctor Jacob Phillips passed out leaflets offering the Foundation as a retreat to rehabilitate young people who were finding life difficult – you know taking drugs, drinking too much alcohol, thieving etc. I took a shine to their leader immediately. He had run a similar successful type of retreat near Sydney in the past.'

'Did he mention the name of the Sydney retreat to you?'

'Yes, he did, but I can't recall the name of it now. I know it was up in the Blue Mountains somewhere. I took

145

the information into work with me, checked out the Blue Mountain retreat and called them. They had nothing but excellent things to say about the Doctor. He didn't own that centre, he was just an employee. But he wanted to start his own community and had purchased property out beyond Manilla. He waited until his place was well established before offering rehabilitation services.'

'You told me Doctor Jacob Phillips was your only point of contact at the Foundation. You didn't ever meet any of the other members?'

'No,' Barbara said, shaking her head. 'I was never present when the Foundation collected the young people from their homes. Doctor Jacob attended an initial meeting with me and the family where we drew up the paperwork. From that point on I wasn't involved except for progress reports that came in the mail.'

Jacko nodded.

'How many people were referred to the Foundation?'

'Not that many. Perhaps about ten in all. It wasn't always an appropriate remedy for some of the young people I worked with.'

'And as far as you are aware, there was only a problem with the one young girl in all the referrals you made?'

'Yes. She was the first one I referred and I hesitated for a while before making any further referrals. Then I just placed boys for a time and that seemed to work out well. Several of the young people I referred ending up staying on there permanently once they reached maturity.'

'What about Timothy O'Leary? His mother doesn't seem to think it worked out too well for him.'

Barbara pulled a face and shook her head. 'His mother

couldn't specify anything of substance about how Tim was treated there, except to say that he'd been used as cheap labour. But one of the conditions of young people attending the retreat was that they contributed to the community in some way, working their keep. It's all part of the programme. Tim certainly didn't have anything to say on the matter, but then he was always a surly, uncommunicative young man anyway. I don't think it worked out too well for him.'

'Are you aware that Tim died in a motorcycle accident last night?'

The surprised expression on Barbara's face was self-evident. 'I heard a young man had died in a crash out on the Manilla Road – it was on the radio this morning, but they didn't state his name. That was Tim? That's terrible. That poor family. They seem to have endless problems. You know their daughter died when she was eleven?'

When Jacko shook his head, Barbara continued. 'Yes, the poor little thing developed leukaemia. Then, because the father took so much time off work to be with his daughter, he lost his job. Later, he was working as a labourer on a building site and had a bad fall. He can barely walk. Both mum and Dad became heavy drinkers, but you can sort of understand why.'

Rachel always wondered how couples like the O'Leary's could afford to be heavy drinkers if they didn't work. Perhaps they received generous disability pensions. She caught Jacko's eye and tapped her watch. It was almost time they were leaving.

She needed the bathroom before they left, so asked Barbara if she could use it.

'Of course dear,' she said. 'The bathroom is the first on the right down the corridor.'

Rachel leapt up and headed towards the bathroom. Unlike modern houses, the toilet was generally in the bathroom. It would have originally been outside away from the house, but then when sewerage reached streets like this, it was squeezed into the bathroom and was the only one in the house. She'd told Andy a prerequisite of their new home had to be a toilet in the bathroom *and* a separate one. In an ideal world they'd also have their own en suite shower room with a loo. But maybe that was expecting too much.

'Well thank you for your hospitality, Barbara,' Jacko said when Rachel re-joined them. He was standing ready to leave. 'If there's anything else I need to know, I'll be in touch. Do you mind if I take the cookies with me? I can eat them in the car.'

'Yes, of course, just let me put them in a bag for you.'

'No, it's okay. They will be disappearing into my stomach pretty quickly. There's no need for a bag,' he said standing and picking up the cookies.

Rachel thanked Barbara and walked towards the door. Barbara followed and stepped out onto the veranda to wave them off.

26

'Pass me an evidence bag from the glove compartment will you,' Jacko said to Rachel once they were in the car. 'And open it for me? Thanks.'

Curious, Rachel complied with his wishes only to have Jacko dump the chocolate cookies into the bag.

'I thought you were going to eat them straight away?'

'It'll spoil my pie if I eat them now and I can't have that. I'll have them for afternoon tea.'

'So why didn't you wait for Barbara to fetch you a bag?'

'I didn't want to waste any more time there.'

'Oh, I see. Worried that the pie shop might sell out of your favourite pies, were you?'

'Something like that. I'd like to finish my pie before meeting with Luc Spinetti. It's tricky asking questions while you're stuffing your face.'

Rachel smiled. Jacko was right about that.

Jacko had downed two pies before the midday meeting. Rachel was halfway through hers before she abandoned it. Eating the two cookies had left her little room to manage a whole pie.

At midday, she stepped out of the pie shop café and waited. A tall young man approached right on cue. 'Luc?' Rachel asked him.

'Yes, that's right. Are you Detective Sharp?'

Rachel nodded. 'We have a booth where my colleague is waiting. If you'd like to place your order then come and join us,' she said re-entering the café.

Luc followed Rachel in and walked over to the counter while she returned to their booth. It had bench seats and Jacko stood to allow her to slide in next to him by the window, while Luc took a seat opposite when he joined them. She introduced him to Jacko and they reached over and shook hands. She hid a smile while they exchanged the male 'g'day mate' business.

'I've ordered mine to take away,' Luc said. 'So I haven't got too long.'

'Your mother tells us you did very well out of your time at the Foundation,' Rachel said as an opening statement to get conversation going.

'Yes, I guess I did. I was lucky. I had an interest in technology and they had plenty of it there.'

'What kind of technology did they have?' Jacko asked.

'Cameras set up all over the place – at the gates, in the barns, outside the main buildings. They had a recording studio – one of the members was a song writer and musician who wrote religious songs. They also had a choir which I recorded a few times. And each week they filmed shows for YouTube which I learned to edit.'

'What kind of shows?'

'Religious stuff. I didn't really take much notice of their content. It didn't interest me.'

'So you spent much of your time indoors? Did you ever do any outside work?'

'Oh yes, everyone had to do a bit of that. Moving cattle and sheep. In the gardens. Or in the slurry pit. That was the worst one – but we all had to take a turn.'

'What's a slurry pit?' Rachel asked.

'It's where the waste goes – human and animal. They had one for the dairy cows – they milk their own cows to make butter, cheese and cream – plus for milk of course. Then they had a slurry pit for the humans. The toilets aren't like ones you're used to at home. We weren't allowed to flush toilet paper down the pan – it had to go into a separate waste bin which was collected each day and burnt in a large furnace they have there. Being vegetarians, they recycle all the human waste.'

'Recycle it how?' Rachel asked, her mind awash with horrendous scenes and smells. She had to swallow a few times to stop gagging.

'It's flushed into the slurry pit and drained. Then used for compost on the garden.'

'It's used as compost for things you then ate?' Rachel asked aghast at the idea.

'Yeah. Or the flower beds. We needed flower beds for the bees. It's not as bad as you'd think. It's perfectly safe and a good way to recycle everything. It's nowhere near any of the water tables.'

'If you say so.' Rachel sat back and decided to let Jacko continue with the questions. She was afraid she would puke up her pie if she opened her mouth again. She knew she was being precious, but even though she'd passed the morning sickness stage, her stomach was rather delicate at the moment.

'So would it be right to say you enjoyed your time there?' Jacko asked.

'It was great experience for me,' Luc said. 'But 'enjoyment' is a bit too strong a word. I had to de-tox first. That was pretty hard.'

'How did they go about doing that?'

'I spent much of the time shut up in one of the cabins with two support people. We went for walks each day to get some fresh air, but I spent a lot of my time alone in my room. They fed me small doses of a heroin substitute then gradually weaned me off it.'

'How long did that take?'

'Three months. It was pretty horrible, but once I came through that I was fine. I was then taken under someone's wing and introduced to technology. From that point on things were a lot easier. I couldn't have lived there long term like the majority of them choose to. Maybe if I had a family – but even then. The life was too narrow. I plan to see a bit more of the world.'

'You were there around the same time as a teenager called Timothy O'Leary. Were you friends?'

Luc shook his head. 'O'Leary wasn't the kind of person I'd ever be friends with. He wasn't the friendly type anyway and not very co-operative at first.'

'His mother claims he was mistreated while he was at the Foundation. Would you know anything about that?'

Again Luc shook his head. 'I didn't hear anything, but it wouldn't surprise me if he was punished in some way. He refused to do anything in his early days there.'

'How would they have punished him?'

'I don't know. I never saw or heard anything.'

'Did you see or hear of *anything* unusual while you were there.'

Luc turned to look out the window as though thinking about Jacko's question. After a minute or so he turned back and spoke.

'Just before I left a mini bus of women arrived. I don't know where they'd come from, but I was told they'd come to live there. There was a shortage of women so it made sense, but I thought it was a bit strange. Then there was the kid from Sydney.'

'What kid from Sydney?'

'About five months before I left some of the guys returned from a trip to Sydney and they brought a teenage kid with them. When I say teenage – he was my age really. Seventeen or so. He was called Benjamin – I don't know if that was his real name. You know that we were all given names from the Bible? Fortunately, I already had one and there was no other Luke there. So I was able to keep my name, but they spelled it with a 'k' and 'e'. Anyway Benjamin disappeared after a few months. I'm not sure Benjamin was the full shilling – if you know what I mean,' he said tapping his head. 'I asked someone where he was and I was told he'd left. But I saw one of the women leaving his shared cabin with clothes I knew were his. Why would you leave and not take your clothes? I thought that was strange. They're pretty closed mouthed there, but I overheard some of the women talking about how Benjamin had interfered with one of the young adolescent girls there and they referred to him as a kiddy fiddler. I never saw Benjamin again. But what I do know was that on the day they said he left, I didn't see anyone leave the grounds at all. It would have shown up on the security cameras and I was on duty with them that day. I'm sure he didn't go out of the main gates.'

'It's a very large property. Could he have got out any other way?'

'I suppose so – I never saw it but I know there's a back gate that leads out onto a different road. There's no cameras set up on that; it's always padlocked and the whole place is fenced.'

'Is the fence electrified?'

'In some places – where they keep the cattle and sheep. Not on all boundaries.'

'Perhaps he got out through a section that wasn't electrified then,' Jacko said.

'Hmm. Maybe.'

'What do you think could have happened to Benjamin if he didn't leave of his own accord?'

Rachel watched as Luc's whole body shuddered. 'I don't know and I didn't like to think about it, so I just kept my head down until I left a few months later.'

'There was no problem with you leaving?'

'No. When I turned eighteen, they asked me if I wanted to stay or leave. When I said leave, they drove me back home to Tamworth.'

'How long were you there in total?'

'Nineteen months.' Luc looked at his phone. 'Look I need to get back to have time to eat my lunch. 'Is there anything else you wanted to ask me?'

'Just one more thing. Have you seen Tim O'Leary since you've returned home?'

'No. As I told you, he wasn't the type I would associate with. He left there after me anyway. Why do you ask?'

'O'Leary died last night in a motorcycle accident,' Jacko said.

As O'Leary's family had been informed, Rachel knew his details would soon be released to the press so there was no problem in Jacko giving out his name.

'That was O'Leary? The dead cyclist mentioned on the news?'

Jacko nodded and Luc whistled. 'Wow. They hadn't said his name. I heard it was a hit and run.'

'Yes, it's being investigated at the moment.'

'Shit. That's bad news man,' Luc said standing and shaking his head.

27

Frank obtained Rawlings' agreement to visit the morgue. An assistant ushered him into the pathologist, a Doctor Pranit Anand, who Frank thought to be of Indian origins.

'DCI Frank Bailey, I assume?' Anand said.

'Yes. Detective Superintendent Rawlings told me you would be expecting me.'

'That's correct. You want to view our motorcycle incident victim?'

When Frank nodded in agreement, Anand excused himself and said he would be back in a moment.

Anand spoke with an obvious Australian accent, so Frank guessed he'd either moved to Australia as a child where he picked up the accent at school, or was born here. He looked to be in his mid-thirties. During Frank's youth the Australian Government had blocked 'non-white' immigrants entering Australia. People from 'non-white' cultures could attend universities for courses of study, but could not settle permanently. Frank couldn't understand why – immigrants from different cultures always made communities more interesting. His grandparents lived in an inner Sydney suburb when he was young and each time the family visited them, Frank looked forward to meeting the 'foreigners' as his father always labelled them. Nana and Pop St. John, (his mother's parents) were Irish immigrants themselves. They ran a small boarding-house packed with people from Europe mainly, who complied with the government's policies. The whole neighbourhood was full of people who had settled from a range of European countries and Frank had loved hearing the different languages and learning about the different foods they ate. His favourite was Italian food which his grandmother learned to cook from one of her lodgers. A couple of times his grandparents had Indian and Malayan lodgers who were in the country on temporary visas. Frank thought them extremely exotic with their colourful clothes. He recalled thinking it was a shame that indigenous Australians didn't dress as colourfully. He felt ashamed when he thought about that now – he had no idea at the time how badly the aborigines were treated by the British and then later the Australian Government. Nor had he understood anything much about their culture. They weren't taught anything like that at school. Kids today probably still weren't. Having since seen and bought a number of aboriginal art works, he learned they did love vibrant colours. One of the artists he bought from explained that each of her works told a story.

Anand returned with an assistant wheeling a trolley, interrupting his thought. 'This is our young man,' Anand announced. 'I've completed the post mortem. He was knocked off his bike and then run over. Had it been a straightforward collision, then I suspect he might have survived his initial injuries. But whoever hit him, then drove over him. Either that or a second vehicle ran over him, after a first vehicle knocked him off his bike.'

'You think it was deliberate?'

'I couldn't tell you that. I can only tell you the facts.'

Frank held his breath for a moment as Anand peeled back the cloth. He'd attended hundreds of post-mortems over the years and remembered most of them. The most gruesome ones often haunted his dreams of a night. In that moment between consciousness and sleep they crept, uninvited, into his thoughts then later might feature in a starring role in his dreams. Beth often told him he'd been shouting in his sleep again and it was always when one of the dead intruded.

'You can see leg injuries from what I would say were the result of the original collision, the impact that would have caused him to be knocked off his bike. He was wearing a helmet which protected his head. He was also wearing a black leather jacket which protected his upper to body to some extent. But it gave no protection when the vehicle ran over him causing considerable internal damage. His ribs were crushed, his lungs ruptured and his heart damaged. Even if he had received instant medical attention he wouldn't have survived.'

The first thing Frank noticed was the shock of thick dark hair. That fitted with the description Collins' neighbour had given him. The man was also quite tall and thin. Another fit. In addition to the stitched 'y' cut running down the man's chest from the pathologist's examination, Frank could see a deep depression in the man's body where the vehicle had clearly run over him. The mere thought of what the man might have gone through made

Frank feel sick.

'Would death have been instantaneous after he was run over?'

'Not instantaneous, he would have struggled to breathe for a bit – but not for long. It would have been over fairly quickly. The victim also has old scarring on his back,' Anand said lifting the body for Frank to see.

Frank released a deep breath. He hadn't realised he'd been holding it for the past few seconds.

Rachel had mentioned Mrs O'Leary's comments about scars on her son's back. She believed he'd been beaten during his time at Babylon. Frank nodded at Anand.

'Do you have his clothes here or have they been sent to forensics?'

'I'm waiting for forensics to collect them. They're still here. Would you like to see them?'

'Yes please. It's the footwear I'm particularly interested in.'

Anand gave him an uncertain grin and asked Frank to follow him. He moved into an office where Frank could see the helmet and clothing items sealed in clear plastic bags. The doctor reached out for a bag and passed it to Frank.

'Is this what you were looking for?'

'Yes, thank you.' Frank could see immediately that the boots had the Cuban style heel described by Collins' neighbour. It was highly likely then that this *was* the man who had broken into Collins' house.

'Would you know if a bag was found in the motorbike storage compartment?'

'No, I wouldn't. Traffic police took the bike. We just

received the body.'

'Okay. Well thank you for your time, Doctor Anand.'

Frank turned to leave and then hesitated. 'Can I ask whether you attended the death of a man called Roger Wilkinson on a rural property called Babylon yesterday?'

'No, that wasn't me. It was our senior pathologist, Doctor Reardon. He's not in today. He only works part-time these days after having suffered a heart attack last year. He's running down to retirement.'

'When might he be in again?'

'Not until next Monday.'

'Would you have a card with a contact number for him as I'd like to have a word with him?'

'I think he still has some cards in his office. Hang on a moment and I'll check for you.'

While Anand slipped out of the office, Frank examined the leather jacket. He could see it was made of a fine, thin leather and was shredded on one arm where presumably O'Leary skidded along the road after the first impact. If he'd landed on his side how come the vehicle was able to run over the middle of his chest? Maybe O'Leary had rolled onto his back in a daze and before he was able to get up, he'd been run over.

'You're in luck. He still had a few on his desk,' Anand said holding a card out to Frank.

'Thank you. And do you have your own card that I could have? There might be a question or two I would like to follow up with you on with our hit and run victim.'

'Of course,' Anand said reaching out for a card from his desk. 'Superintendent Rawlings tells me you're from Newcastle Police Area Command.'

'That's right.'

'What brings you up this way then?'

'An escaped prisoner.'

'Right. Not our young man in there?'

'No. Thanks for your time, Doctor Anand. I'd best get on.'

Frank met up with Rachel and Jacko back at headquarters and exchanged information.

'I'll ask Rawlings whether anyone has been put on the case yet and see if she will put me on the team dealing with O'Leary's death,' Jacko said.

'Can you also look into records and see if there was an official recorded death from Babylon of a teenager around the age of the kid they called Benjamin.'

'You think they might have killed him?' Rachel asked.

'It's quite possible,' Frank said. 'But they would have disguised it to look like an accident if it was recorded. Otherwise, they might have made him disappear.'

'We know they have a graveyard on the property, and Luc Spinetti told us they also have a large furnace. That would be a handy way to dispose of a body,' Rachel said shuddering at the thought.

'I'd like to call on the RTA division who collected the bike and see if they recovered the black bag O'Leary was seen leaving Collins' house with. I'll run it by Rawlings first.'

'If Rawlings lets me work on the case, I should check it out with you,' Jacko said.

'I could look into official deaths while you two do that,' Rachel said.

'Sounds like a plan,' Frank said. 'Let's meet up again later.'

28

Once she'd unpacked and made a cup of tea, Beth relaxed on the couch. She sent a message to Matt to tell him she'd arrived home safely.

The land line rang a few minutes later and she guessed correctly it would be Matt. The mobile signal strength wasn't always great where she and Frank lived and they could be cut off.

'How did you and Steve get on at the Horse Stud? Was the owner welcoming?'

'*Couldn't have been more welcoming,*' Matt said. '*He and his wife were very sympathetic about Harry and filled us in on what they'd seen. We've only just arrived back from there. Dad's resting now.*'

Beth imagined Matt sitting outside the room or on a bench in the motel's garden area near the pool, drinking a beer.

'Did Steve get to travel out to the boundary of next door's property?'

'*Yes, the owner – also called Matt, drove us down to the boundary in his jeep. He's lived there all his life and inherited the property from his parents. He told us before the Babylon*' *place was set up, there were wooden fences on the boundary — as you'd expect to see on most country properties. Then they erected a huge wire fence, which they electrified. Matt told us it had caused problems with his horses, so he approached the Foundation and they no longer electrify it there, but they still have a bloody huge wire fence.'*

'I hope you and Steve aren't thinking of attempting to climb in there.'

Matt laughed. *'No way. After we left Matt's place, we drove further down Rushes Creek Road where he told us there was a back entrance to the property. But it was padlocked. I suspect if it hadn't been, Dad would have wanted to drive in there.'*

'Is he giving up now then?'

'I doubt it, but I told him I couldn't stay down here with him indefinitely. Matt, the stud farm owner, gave us an email contact for the Foundation. It's more than the Manilla bloody police did. Dad's sent them an email, but they haven't replied yet.'

'I presume there's been no news on Felix or his car. He hasn't arrived home?'

'No, he hasn't and we still can't get any response from either of their phones. Dad's pissed off that the police are doing nothing about looking for the two boys. I rang Frank again earlier to ask him if they could put an alert out on Felix's car. Apparently once the police learned the car had been collected, all interest in locating them was dropped. We can't seem to convince them that Harry and Felix wouldn't take off like that. It's been almost two days since the car was collected so if it was them, they should have been in contact with someone by now.'

'What did Frank say?'

'He said he'd have a word with someone up there and see what he could do.'

'Well, I'm sure he *will* do all he can to help.'

'I'd better get back and check on Dad then. I'll update you tomorrow.'

'Okay, Matt, but don't let Steve do anything foolish.'

'I won't.'

In Tamworth Frank and Jacko were on their way back to Headquarters from the depot where O'Leary's bike had been taken for examination. O'Leary's wallet had been found in his jacket which is how they were able to identify him, and an old pay-as-you-go mobile phone was found in one of the pockets. So far analysis of the phone had shown no recent calls or messages that gave any clue as to what O'Leary had been doing out on the Manilla Road. Jacko told him there was a closed petrol station nearby and suggested that might have been where O'Leary was heading.

Witnesses who had come across O'Leary shortly after 11pm confirmed his body was still warm to the touch and that they saw the lights of a vehicle disappearing into the distance. Manilla police were looking at camera footage to see if they could track any vehicles entering the town area soon after the accident.

When he asked, Frank was told that no bag had been found in the bike's storage compartment. But a piece of information which caused Frank concern was that the bike was showing evidence of paint scrapings from the vehicle they believe caused the accident. Similar paint scrapings had been recovered from the Manilla Road at the site of the incident. It was a metallic lime green paint which had been traced to a Hyundai Elantra model. Frank was worried because when he and Beth had spent the night together in Tamworth, she'd mentioned the 2002 Hyundai station wagon that Felix owned and it was the same unusual colour. What were the odds? Matt had phoned Frank just before he left the depot asking if it would be possible to put out an alert on Felix's car. Matt had given him the rego details and confirmed the make, model and colouring. Frank was sure an alert would be put out for all vehicles of that colour, but not for the reasons Matt had supposed. He hadn't mentioned the paint scrapings to Matt.

He shared his concern with Jacko.

'You think it could be the glider's car that knocked O'Leary off his bike?

'I don't know. I don't know how common that model and colour are. But it is an unusual colour. If it was Felix's car, I doubt very much he or Matt would have been driving it. From everything I've heard they don't sound like the type of young men who would knock someone over and not report it. But I couldn't be sure about that.'

'O'Leary's parents told me he received a call before he went out. I assumed it was on a mobile, but if the one he was found with hadn't received any recent calls, then that means the call came in on either a land line or he had a second mobile.'

'That's something that needs to be checked out then.'

'I could drop you at the station, then call around to O'Leary's house quickly to check with his parents if you like,' Jacko suggested.

'Yes, okay. I want to speak to Senior Sergeant Richards.'

'No, the call Tim received didn't come through on our

166

land line,' Mr O'Leary told Jacko. 'It was a mobile call.'

The couple had invited him into the house and Jacko did his best to ignore the strong smell of alcohol in the room – which tapped into unpleasant memories of his father. On the coffee table there was an empty whisky bottle and another one half full. This couple were serious drinkers.

'Do you know if he had more than one mobile phone?'

'I wouldn't have thought so. He hasn't been earning a lot of money recently so I can't see how he could afford two phones but Tim didn't exactly fill us in on everything about his life.'

'I heard the ring,' Mrs O'Leary said. 'It was different to the ring I'd heard on his phone before. But Tim was always playing with it making changes. So, it might have been his usual phone – or another one.'

'There were no recent calls showing on the mobile we found on him. Until we pick up the records from his provider we won't know if he deleted the details. Would you mind if I did a quick search of his room?'

'No, go ahead. It's a bit messy in there though,' Mrs O'Leary added as she moved off to the hall.

Jacko thought "a bit messy" was a huge understatement. He'd had to put the light on as the blackout blind cloaked the room in complete darkness. The floor was littered with dirty clothes and empty beer cans. An overflowing ashtray sat on the bedside cabinet and there were motorbike magazines lying on the desk and floor. The room stank of a mixture of unwashed sheets, dirty clothes, stale beer and cigarettes. He donned a pair of latex gloves – an essential item he always carried in his pockets, before he started the search.

The wardrobe and chest of drawers yielded nothing, so he lifted each item of clothing off the floor and shook it. No joy. He pulled back the top sheet and lifted the pillows. Nothing. He felt all around under the mattress edges and even lifted to see if anything was underneath it. The floor had fitted carpet and there were no obvious signs of it being lifted on any exposed corner. There was no mobile phone in the room.

After asking a few more questions, he thanked them and left the sad couple as quickly as he could, saying he – or another member of the team would be calling back another day to take formal statements from them.

At Tamworth Police Station Frank sought out Senior Sergeant Richards and asked him to put out an all-points bulletin on Felix's car. Richards readily agreed to it as he had already received information regarding the Hyundai Elantra model they were seeking.

'We've already started checking out Elantra models of that colour in and around the Tamworth area. There are exactly two. Uniforms are checking them out now. But with this registration and the fact that there are suspicious circumstances around the car, it would be good to trace the whereabouts of that particular one. I'll get on to Police Queensland also and ask them to put out an alert in case the gliders are still on the road and are heading home. Felix McMurray's family haven't heard from him?'

'No. No one has seen or heard from them,' Frank told Richards. 'If they were going to head home it would have been on the Monday when the car was collected. Or

Tuesday morning at the latest. Why would they be out on the Manilla Road heading *towards* Manilla on Wednesday night? It makes no sense.'

'I don't know,' Richards said. 'But it would be good if we could find the young men in question.'

Frank agreed. It would be very bloody good if they could find Harry and Felix.

Frank, Rachel and Jacko met up to exchange information. Jacko filled them in on his unsuccessful search for a mobile phone in Tim O'Leary's bedroom.

'Could O'Leary have hidden a phone in any other part of the house?' Frank asked.

'They were my thoughts. I took a quick look in the bathroom and I checked out the drawer in the telephone table where the land line sits. I also asked the couple if they thought Tim would hide a phone anywhere else in the house. They said no – but unless we do a detailed search of the whole property, we can't be sure of that.'

'What's your gut feeling say?' Frank asked him.

'That if he had another phone, it was on him at the time he was hit and someone removed it.'

Frank nodded before turning to Rachel.

'There were no recorded deaths linked to the Mark Foundation around the time that Luc Spinetti said that the young man called Benjamin went missing,' she said.

'So they either dropped him back into Sydney, or they got rid of him on their property,' Jacko surmised. 'It's a shame we don't have his real name.'

'I've done a search through birth records of boys named Benjamin around the years he would have been born,' Rachel said. 'I found seventeen recorded across New South Wales. No deaths listed for any of them. Do you want me to try and track them all down?'

'I doubt you'd have time to do that today,' Frank said. 'Let's take all that information back with us to Newcastle tomorrow and follow it up there.'

'We're definitely going home tomorrow?'

'Yes. But I'd like to call on Wade Collins once more before we do. You said you had his agent's number Jacko? It's likely he will be performing somewhere tonight.'

'Okay. I'll give the agent a call. I think it would be good if we turned up at the venue. If his lover is there, we could have a quiet word with her.'

'That's what I was thinking.'

Rachel didn't fancy listening to live country and western music. She hoped Frank would give her the night off. But she *was* feeling hungry.

'Are we going to go out for something to eat before you two head off there,' she said, hoping Frank would take the hint.

'I think we should. We don't want to turn up at the venue too early. They often don't start playing until after nine.'

Rachel would like to be soaking in a bath by then, curled up in bed with a book, or talking on the phone to Andy.

'I can't join you for a meal tonight. I'm on cooking duty at my sister's to give her a break from the nippers – otherwise she won't get to eat a decent meal.'

'Her husband doesn't cook or help her out?' Rachel asked.

'He did very little anyway, but the bastard took off a

few weeks' back. With someone he met up with at this year's festival.'

'That must be tough on her. Especially after recently having another baby.'

'Mmm. It was – especially when he announced it was a *man* he was leaving with and that he'd always been that way inclined. He failed to mention that little nugget of information before they married. It's a good thing he's no longer around or I wouldn't be answerable for my actions. I never liked the bastard anyway.'

Rachel looked at Frank and could see he was as embarrassed as her with Jacko's announcement.

'Right. Well, I'll let you know where Collins is performing tonight and then we can arrange a time to meet up. I can pick you up at your motel, then you can have a drink tonight if you want,' Jacko said addressing Frank.

29

Shortly after nine Rachel was relaxing in a warm bath when she felt her belly move. She looked down and saw it was changing shape. The baby was kicking! It was the first time she'd experienced it and it felt so weird. Perhaps it liked the water. It was the first bath she'd taken since discovering she was pregnant. Normally she showered but she'd been desperate for a bath tonight to ease her aching limbs and to hopefully help her sleep. She just hadn't been able to get comfortable in the strange motel bed. It was rare for motel rooms to have a bath, but she'd been lucky to have landed in a family room where they did provide baths for children. She watched in fascination as the baby inside her moved from one position to another and her stomach altered shape. It made her pregnancy seem all too real now. She'd spoken to Andy after returning from her meal with Frank, but she'd have to phone him again with this exciting news.

Wade Collins was on the stage when Frank and Jacko walked into the lounge, greeting the audience. It looked as though he was about to start his performance. There was an empty dance floor in front of the stage and Frank wondered if the audience would venture on to it or listen to Collins looking like love-sick puppies. Collins, Jacko had learned, had been booked to appear at this Tamworth club for a full week and had made his first appearance last Sunday night. Frank could see tables full of 30 something year old women looking at him adoringly. There were tables with older women who looked to be in their 60s with similar expressions and only a handful of mixed tables. Two tables contained groups of men. A lone woman sat at one table looking like the cat who had got the cream and Frank suspected she was Collins' lover. He nodded to Jacko and suggested they sit at the empty table right behind her. There was a pillar between the woman and the table they chose so Frank would be partially obscured. He didn't think Collins had seen him and he wanted to keep it that way. Collins might of course recognise Jacko, but they'd have to take that chance. He could see Collins wasn't wearing his glasses – probably out of vanity, so unless he was wearing contact lenses, with any luck he wouldn't be able to make out facial details.

Frank nursed a single beer throughout Collins' 45-minute performance. He recognised some of the songs Collins sang – they were old country classics, but there were many he didn't recognise. The audience converged onto the dance floor for a couple of the faster numbers and started line dancing.

Collins finished his set to uproarious applause. He thanked the audience and placed his guitar on a stand, which indicated he might be doing a second performance. Jacko rose and headed off to the bar to replenish his water and buy Frank another beer as they'd agreed.

The woman in front of him sat up, preening herself expectantly, but Collins didn't head straight to her. Grabbing the half full glass of beer which had sat beside him on a small table on stage (and which Collins had taken sips from throughout the performance), he circled around many of the tables stopping for quick chats; offering handshakes to the men and cheek kissing many of the women. Just when Frank thought he'd been wrong about the woman in front of him being Collins' lover, he turned and walked towards her, leaning over and giving her a full-on mouth kiss before sitting down and taking her hand.

When Jacko returned with their drinks, Frank stood and they moved in to occupy the two vacant seats at Collins' table.

'I enjoyed your set Wade,' Frank said nodding to Collins' and smiling at the startled couple.

'What are you doing here?' Collins growled.

'Who are these men?' the woman asked looking from Collins to Frank and Jacko.

'My apologies, we haven't been introduced,' Frank said. 'I'm Detective Chief Inspector Bailey and this is Detective Constable Jacko.'

'Wade?' the woman said turning to Collins.

'It's nothing,' Collins said. 'I had a break-in last night. The detectives are here about that, aren't you inspector?'

Frank nodded. 'That and a little more,' he said turning to the woman. 'You know our names, now I would like to know yours.'

'My name? Why do you want to know my name?' she

asked with a look of panic of her face.

'It will help us with our enquiries,' Frank said.

'I tried to keep your name out of things love, but you'd better tell him,' Collins said, looking daggers at Frank.

'My name's Leoni Chapman and how can I possibly help you with Wade's break-in? You don't think I had anything to do with it, do you?'

'We'd like confirmation of your movements every night since Sunday.'

The woman laughed. 'This is absurd. I was here on Sunday night with a couple of friends to see Wade's show. And every night since.'

'And after the show?'

'We … we've stayed at my place every night since Sunday.'

Frank nodded. It more or less backed up Collins' claims about being with her. 'And where might your place be?' Frank asked.

'It's within walking distance of the club. We went there so Wade didn't have to drive and he could have a few drinks. When did the break-in happen?' she asked turning to Wade.

He shrugged.

'Last night,' Frank filled in for her. 'Around ten thirty.'

'Well Wade was here at the club then.'

'We're aware of that,' Frank said.

'Oh, I get it, you think Wade is trying to pull some insurance scam,' she said with a smirk on her face.

'On the contrary, I was concerned because Wade didn't want to report the break-in.'

'What? Why not Wade?'

'The only thing that was taken was a bit of money. I had to get the door fixed before I came here tonight. That was my priority so it didn't seem worth the hassle.'

'Don't forget the bag Wade. The burglar removed a bag as well. And within an hour of leaving Wade's place a young man was lying dead on the Manilla Road. Murdered.'

'Murdered? I thought it was a hit and run accident,' Wade said, looking genuinely shocked. 'You're calling it murder now? And you don't know that he was the one who burgled my place anyway.'

'We believe the man was deliberately knocked off his bike and then run over for good measure. The bag he'd stolen from your house was not with his bike. He could have dropped it off somewhere on the way to wherever he was going that night. But the estimated time of death would have left him little time to do that. We think he had a rendezvous with someone at the defunct garage near where he was found.'

'I know nothing about that,' Wade said shaking his head. 'And I told you I've never owned a small black bag as you described. The small bag I have which I use for hand luggage on overnight stays, is navy blue and red.'

'*You* might not have owned the black bag, Wade, but you may know who did.'

'What?'

Collins had a panicky look on his face. Frank knew he would be aware that, if he was caught up in the middle of another crime, his parole would be rescinded and he would return to jail.

'I asked you who owned the black bag.'

'I have no idea. It wasn't mine, that's all I can tell you.'

It was obvious that Collins was not going to budge. 'Now I know you weren't too keen on reporting the break-in Wade, but now this is a murder investigation, we're going to need you to make a formal statement about exactly what was or wasn't taken from your place and any damage that was caused when O'Leary broke in.'

'You don't *know* it was O'Leary who broke into my house. It could have been anyone.'

'We do know it was O'Leary, Wade. He was seen leaving your house.'

'But … I told you I had nothing to do with O'Leary,' Collins said looking confused.

'Nevertheless, we're going to need you to come down to the station tomorrow morning. Say about ten am. Would that suit you Detective Jacko?' Frank asked turning to him.

'That suits me fine.'

'You're not going to put my name into any police reports, are you?' Leoni asked.

'Wade has explained the circumstances of your relationship which is why he was reluctant to give us your name. We will have to put your name in our reports to confirm his alibi.'

Even in the club's dull lighting, Frank could see the blush creeping up the woman's face.

'Why would Wade need an alibi?'

'To exclude him being involved in the murder.'

'Shit. What if there's a court case. Will I be called to testify?'

'No, that's unlikely. And the reports will remain as confidential police files.'

He could see the visible relief on the Leoni's face. He didn't know about her circumstances or what her marriage was like, but extra-marital affairs troubled him. They often led to tragic crimes of revenge disguised as passion and there'd been many of those he'd had to investigate over his years in the force. Even during the sexless years of marriage to his first wife, he didn't seek sex outside it – always hoping his wife would change. But he had been tempted many times. As though reading his mind Leoni made an announcement.

'Ricky, my husband, and I are separated. But I don't want him finding out about Wade and using it against me. I've started divorce proceedings. It was him who first played away having affairs with lots of young women. Wade is the first man *I've* had an affair with.'

Frank didn't know if she was telling the truth – but she seemed genuine. It wasn't his business anyway.

'We will need your address and Detective Jacko and someone else from the team will need to call on you to take your statement. Unless you'd like to accompany Wade to the station in the morning?'

Leonie looked to Wade who nodded.

'I guess I could come in with Wade and give my statement then.'

Frank nodded and signalled to Jacko it was time for them to leave. 'We'll see you both at ten am then.'

30

Friday

'We'll head off once we've taken Wade Collins and Leoni Chapman's statements,' Frank told Rachel. 'Can you take Leoni Chapman's statement with one of Jacko's colleagues, while he and I do Collins? It would help speed things up a bit. Jacko's just asking who might be available.'

'Okay, I don't mind. The sooner we get on the road, the better. It's Friday don't forget and the traffic heading to Newcastle will be heavy.'

'I know. I'm not looking forward to it.'

Jacko re-appeared with a colleague he introduced as DC Alan Williams who would be taking the Leoni Chapman statement with her. Turning to Frank he added, 'We have a few sightings of the Hyundai Elantra. It wasn't spotted in Manilla, but it was picked up on the Freeway heading towards Sydney late on Wednesday night. It stopped at the services in Wyong and a man was caught on camera at the petrol station pumps. There was someone else in the car, but the image was too blurred to make out who it was. Sydney police also clocked it last night in the Petersham area of Sydney and then it just vanished.'

'Any chance of getting the footage from the petrol station sent to you here. I know the father of one of the boys is still in Manilla. He could drive over to Tamworth to look at the footage and see if he recognises the man filling the car up. They're staying at the Manilla Motel. The father's name is Steve Meredith and my stepson is Matt Meredith. I have both their mobile numbers as they've called me a couple of times while I've been up here.'

'Okay, I'll organise the footage and if you give me their numbers, I'll contact them.'

The phone on Jacko's desk rang. He answered it, listened for a minute, thanked the person on the other end and hung up.

'They've both arrived. Shall we get this over and done with?'

'I'm pleased to be heading home,' Frank said as he drove down the New England Highway towards Newcastle. 'I can't help but think that our trip has raised more questions than we have answers to though. And I think caught up in it all somehow are those two unfortunate young gliders.'

'I gathered that your final conversation with Rawlings was unsuccessful.'

Frank had popped in to speak to the Detective Superintendent before they left Tamworth and he'd come out of her office with eyebrows furrowed and a scowl on his face. Rachel hadn't liked to ask him about the conversation and focused instead on lightening Frank's mood before they set off. Ten minutes into the journey Frank started talking.

'I just know in my gut that the Mark Foundation are at the centre of it all: the glider's disappearance; possibly shielding Lee Wells, and that Tim O'Leary's death is also somehow connected to that place. Rawlings believes the links are too tenuous to act on. She claims the photographs that were taken from the aircraft Steve Meredith hired proved nothing and were too blurry. I'm feeling bloody frustrated by it all.'

'At least the Super was willing to put Jacko on the team dealing with O'Leary's death. Apart from trying to find out more about this Benjamin character, there doesn't seem to be a lot more we can do.'

'We could try squeezing Nick Pollard again. You said you suspected he knew more than he was letting on.'

'I guess. I hope you're not suggesting we do that today though. I was hoping we'd have the rest of the day off when we arrive back.'

'No, I didn't mean today. You can visit him tomorrow. I'll have to pop into the station this evening but I'll be heading home again as soon as possible. We can type up our reports tomorrow.'

'I've already done mine,' Rachel said, trying not to sound smug. 'Most of it was for Tamworth's records anyway, although I kept a copy of it for our files.'

'I managed to type up all my notes on the Tamworth end for Rawlings and the O'Leary investigation, but I haven't completed the ones for our records,' Frank sighed. He reached out and pushed a DVD into the player, signalling that he didn't want to talk anymore. That was fine with Rachel. She trusted Frank's driving, unlike Detective Jacko's – he drove too fast and she couldn't relax at all.

With Frank she could take the opportunity to have a little nap if her bladder didn't force them to make a stop.

Steve and Matt arrived at Tamworth Police station shortly after 1pm only to be told that Detective Jacko hadn't returned from lunch yet. Their appointment wasn't until 1.30 anyway, so Matt suggested they go for a walk while they waited.

Steve didn't believe for a minute that Harry and Felix had headed off to Sydney and he kept repeating this like a mantra. Matt didn't know Felix, so felt unable to comment on him but he was certain that Harry wouldn't have been so irresponsible as to take off to Sydney without making contact.

'It's those religious nutters,' Steve said once again as they ambled along. Steve was unable to walk fast and since they'd been away Matt had had to adjust his normal pace to move much slower. 'Someone from their mob must have taken Felix's car.'

'If it had just been the car that was taken, I'd say it could have been anyone. But with all their belongings gone as well … it must have been someone who knew they'd been staying at the cabin. If Harry and Felix landed on someone's property out in the sticks, it had to be one of them who passed on the information,' Matt said.

'Exactly. I reckon they landed on the Foundation's property, explained their situation and asked for help. Which means they're still alive. But instead of helping the boys, that lot are keeping them prisoner. I'm sure it was one of *them* who collected the car and the boys' stuff.'

It all sounded a little too far-fetched to Matt. There had

to be more to it.

'Why take the car to Sydney then?'

'To put us off the scent. They want us to think that Harry and Felix took off to Sydney. You know, young men heading for the bright lights to have a good time. Something like that.'

'And why would they keep Felix and Harry prisoner? Why not send for help?'

'I don't know but it has to be because they are doing something dodgy on that property that they don't want outsiders to see.'

'Frank said the Foundation have a clean record and haven't been in any trouble with the police. It could be the boys landed somewhere else and it's nothing to do with them.'

'I don't care what bloody Frank says. It's that mob. We saw what looked like the glider from the plane and they found a piece of the glider there didn't they?'

'Yes – but the police in Tamworth and Manilla said the piece they found could have blown in. They could have landed further over towards Gunnedah. In fact, they could be anywhere in the region. You heard what Sergeant Booth said. That dust devil travelled for miles. When Frank searched the property there was no sign of what we saw from the plane.'

'That's because they saw us and the police helicopter flying over the property and moved it. They've hidden it somewhere. All their buildings should have been searched.'

'Frank wanted to, but the top bosses at the police in Tamworth wouldn't allow it. "No probable cause",' he was told.'

'The police will have to do something. It's almost a week since Harry and Felix took off on the glider. They have to be somewhere.'

'It's not Felix and it's definitely not Harry,' Steve Meredith told Jacko.

'Can you tell me how you can be so positive about that when the man in the images is wearing a jacket and a cap and you can't make out his features?' Jacko asked.

'I can see he's too short to be either of them. Harry is six foot two and Felix is six foot or thereabouts. That man is much smaller. I can tell by the pumps. I'm nearly six foot and I stand taller than that next to the petrol pumps. That's how I know.'

After doing metric conversions in his head, Jacko was pretty sure Meredith was right, but the only way to be absolutely sure was to measure the actual height of the pumps at the petrol station. The pumps were also mounted on a raised plinth; that had to be taken into account. He could phone the oil company and find out that information. Would they have standard size pumps for all their franchises though? The best way would be to get someone to actually drive down there and measure them. Then they'd be able to work out the height of the man in the shots. He hadn't told Meredith that the car might have been involved in a hit and run incident. What had been established was that O'Leary had been knocked off his bike by an Elantra that was the same colour as the one in the video which belonged to one of the missing men. They were also looking for a larger four-wheel drive vehicle like the one that was driven over O'Leary, causing his death.

Faint tyre marks had been picked up on O'Leary's leather jacket. It had been confirmed that the tyres in question were commonly fitted to four-wheel drives and that there were several brands which would suit. The problem was that there were thousands of four-wheel drives in the region.

'So now you know it's neither Felix nor Harry driving the car, will you resume your search for them up here?' Meredith asked him.

'That won't be up to me. I know Sydney police are still trying to locate the station waggon. If they do locate it then it might help provide some answers as to the whereabouts of your son and his friend.'

'They weren't in the car. Someone is holding them somewhere. My son Matt here thinks they could be anywhere from Manilla to Gunnedah. But I think it's that religious mob. Who the hell is in charge of this investigation? I want to speak to them. Talking to Sergeant Booth is a waste of time. Who can I speak to here?'

'I know Senior Sergeant Richards was in charge of the search. However, the decision to abandon it wouldn't have been his.'

'So who made the decision? I want to speak to them. And I'm not bloody budging from this station until I do.'

Jacko looked from Meredith to his son Matt, DCI Frank Bailey's stepson. Matt shrugged and held up his hands as though in surrender. The look on his face suggested he was helpless to control his father's demands.

Jacko suspected it was the Chief Super who had made the decision, but he decided to speak to Rawlings in the first instance. 'I'll see what I can do for you,' he said before heading off towards her office.

After explaining the situation, Rawlings erupted in anger. 'Not another bloody person who thinks the Mark Foundation is behind everything. I hope DCI Bailey hasn't put these ideas into his head.'

'I don't think so ma'am. I heard DCI Bailey talking to Steve Meredith on the phone saying we'd found no evidence that pointed to the glider landing on the Foundation's property. Steve Meredith believes it landed there because they *spotted* something from the plane they hired and took photos of it.'

Rawlings waved her arm in the air dismissively. 'Those photos could have been of anything. And you found nothing there when you went to investigate – except for a tiny piece of fabric that *might* have come from their glider. And you know all too well that was not enough to take matters further. The problem is that DCI Bailey also *believes* the glider landed there.'

'To be fair to DCI Bailey – it is possible. The people at the Foundation would have spotted the aerial searches and if something had been there, they could have removed it.'

'Hmm. Bailey said the same thing.'

'There are links back to the Foundation with Lee Wells and Timothy O'Leary. And both men are connected to Collins.'

'But we have no concrete evidence that would enable me to obtain a search warrant,' Rawlings sighed. 'My hands are tied. I hope you haven't mentioned the glider's car is suspected of knocking down O'Leary?'

'Of course not. Steve Meredith thinks we're searching for the car in the hope that it will lead to the young men'

'Righto. You'd better send him in to see me then.'

'I know you're not happy with what the Superintendent said, but can you see her point of view Dad? They can't spend thousands of dollars looking for two missing paragliders when their car and belongings have been collected.'

'I do understand that. But *we* know it wasn't Harry or Felix who collected them.'

'They've at least agreed to put a broadcast out on the radio along with photos of the boys and their car on television. I thought it was quite generous of them.'

31

Saturday

Frank arrived at the station shortly after 9am. He'd breakfasted with Beth, then apologised, explaining that he had to go into work today. It would give him time to finish typing up his reports before Rachel arrived. He'd told her that she could have a sleep-in and arranged to meet her at the station at 11am. Once he'd settled into his office, he found himself staring at the blank computer screen for ages, mulling over everything in his mind. After a while he checked his watch. Almost an hour had passed. How had that happened? He switched the computer on and berated himself – he'd have to get a move on.

Andy had spoilt Rachel rotten last night and again this morning, and they were enjoying a leisurely breakfast he'd cooked out in their back courtyard. He'd lined up some properties for them to see today and was disappointed that she had to go to work.

'You check them out Andy. You know what we're looking for. If there's anything you think worth following up on, we can make another appointment.'

'It's not the same looking at them on your own. I'd rather you were with me.'

'Well we could leave it for another week then. They're only open house viewings. It's not like you have to cancel appointments. I should be able to have tomorrow off and we can drive around some of the locations and see what we think.'

'Okay, I think that'd be best. I'll give Brian a bell, he's bound to have one of the English football matches recorded and I know that's what he likes to do on a Saturday afternoon. I really hope we find a property that has outside covered areas like he has with the TV and barbie. If we can't find a house that already has it, we'll have to build it.'

'Great, so then you can spend Saturday afternoons watching a match and drinking beers instead of interacting with your family.'

'No – well, it wouldn't only be for that. It would have a multi-purpose use. A place for the kids to play out of the searing heat, or when it's raining.'

She noticed he said kids. Plural. Rachel knew Andy was keen to have more than one child. As an only child he'd hated growing up without siblings. Rachel had a brother and a sister – not that they'd been especially close. Her twin siblings were twelve years older than her and seldom spent any time playing with her as a child. If Rachel spoke to Laurel or Leo, they'd pat her head dismissively and walk off. If she didn't make her presence known it was as though she was invisible. She may as well have been an only child. They'd have to think about age gaps between any children they had. If Andy had his way, they'd have one after the other. Looking after two very young children close in age would be a nightmare in her view. She'd prefer a reasonable gap so that she didn't miss out on promotions at work. Fortunately, she'd been promoted to her current rank before she discovered she was pregnant. She didn't have great ambitions – she wasn't looking to become a Superintendent or Chief Superintendent – not if she had children. She'd be happy to make it to a DCI rank. Rachel sighed, thanked Andy for the breakfast and headed off to the bathroom.

He was rinsing plates preparing for washing them when she returned, ready to leave.

'Right, well I'm off then. Enjoy your afternoon and I'll see you tonight,' she said leaning over to kiss him.

'Mm. Love your minty breath,' he murmured. 'It doesn't exactly mix well with bacon and eggs though, does it?'

She punched him on the arm and gave him a huge grin before turning and leaving.

'Ryan's on duty this morning. I've warned him that he will be going to visit Nick Pollard with you again,' Frank said. 'He didn't seem too keen.'

'I'm not surprised. The smell can't be any worse than last time though. At least, this time, we'll know what to expect. I didn't see Ryan when I arrived.'

'I think he's popped up to the canteen to get a sandwich.'

'Okay, we'll head off as soon as he gets back. Any news from Jacko?'

'Yes, Steve Meredith claimed it wasn't his son or his son's friend who was caught on camera at the services.

190

Meredith insisted the man was too short. Jacko's asked if someone can go down there and measure the petrol pumps.'

'Surely he could get that information from the garage itself?'

'Jacko doesn't trust them to give us accurate measurements.'

'Right. Do you have someone in mind for the job?' Rachel asked, hoping he wasn't about to say she could do it.

'I thought young Ryan could do it after you've been to Pollard's. It doesn't need two people for the job. I mentioned it to him and he's quite willing. It'll be a nice mindless task for him.'

'Any news on the glider's car?'

'The boys and the car were featured on the news last night in Tamworth. Sydney ran it also apparently, as the car was last seen down there. A few reports have come in on the car. Nothing on the men. They're looking into the car sightings and Tamworth are still trawling through CCTV looking for it from the time it left the Glider Club to when it potentially hit O'Leary.'

'Why hadn't they done that already?'

'They only started looking at the CCTV yesterday after the reports came in about it being the possible vehicle involved in the incident with O'Leary. It wasn't considered necessary when they thought Harry and Felix had collected the car and their belongings.'

'Has Harry's father been told about the car possibly being the one which hit O'Leary?' Rachel asked.

'No, and I haven't mentioned anything to Beth either,

in case you're wondering.'

'I didn't think for a moment you would have.'

When there were on-going investigations, they weren't supposed to discuss details of it with anyone outside the team. Press publicity might reveal basic information that they could mention to family. Andy never pressed her for any details but would often ask her if she was involved in the investigation of a particular crime. Her response was only ever 'yes' or 'no'. She imagined Frank would do the same with Beth or other family members.

'They'll have to tell Harry's father and young Felix's family at some point, if, or when the car is found. Ah, here's Ryan. Best get off and see Pollard, then you can go home after.'

When they reached Pollard's place, a couple of people were standing around the residents' car park out the front, one of them pointing towards Pollard's flat. The block was a low rise with a total of three levels. A stairwell ran up beside Pollard's flat on the ground floor. Each flat on the upper levels was entered from a long walkway that ran across the front of the building. The ground floor flats opened on to a narrow footpath in front of the residents' car park.

'Have you come to deal with the smell in that bastard's place?' one of the group asked Rachel as they approached them.

'Um, not especially,' she said.

'Well something should be done about it. He's a disgrace, the dirty bugger. He has all the windows closed but you can still smell it out here.'

Rachel was instantly on the alert. When they'd visited Pollard last Monday, the smell of his place only hit them once the door was opened. It was unusual for it to permeate through closed windows and doors unless … She walked towards Pollard's flat and as she was within a few feet of it the smell hit her causing her to gag. Clamping a hand over her mouth she stepped back and warned Ryan not to come any closer.

'You can't see anything in there. I've looked,' a woman from the group called out. 'He's got all the curtains and blinds shut. I've checked around the back as well. And he's not answering the door. I don't think he's home and I suspect he's left some food rotting in there. It'll attract vermin.'

'How long has it smelled this bad?' she asked the woman.

'It started yesterday morning. And it just seems to be getting worse. We were just discussing whether to call the police or someone who deals with health hazards.'

'We are the police,' she informed them. 'We'll deal with it.'

Rachel pulled out her phone. They'd need back up, a pathologist and forensics if what she suspected was correct. The smell wasn't rotten food – it was a decomposing body. She'd smelled enough of them in her time.

Frank arrived the same time as a group of uniforms. Masked uniformed officers smashed the front door in and entered. Swarms of flies followed them out as they retreated nodding at Frank and Rachel.

Rachel turned away and made a call.

'He's dead sir,' a sergeant confirmed.

'Could you see any obvious injuries?'

'No sir. He's just lying there on his couch as though he's gone to sleep – but there is a needle on the coffee table next to him. Looks like an overdose.'

'Or perhaps that's what someone wants us to think. Damn. Forensics need to go over the place – I want a thorough search done. You've called them and the pathologist haven't you DI Sharp?'

'Yes sir,' Rachel said. 'They were just waiting for my confirmation which I've now given them. They'll be here shortly.' She and Frank used a more formal address in the presence of others.

Frank sent Ryan off with a couple of uniformed officers to collect a car from Headquarters so he could drive to the services on the M1. He'd asked Rachel to remain with him and while they'd been waiting for the pathologist to complete his examination, she'd been taking details from some of the neighbours. Doctor Hayes joined them in the car park, a large section of which was now cordoned off.

'Looks like a classic overdose case,' Hayes said. 'But I'll know more when I get him on the table and his bloods have been analysed.'

'How long has he been lying in there like that?'

'A couple of days plus. I'd say approximately 55 – 60 hours. Rigor mortis has been and gone. The maggots have hatched. But decomposition will have been accelerated by the heat in there as all the windows were closed.'

Frank nodded. That placed time of death very late on Wednesday night or in the early hours of Thursday morning.

'When do you think you might be able to do the post-mortem?'

'I'm off tomorrow and I have a couple to complete this afternoon. Shall we say Monday 10am? Will you be attending?'

'I might accompany DI Sharp, but one, or both of us will be there.'

Hayes nodded and left.

The techs had given them a couple of protective suits so once the body was removed Frank persuaded Rachel to suit up and join him in the flat. With the body gone, the worst of the smell had dissipated. But even with strong eucalyptus oil under his nose and the mask, he could still smell it. He knew Rachel was sensitive to smells – particularly so since her pregnancy so he turned to see if she was okay. She gave him a thumbs up so he continued into the flat.

One of the techs who'd been photographing everything, showed them the images of Pollard.

'He died with a smile of his face,' he said.

Even with decomposition of the body, and an open mouth, a faint smile was still visible on Pollard's face.

'What's this?' Frank asked pointing to one of the evidence bags the tech had on the coffee table.

'An envelope of money. I say that – there were a few fifty-dollar notes at the top of the pile, but the rest were sheets of cut up blank paper – I suspect made to look as if it was full of notes.'

'Hmm. Did you find any drugs on the premises?' Frank asked.

'A small amount of cannabis leaf in the kitchen and, here on the coffee table, an empty wrapper of what might be heroin which we suspect is what he injected into himself. That's all. Plenty of empty bottles of spirits and tins of beer though,' the tech said.

'Once you've analysed the remnants in the wrapper, can you get onto the drug squad to see if they are able to match it to any batches they've picked up in the region?'

'Sure.'

'Was there a mobile phone?'

'Yes. We have it bagged up.'

'Right, well I don't think there's a lot more we can do here,' Frank said turning to Rachel. 'I think we should head back to the station. We need to track down Pollard's next of kin. Prison records should have those details.'

He could see from the way Rachel's eyes lit up and her eager nod that she welcomed the idea.

32

Frank asked Rachel to join him in his office. He wanted to know her thoughts on Pollard's death. They'd spoken little on the ten-minute drive back to the station, except to comment on the smell and state of Pollard's place. Before Rachel made it through the door, she held up a hand and rushed off, excusing herself.

'Are you okay?' he asked her when she reappeared. 'You haven't been sick, have you?'

'No. I desperately needed the bathroom – it's one of the problems I've encountered since being pregnant that I need to go more often. Plus, I needed a glass of water. The smell at Pollard's was stuck in my throat.'

'Hmm. I've made us some coffee. Thought we could do with it after Pollard's place. I made sure they were clean mugs – pulling them straight out of the dishwasher,' he added. Fed up with team members not taking the time to wash their dirty mugs, Frank had used part of their budget to have a dishwasher installed when the kitchen was refurbished. He'd argued the case on health and safety grounds with his superiors. It was paying off. The number of sick days among members of the squad had dramatically reduced.

'I was thinking that Wade Collins' life might be in danger if he has had any involvement in whatever is going on,' Frank said.

'Yes, you're probably right. We should ring Jacko and get him to pay Collins another visit. See if a second death of one of his fellow inmates might scare him into talking.'

'I've left a message for Jacko to call me.'

Rachel nodded. 'Before you arrived Ryan and I checked for cameras that might be in the area. Unfortunately, there aren't any outside Pollard's flat or in the residents' car park, and we couldn't spot any CCTV nearby. But when Ryan walked around the block, he found a security camera attached to a business premises in a nearby street. They weren't open today and it might not give us anything, but I can send Ryan back there on Monday to check it out.'

'Okay, that's good. We know approximately *when* Pollard died, but what we don't know is when the heroin – if that's what it was, came into his possession. He could have had it for days, saving it as a special treat. Or it might have been delivered to him with the envelope of money any time on Wednesday during the day or late that night.'

'Neighbours we spoke to didn't see anyone at his door. With Pollard being a former addict, I would have thought he would have been keen to sample the goods pretty soon after receiving it.'

'Hmm. You may be right – and *sample* might be the key word here. Maybe what he injected himself with was a sample of a larger delivery he was expecting. And that envelope of money and blank sheets, indicates payment for something – either to buy goods or for something he did on behalf of someone else. I'm inclined to think the latter is more likely as the envelope wasn't full of notes. I suspect he was fooled into believing it was. Which makes Pollard's death highly suspicious.'

'Yes,' Rachel agreed. 'A killer wouldn't want to waste a large amount of money on someone who they knew would soon be dead.'

'Hmm. I was working out the time frame as we drove back to the station. It would have been possible for whoever killed O'Leary to then drive on to Newcastle and take care of Pollard.'

'Tying up loose ends you think?'

'Quite possibly,' Frank said nodding. 'I still think that Pollard had something to do with supplying the drugs that Wells used on his sister and brother-in-law. So that leads us back to Wells again.'

'I can't imagine Wells would take the risk of travelling to Newcastle to deal with Pollard. He must know that we'd be looking for him and possibly watching known associates' places.'

'He would be aware of that – but he might have sent someone else to do his dirty work. Characters like Pollard aren't very reliable. Perhaps he couldn't be trusted. It was an oversight on my part – I should have put surveillance on Pollard's place. But I was caught up with the sighting of Wells in Tamworth. Whilst I believed Pollard might have aided Wells in his escape plan down here, I thought him too insignificant a player to be of any further use to Wells. I took my eye off the ball and now a man is dead.'

Rachel was tempted to say that men like Pollard seemed

to have a death wish anyway – but she knew it wouldn't be helpful. Instead, she said, 'There's no point in beating yourself up about it. It won't help us move our investigation forward.'

'No, you're right. I'll try Jacko again. You may as well go home. Have tomorrow off. We won't get the lab reports until Monday at the earliest anyway; the post-mortem is then. I'll wait here for Ryan to return with his measurements and pass that information onto Jacko also.'

'Are you sure Frank? What about notifying Pollards next of kin? I can stay longer if you want.'

'No, there's no need for both of us to stay. I *have* to stay to check in with Tyler and Rogers to see what progress they've made with the investigation I put them onto on to before we headed up to Tamworth. I know you were planning to look at houses this weekend. If you're going to find one and settle into before the baby is born, then you need to get a move on with your search. I'll check out Pollard's next of kin and get some uniforms to notify them of his death.'

'Okay. Thanks Frank. I would like to be in our new house before the baby comes. I'll see you on Monday then,' Rachel said, standing to leave.

When Harry woke, he could tell that the plaster cast on his leg had been removed and his leg was no longer elevated. When had they done that? He couldn't remember a thing. Pulling back the sheet he saw that his leg below the knee was covered with a bandage. His arm was still encased in plaster so he wondered why the leg cast had been removed. Normally they stayed on for about 6 weeks if his memory served him correctly. Felix had broken his foot last year on a bad landing and his plaster had stayed on for 6 weeks, driving him mad because it was so itchy. He kept borrowing his mother's knitting needles to scratch inside the cast.

With the plaster cast gone, movement was easier. He swung himself out of bed and practised standing on his good leg. Apart from the twinges of pain that still plagued his side, standing proved to be no big issue. Good – that meant he'd be able to make use of the bucket without assistance for at least one of his needs. He reached out to make use of it right away not caring if someone was watching him on camera.

After carefully placing the bucket back down, he decided to try and put weight on his damaged leg. The pain was excruciating and the leg collapsed under him. No, he definitely wasn't ready for that. He sunk back onto his bed, moaning and feeling sorry for himself. He could see daylight through the slits of wood in the barn but it was still dark inside with the barn doors shut and so little natural light. He wished they'd leave him with one of the lamps at night, but Dee said it was too risky. Risky for whom?

Speaking of Dee, he saw her hurrying in towards him and this time she had a wheelchair with her. It gave him a spark of hope. She stood outside his cage while she addressed him.

'Now your leg plaster is off I thought you might like some fresh air,' she said. 'Jacob said it would be good for you.'

Harry was sick to death of hearing Jacob's name. The

ghostly figure who controlled everything about him, whom he still hadn't met. Although he *had* received a visit from the man called Ethan who emphasised that Harry had to show a willingness to remain on the farm when he did meet Jacob. To ensure his *safety* was how he'd put it. But Harry had read an implied threat in Ethan's words and body language.

'I would like some fresh air, but tell me why did you remove my leg plaster? I thought they stayed on for about six weeks.'

'If you had just had a broken bone, then that would have been the case. But you have a nasty wound and Jacob had to perform surgery. We had to remove the cast to be able to check the wound and apply fresh dressings. It really should have come off days ago.'

'So why put the plaster on in the first place?'

'To ensure you didn't damage your leg further.'

'Right. And my arm?'

'No that cast needs to remain on. Would you like to go for a walk?'

'Yes, I would, thanks. And maybe meet some of the other residents who live here with you.'

'Most of them will be busy this afternoon. It's John's burial service.'

'He's being buried on your farm?'

'Yes, there's a graveyard that's been here for a very long time. We're allowed to bury our people there.'

'And how many have you had to bury since you've lived here?'

'Only a handful. We live a very healthy lifestyle.'

'Right. I know. No meat except at Easter and Christmas,

or wedding celebrations – if people want it. I can't see how eating meat so rarely can be good for you. Surely your bodies wouldn't be used to it?'

'Many people opt not to eat it.'

'Do you?'

'I can't bring myself to eat the chicken or lamb. I always become too attached to them. But beef – I'll eat beef when it's on offer.'

'You don't get attached to the cows then?'

'Only the ones we use for milking and breeding. But we don't eat *them*. So, do you want to come for a walk or not? We need to go while the burial service is on.'

'Okay. If you unlock my *cage*, we can get going.'

Harry was astonished to glimpse a large number of buildings when Dee wheeled him out of the barn. She turned right, then right again so he only managed a fleeting look, but it all seemed so huge. They passed the end of the barn and she turned right again, following a track amongst what looked like food crops.

'Why is it so important for you to take me on this walk while no one is around?'

'The community is angry about the aerial searches for you and your friend when he had already been dropped in Manilla. They thought there was no need for it. It caused John's fall and his death. Your friend should have reported that you were safe and sound.'

'But my family would still want to look for me. What's wrong with that?'

'Your friend was supposed to tell them that you had decided to stay here.'

'But I haven't decided to stay here. And my family wouldn't have believed that anyway. Not without having confirmation from me.'

'You need to at least *pretend* that you want to stay here. It will be the best way to ensure your safety,' Dee said.

Dee was repeating what Ethan had said to him.

'Are you saying my life is in danger if I *don't* pretend?'

Dee shrugged. 'I'm just telling you what I think.'

'What aren't you telling me Dee?'

'We need to be careful what we say in the barn. Very careful. Out on a walk like this we can speak our minds, but not in there.'

'You've organised this walk, haven't you?'

'Yes, I persuaded Jacob to let you get some fresh air.'

Harry wondered what her motives were. Was it because she felt attracted to him? Or was she looking for a friend who might help her to leave the community?

'Are you willing to help me escape Dee?'

'We can't. Well not for a good while yet anyway. You're too incapacitated with your leg injury.'

'But you might help me if I was able-bodied?'

'We could only consider doing that if we were married.'

'*Married*?' Harry was alarmed at the very idea. He was far too young for marriage and so was Dee. But he didn't know what age people typically married in the *community*. He voiced his concerns to see what she'd say.

'We're both too young for marriage Dee.'

'Not here, we're not. Most people my age are already married.'

'Why aren't you married then?'

'No one wants me because I'm soiled. I'm thankful

for that otherwise I might have already had a couple of children. Then I'd never get out of here.'

'What do you mean soiled?'

'I was raped by one of the other residents when I was thirteen, so many of the male residents consider me soiled goods when it comes to marriage.'

Harry was shocked to hear about the rape, but not the attitude. At his university one of the female students had been raped on her way home one night and he'd heard some of the male students call her a "slut" when she returned, saying she must have been "asking for it". He'd argued against their attitude but it did little to shift their thinking. In the end the girl dropped out.

'How old was the man who raped you?'

'He was only a teenager himself. Benjamin. I think he was seventeen or maybe eighteen. He was living on the streets of Sydney before he came here and he told the elders that there everyone just took what they wanted.'

Harry whistled. 'And how did they react to that little revelation?'

'They expelled him. Took him back to Sydney and dumped him on the streets again.'

'Well that was wrong. With that attitude he would have gone on to rape other women or girls. They should have reported it.'

'They don't like the police coming here. One of the community was unjustly accused of assaulting a teenage girl many years back and it caused all sorts of problems for them. Since then, they've wanted nothing to do with the police.'

'What happened about the allegation the girl made?'

'She dropped it. Admitted she was lying. She just didn't want to be here. She was a drug addict.'

'How did she manage to report it if she was stuck out here?'

'She escaped.'

'Escaped how?'

'We're not sure. One of the local dairy farmers came to buy a load of heifers for expanding his breeding and milking stock. She must have heard about it and we think she hid somewhere in his truck. Since then, we *deliver* stock anyone buys from us.'

'So because they think you're soiled – which I think is a load of bollocks by the way, no one in the community will marry you.'

Dee shrugged. 'Although one man ...'

Dee stopped talking and shuddered. What was that about?

'Anyway, Jacob had a dream about you and that's why he thought God had sent you to us – for me. He knows most outsiders don't think like that about women. Here in this community young females have to be virgins before marriage. It's only those who come here as more mature women or widows who are excused. Anyway, Jacob doesn't want to see me be alone for the rest of my life. I'm his step-daughter. My mother is married to him.'

'And what does your mother think about all this?'

'Oh she worships the ground Jacob and Moses walk on. She believes *anything* they say.'

'Who is Moses?'

'He's one of our Elders.'

'When you say Elders – do you mean they are the ones

in charge here?'

'Yes. Sort of. The Elders make most of the decisions – but everyone is consulted of course. We hold daily gatherings. If there's any new decisions to be made it's discussed then.'

'Do people get to vote? Is it a democratic process?'

'I'm not sure what you mean by democratic. If you're asking me whether people have a say, then yes, they do. But the elders make decisions without consultation on some matters and just tell us. Then there are a couple of others who are in charge of security who do the same.'

'Right.'

As they'd been talking Dee had continued pushing him past the crop growing fields. Now they were clear of them she stopped at a bench and parked the wheelchair. Harry could see the land sloped down from their position. As far as the eye could see it was an open landscape without any buildings.

'Is this all part of the farm's land?' he asked her.

'Yes. Beautiful, isn't it?'

'It is, but I can't imagine living in a place like this. It's too remote.' He could just make out a herd of cattle in the distance. Flies had been bothering him as they walked and now little buggers really honed in on him. Every second he was swiping them away. He could do with one of those hats he'd seen on telly with a wide brim and dangling corks. He'd always thought they were a bit of a joke, but he could see why they might be very handy in the countryside. The place seemed full of flies.

'Why are there so many bloody flies?' he asked Dee.

'It's the livestock which attracts them I think.'

He thought about that for a minute and guessed it made sense. He imagined flies would categorise humans in the same way they did sheep or cattle which is why so many were hanging around them. Dee had a wide brim hat on but was still being pestered by the persistent little buggers. She looked quite beautiful as the light fell on her. Like a wispy fairy.

'So what difference do you think it would make if we were married?' Harry asked her, curious as to what she might say.

'When you marry, you can have your own house. If you're single, you have to share quarters. Other people see what you are doing then. You wouldn't be able to move about so easily without someone wanting to know what you were doing or where you were going.'

'You don't have freedom to move about the place?'

'We do. But everyone has their allocated jobs each day. We eat our meals in a big hall. Living quarters have facilities for making snacks or drinks, but not a functioning kitchen. Married couples have the privacy of their own houses. In shared quarters you only have your own room, then there's a shared seating area off the kitchenette and a shared bathroom. At least we do have our own rooms now. When I was younger most of us slept in dormitories, but they built more houses so we don't have to sleep in those anymore – thank goodness.'

'But surely once you've finished your daily chores and had your evening meal you can do what you want?'

'You can – sort of. It's just that someone might be monitoring you. And there are cameras about the place. If someone was suddenly to start doing something out of

33

Sunday

Jacko was pleased to see Collins' car was parked in his driveway when he pulled across the entrance blocking the possibility of the man driving off. He wondered how Collins would take the news of Pollard's death.

Collins opened the door sporting a great big grin, which turned to a frown. 'Oh, it's you. I thought ...'

'You were expecting someone?' Jacko asked.

'Leonie said she might ... never mind. What do you want now? I've given you my statement.'

'Yes, you have but I'm here to give you some news.'

'What news?'

'I think it's best if we talk inside, don't you?'

Collins pouted and hesitated for a moment before he unlocked the fly screen door and opened it for Jacko to enter. Jacko managed to grab the door before it slammed shut again and followed Collins into the living room. Not inviting Jacko to take a seat or offer him any refreshments, he swung around and said, 'Well what is this news then?'

'Nick Pollard was found dead in his flat in Newcastle

yesterday. He'd been dead for some days – it's estimated he died in the early hours of Thursday morning.'

Jacko watched as Collins' face turned pale and he seemed to stagger back a little.

'Why don't you sit down Wade? You don't look to steady on your feet there.'

Collins stepped back and dropped onto the couch. Jacko took a few paces towards him.

'Now we're concerned for your safety Wade. Two of your old prison chums dead within days of each other. Who's to say you won't be next.'

'What? … Why would … I haven't done anything,' Collins said almost shouting. He slumped back onto the couch and in a quieter voice said, 'How did Pollard die?'

'It's looking like a drug overdose at the moment.'

Jacko could see the visible relief on Collins' face at this piece of news.

'He was always a druggie. Even inside he managed to obtain supplies,' Collins said.

'What type of drugs was Pollard partial to?'

'I wouldn't have a clue. Anything he could get his hands on I imagine. I'm not very familiar with drugs – I've never taken them. Alcohol is my poison.'

'You mean the only drug you indulge in is alcohol.'

'What? No, alcohol isn't a drug.'

'It's classified as such.'

'Bullshit. Alcohol is completely different.'

'If you say so.' Jacko didn't want to get into an argument with Collins about alcohol – he'd been down that road many times with family members and colleagues. 'Now, as well as ingesting a lethal dose of whatever drug he took, an envelope full of money was found with Pollard. What can you tell me about that Wade?' He didn't clarify that there were only a few real notes in the envelope.

'What? Why would I know anything about what Pollard was up to? He was probably dealing drugs or something.'

'Hmm. Maybe, but we don't believe that was all there was to it. You see it's possible that whoever murdered Tim O'Leary then drove straight to Nick Pollard's place and paid *him* a little visit. That's why we're concerned for your safety. You see the pattern here, don't you? Two of your ex-prison mates are now dead. You might be next.'

'O'Leary was *not* a mate of mine.'

'Each of you are connected to Lee Wells. Could Lee Wells be dead also? Or could Lee Wells be behind these deaths?'

'Lee? No. I can't see him being involved in anything violent. He could be intimidating and he scared people with his God rantings, but no, I can't imagine Lee killing anyone.'

'But he might know people who would kill?'

'I really don't know,' Collins said, shaking his head.

'Okay Wade, let's go back to your statement then.'

'I told you the truth in my statement.'

'Hmm. I've been going over it Wade and there's a couple of things that stand out for me. You take great pains to point out that you had no contact whatsoever with Tim O'Leary once you were released. You also wrote – and I'm quoting it from memory here, "I didn't own the black bag that O'Leary was seen leaving my house with and I don't know what was in it." Unquote.'

'Yes. All that's true. I didn't lie.'

'I've no doubt about that Wade. It's the wording that concerns us.'

'What do you mean?'

'The way you wrote your statement indicates that you *knew* there was a black bag in your house but you didn't know what was in it because you hadn't looked? Would that be right?'

Collins paused for a second too long before replying – the surprise on his face giving him away.

'No. Detective Bailey asked me about the bag and so I thought I should say something about it in my statement.'

'No that's not quite right Wade. We asked you to write a statement regarding events leading up to your burglary and what you discovered when you returned home that day. I know DCI Bailey mentioned the bag to you, but when you came in to give your statement, we didn't ask you about the bag. You volunteered that yourself.'

'Yes, because Bailey had *asked* me about it.'

'Hmm. Our theory – that is DCI Bailey's and my theory is – that you *were* in possession of the black bag. Perhaps someone asked you to look after it until it was collected. Someone like Lee Wells. Perhaps you were told not to look in it. That way you could say with total honesty, that it wasn't yours and you didn't know its contents.'

'What? No—'

'Come on Wade. This is *serious*. Two men are dead. Two men you knew in prison. Your life could well be in danger. You need to come clean with us.'

'If my life is in danger then wouldn't that be all the more reason to say nothing – even if I knew anything,' Collins said in a quiet voice.

Jacko sighed. He didn't think he was going to get anywhere with this fool. He'd give it one last go.

'Whoever killed O'Leary and supplied Pollard with a lethal drug, could be watching you. If they are, they would have seen you receive several visits from the police. They may well have seen you entering the police station when you gave your statement. They might believe you've already spilled the beans to us. I really think it would be in your best interests to tell us the truth.'

'*If* my life was in danger, what could you do to protect me? Nothing, that's what. I can't afford to put my life on hold because of what you *think*.'

'Don't say I didn't warn you Wade.' There was resignation in Jacko's voice. Taking a card out of his pocket, he placed it down on the coffee table. 'Here's my card. If you decide there's anything you'd be willing to tell me, give me a call.'

Collins nodded without speaking, so Jacko let himself out. 'Don't forget to lock the door behind me, will you?' he said, as a parting shot.

Wade had put on a brave front with the detective, but as soon as he'd closed and double locked the door, he went into the kitchen, pulled a bottle of scotch out the cupboard and, with shaking hands, poured himself a glass. Perhaps he should have told the detective everything. But what did he know? Not much when it came down to it. And he hadn't done anything illegal had he? He had to be super careful or his parole could be revoked. If he told the detectives what had happened then would he be sent back to jail? But if he didn't tell him, then could his life be in danger? He wasn't sure what to do. Perhaps he should move into Leoni's place. She'd suggested it as a possibility. Maybe that was taking things too far though – and would be putting her at risk. He was enjoying their affair – she was a good sport. But he wasn't interested in settling down with one woman. There were too many gorgeous females out there. Needs must though.

He pulled out his mobile and called Leonie.

'Hi Darl, I thought I might take you up on that offer to stay with you. Why don't we give it a few weeks' trial run?'

34

Monday

First thing on Monday Frank placed a call through to Alex Reardon, the senior pathologist in Tamworth. The phone was eventually answered by someone and he was told Reardon hadn't arrived yet. He said he would call later and hung up. Checking his watch, he saw it was time to head off to Pollard's post-mortem. Rachel was meeting him there.

At 2pm Frank called a meeting in the squad room. Rachel looked around noting that Stuart Tyler was not present – that meant Tyler and his new dogsbody DC were still working on their case. Phil Rogers had joined them and there were a number of others present who were on the squad, including Ryan Pullman.

Pollard's image was up on the board, together with Tim O'Leary's and Lee Wells' plus images of the Elantra station waggon. To the side there were also images of the two missing gliders with an arrow linking them to the Elantra.

'DI Sharp and I attended Pollard's post-mortem today. He died as a result of injecting himself with a dose of pure heroin. The purest that the technicians have ever come across. Normally, as you might know, heroin is cut with other substances. Even a seasoned heroin addict would have died from the dose he'd injected. We don't believe he had any idea of its strength, but we suspect the people who supplied it to him did. We're therefore considering this as a suspicious death.'

Rachel took over to update the squad with the details of O'Leary's death and Pollard and O'Leary's connection to Lee Wells.

'It's possible that whoever murdered O'Leary then travelled down to Newcastle to see Pollard,' she concluded.

'What about the Elantra and the missing gliders? Any more news on that?' Rogers asked.

'There were only a couple of other Elantra's of the same colour in the Tamworth region. They've all been excluded and unless another unknown vehicle was in the area, we believe it *was* the glider's station waggon that hit O'Leary,' Frank told them. 'On Thursday, the vehicle was picked up on camera at various times around Tamworth and at the services on the M1 heading to Sydney. Fill the team in with what you know Ryan,' Frank said.

Ryan stood up and explained the purpose of his trip to the Wyong services. 'We've ascertained that the man seen filling the Elantra with petrol was neither the owner, Felix McMurray, nor his friend Harry Meredith. As yet we've been unable to identify the driver. He had his back to the cameras and his head covered with a cap. He paid for the petrol at the pump using Felix McMurray's debit card. The vehicle was sighted in Sydney an hour later, and again the next day but it then disappeared and hasn't been seen since.'

'So the Elantra was stolen then?' Rogers asked. 'If so, what's happened to the gliders?'

'Good question. We believe the Elantra *was* stolen,' Rachel said. 'Of course, it's possible the gliders were also in the Elantra, but from CCTV and security shots of the vehicle at the services and traffic cams around Tamworth, it seemed there were only two occupants. As to the fate of the gliders, DCI Bailey and I have some theories, but we can't, as yet, prove it.'

'We travelled up to Tamworth as there had been a reported sighting of Lee Wells. Then we picked up a connection to the gliders – all of which leads back to Wells and the Mark Foundation – a religious group who live on a large property outside Manilla, a town not that far from Tamworth. We searched a particular part of the property after relatives of one of the missing boys spotted what could have been glider debris on the property.'

Frank went on to explain everything they had learned in Tamworth, including Jacko's recent visit to Wade Collins.

'So, we have nothing much to go on,' Rogers said.

'There's plenty we can be doing. I want all CCTV in and around the area of Pollard's home checked. Look for the Elantra or any other vehicle seen entering or leaving the area near Pollard's flat. We also need to check all traffic cams, and any CCTV in other areas of Newcastle in the early hours of Thursday morning to look for the Elantra. Being a station waggon, it should stand out. They were produced as a limited edition. We need to do a door to door in the area and see if anyone saw or heard a vehicle anywhere near Pollard's place – or spotted an unfamiliar vehicle in the residents' car park. Liaise with Sydney to see if there's been any more sightings of the Elantra. Go over Wells known associates both here and in Canberra – but not his family. DI Sharp and I have met some of Wells' family – we'll follow them up. When you're looking into his associates, see if there's something we've missed there. We know for example, the man who died on the Mark Foundation property knew Wells in Canberra. Phil, I'll leave you to organise teams on that. Requisition uniforms to assist if you need to,' Frank said.

'One more thing,' Rachel said, jumping in. 'A mobile phone was picked up at Pollard's flat. Ryan, can you follow through on that? And, could you pass onto Phil the details of the company with the security camera that you spotted on Saturday near Pollard's.'

The room started buzzing with activity. Frank indicated he wanted a word with Rachel and signalled for her to follow him to her office.

'We need to pay a visit to Sarah Harper and her mother,' Frank said once they were seated in his office. 'I'd like to see them separately. We haven't met Lee Wells' mother as yet. Perhaps she might have some interesting things to tell us. But before we go, can you look into the father's death? If I remember correctly Sarah Harper said he was killed in a car accident. See if you can find out any details and whether it happened locally.'

'You think there might be something suspicious about his death?'

'No idea. At this point I'd just like to know all the

details.'

Rachel nodded and got up to leave. 'I'll see if I can get hold of both women and make an appointment,' Frank said. 'I know Sarah Harper works, so it might have to be an evening appointment – depending on what she does. I'll let you know.'

Rachel made an interesting discovery when she looked at Lee Wells' birth records. His given name on the birth certificate was Levi Joseph Wells, born to a John and Mary Wells. According to records Wells changed his name officially to Lee when he was 21. Levi wasn't a common name at the time of his birth – perhaps he was ribbed about his name being linked with the jean brand or Jewish associations. As far as she was aware the family weren't Jewish. She knew from her bible reading days as a child, there were references to a Levi in the Old Testament. She couldn't remember in connection to what though.

Further searches into John Wells' death brought no results. He wasn't on the register. She recalled Sarah Harper mentioning that her father took a sabbatical and went travelling. Perhaps he'd been killed in another state or overseas. A quick search into state registers across Australia also turned up no results. That indicated that he'd died overseas. But why wasn't his death registered in Australian records if he was an Australian citizen?

'We're seeing Sarah Harper at 3.30pm. She only works part time and will be home by then. I've arranged to see Mary Wells at 4.45 pm. It's only a ten-minute drive to her house from the Harper's place. We need to head off now if we're going to make it. Grab your bag,' Frank said.

On the drive to the Harper house, Rachel filled Frank in on what she had learned.

'Hmm. Interesting about the father. Presumably Mary Wells can shed some light on the mystery for us.'

35

The Harper home was an impressive modern two storey cement rendered house with a double garage set out on a large plot in Wallsend. Rachel knew from her house and land searches with Andy that the area had been subdivided into generous sized plots for new housing some years back. And they were costly. Not all lots had been developed. She and Andy had considered buying a plot and building from scratch, but decided against it for now. Most available building plots tended to be further out of the city and she didn't want a long commute to work. The larger Wallsend ones would have been out of their price range anyway.

'If Nick Pollard paid a visit to this neighbourhood, he would have stood out like a sore thumb,' Rachel said as they walked up to the front door.

'Hmm. I was thinking that. Maybe he came with mates and they were disguised as workmen. People tend not to notice tradies.'

Sarah Harper greeted them warmly and ushered them into a spacious lounge with folding doors opening onto a patio and large back yard. Frank noticed that the garden was well established with small trees, bushes and flower beds. There was also a pool area off to one side with what looked like a pool plant room. Plenty of places to hide small vials of drugs. The garden also backed onto open countryside – another possible point of entry.

Sarah Harper offered them refreshments and they accepted glasses of iced water.

'You have a beautiful home Mrs. Harper,' Frank said when she returned with the water. 'How long have you lived here?'

'We bought the plot when they first came on the market while we were still living in Perth, with the intention of returning here and building one day. We'd had plans drawn up for one of those factory-built houses – you know the type the structure can be assembled in days. I saw a program called Grand Designs in Britain where some absolutely fantastic houses were built that way.'

'Oh a flat-pack home? You'd never know. It's very impressive. My wife and I were considering one for an annex on our property.'

Sarah Harper was wearing a low-cut loose-fitting top over a pair of linen trousers. She'd been leaning forward exposing her cleavage to Frank in a flirty manner until his last comment. Not that Frank would notice that, Rachel thought. With Frank's last comment about a "flat-pack home" she sat up and bristled.

'It's a bit more than a flat-pack,' Sarah snorted. 'It's custom designed to our specifications. We decided to have a rendered façade and the company supplied and fitted everything for us. So we were able to rock up and just move in with our furniture. It wasn't easy planning it from the other side of the country – we had to make decisions on every single little thing.'

'Well I have to say you've sold me on the idea of it,' Frank said looking around, oblivious to her reaction.

'After dad's death we decided we had to make the move sooner than planned. We've been here almost two years now.'

'Last time we spoke you mentioned your father had died in a car accident. Could you tell us where that happened?'

Rachel pulled out a notepad and prepared to make notes.

'My father was in the UK at the time. He'd been travelling in America, then flew to London. I'm not sure where he was – somewhere in the countryside there. He was visiting a community of people who have a similar religion to Dad's. You know he was one of the leaders of his local church here?'

'No, I didn't know that.' Interesting, Frank thought. Was that who the son picked up his religious beliefs from?

'And what was your father's church called?'

'It's called The Liberal Christian Church.'

'And how does this church differ from most religions, such as Church of England, Presbyterian, Baptist, Catholic etc.'

'The Liberal Christian Church follow a Dual Covenant Theology.'

'What does that mean exactly?'

'They follow parts of both the Old Testament and the New Testament, whereas most Christian religions follow only New Testament teachings.'

'I see,' Frank said, although he didn't really. He knew that the Jewish religion followed teachings from the Old Testament, but he thought Christian churches did also. When he went to Sunday school as a child, he was taught about things from both the Old and New Testament at his Church of England classes. Didn't the Ten Commandments come from the Old Testament? He remembered having to recite all the books of the bible in order – both the Old and New Testament.

'Was the church a full-time job for your father?'

'Good heavens no. He wasn't a minister or priest. They only have Elders.'

'What did he do for a living then?'

'He used to own a chain of electrical stores across the region selling things like home appliances. In fact, the shops were called 'Appliances.'

Frank nodded. He'd bought products from their stores and the last time he'd been in one he wondered how they'd survived with all the competition from the bigger chain groups.

'It was a thriving business. But he sold them some years back and carried on managing one of the local stores for the new owners until he took his sabbatical.'

'Why did he sell if it was a thriving business?'

'I really don't know. My father inherited two shops from his father and then gradually expanded the business over some years. I guess he thought neither of his children would be interested in taking over the reins when he retired so decided to sell. I was living in Perth at the time. I didn't even know he'd done that. Mum could tell you more. She wouldn't discuss it with me. I only found out that he no longer owned the stores after he died when I asked Mum what she planned to do about the businesses.'

'If you don't mind me asking, were you left any money in your father's will – say from the sale of the businesses?'

Sarah shook her head. 'I asked mum about a will and she said he didn't have one. She told me she had inherited money and that it would come to Lee and me in due course. She didn't really want to discuss it. I raised the subject with Lee on that weekend he was out asking whether he'd been left any money. He was always closer to our father than I was. But he claimed he hadn't.'

Frank nodded. He'd have to ask Mary Wells more about what had happened to the money from the sale of the businesses.

'Were you brought up in the teachings of your father's church?'

'Yes. It was a very small congregation back then, but it gradually grew. I became disillusioned with the church and my parents' beliefs in my teenage years which caused friction in our household – particularly with my father. I made a complete break from the church after Ted and I married. Lee was well and truly entrenched in it though. I'm not sure if you know but he ran his own branch when he lived in Canberra.'

'As far as I'm aware that was called 'The Wisdom Foundation', not the Liberal Christian Church.'

'Yes, I know. But he generally ran it along the same principles as the one here.'

Frank wanted to ask more questions about her father, but decided he'd save them for Mary Wells.

'Were you aware that Lee changed his name officially

when he was twenty-one?'

'Yes, I discovered that from reading details about his trial in the newspaper. I hadn't known before that. As a child, he was always called Lee by his friends and teachers at school.'

'Have you heard from Lee since he disappeared?'

'No,' she said shaking her head. 'I would have been in touch with you if I had. I'm not likely to hear from Lee – especially after what he did to us. We weren't exactly close. We offered to spend time with him on his day releases because I thought it would be too much for mum to deal with.'

'Why do you think it would be too much for your mother?'

'Lee looks a lot like our father. Every time mum went to see him in prison she left in tears. I just thought it would be better if she didn't have him around the house for too long. Taking him for a visit to see her would be more than enough. She … mum hasn't coped with my father's death all that well.'

'Right. Well thank you so much for your time, we'll leave you in peace then,' Frank said standing and nodding at Rachel, who was shoving her notebook back into her bag.

'Did you notice that the back yard opened onto countryside,' Frank said as they drove away. 'Pollard could have gained access to it from the rear. It would be useful to look at a street map and see exactly what else is behind there. I don't suppose it matters all that much now and we're unlikely to find out. I just like slotting all the pieces into the puzzle.'

'I know what you mean. I'm pretty sure there's a canal runs around the back of the houses there. I remember that from when Andy and I looked at the building plots and considered whether the area was a potential flood risk.'

'With the dry weather we've been having, a canal would provide another point of entry then and would have made it easily accessible on foot.'

'Yes.'

They drove on in silence for the remainder of the journey until Frank pulled up at an older looking single storey brick house in Jesmond.

Mary Wells greeted them with a disingenuous smile that quickly turned into a frown. Frank thought her face carried a look of bitterness he'd come across on many older women. Above her thin lips were ridge lines as though she wore a permanent drawn and angry face. He knew from checking that she was 70years old and unlike many women her age, she'd left her thinning, grey, curly hair undyed. They were shown into an overcrowded front living-room where the thick heavy curtains were open but the nets covering the windows meant you couldn't see anything outside. They also prevented anyone being able to see in. He noticed there were a few family photographs dotted about on a sideboard. One wedding photograph – presumably of Mary and her husband. One of two young children which, judging by the age of it, were Sarah and Lee. The final one showed two young boys. No doubt Sarah's two boys when they were younger. No refreshments were offered and Mary Wells did not appear happy about having them in her house. Despite the clutter of furniture there was something harsh and austere about the room. Frank felt a shiver run down his spine as he settled onto the brown velour couch which didn't look like it had been replaced since the 70s.

'Thanks for seeing us Mrs Wells.' He was tempted to make a comment about her married name being the same as the Motown singer – most famous for her hit *My Guy*, but didn't think this Mary Wells would appreciate it. She didn't look like the type to follow any popular music. Or have a sense of humour.

'I don't know how you think I might be able to help you,' she said. 'I have no idea where Levi is and I haven't heard from him. He's just like ...'

She stopped speaking and Frank would swear that she was about to say Lee was just like his father.

'We're trying to piece together a broader picture of Lee and would also like to ask you some questions about your husband John.'

'What's my husband got to do with anything? He's dead. He died shortly after Levi went to prison.'

'Yes, your daughter was just telling us that.'

Mary Wells bristled and shifted forward in her chair, a look of unease on her face.

'He died while he was in the UK, Sarah was telling us. Can you tell us more about that?'

'Why do you want to know?'

'It's just that we were unable to find any record of his death. Why is that?'

'Well, he died in England.'

'Yes, but his death should still have been recorded here in Australia. You haven't done that?'

'I didn't know I had to.'

'Surely your husband had an estate that had to pass through probate?'

Mary sighed. 'He'd already put this house in my name. And settled some money on me. If you must know we were separated. He planned to divorce me. I never told Sarah or Levi that. Levi might have known. His father went to see him before he left for overseas.'

'I see.' Was that why John Wells had sold his business? He needed money to settle on his wife?

'Did the divorce ever finalise?'

'No,' she said shaking her head. 'I didn't receive any papers, so he's ...'

Again, she stopped speaking. Frank was sure there was something important she wasn't telling them.

'So how did you become aware of his death?'

Mary seemed to become agitated. She was wringing her hands and wriggling about in her seat. 'I was his next of kin, wasn't I?' she eventually said.

'Was he buried in England then, or did you bring his body back here?'

'We erected a plaque in his memory at our church.'

Frank noticed she hadn't answered his question. 'Can you tell us the details of when and where he died then? We will need to follow up on it.'

Rachel had been sitting making odd notes while Frank questioned Mary Wells. She noticed the woman becoming more and more agitated. She was wearing a pale pink short-sleeve jumper that Rachel would bet was part of a twin-set, a set of pearls around her neck which she kept fingering nervously, a pair of fawn 'non-crease' synthetic looking trousers that her grandmother referred to sneeringly as "slacks", and a pair of beige flatties with stocking-type socks. Nan, who would be turning 80 next week wouldn't have been caught dead wearing clothes like this. She wore either bright coloured jeans and dresses or shorts in hot weather. Rachel doubted that Nan had ever owned a twin-set or that Mary Wells ever wore shorts. Just looking at her outfit made Rachel feel hot, uncomfortable and itchy. It must be still in the region of 30° and was very humid. Yet Mary Wells hadn't looked hot until Frank's question about her husband's death.

Now sweat broke out on her face and Mary exploded out her seat, nostrils flaring, fists clenched, shouting at Frank. 'John's betrayal has *nothing* to do with Levi. He's … *why* are you asking me all these questions? Why can't you leave me alone? Haven't I suffered enough humiliation?'

Rachel thought she made a frightening spectacle and stared in silent fascination at the dramatic change in the woman. Frank had *really* pressed her buttons. She felt butterfly movements in her stomach. Was the baby reacting to the shouting?

Frank cleared his throat. 'I can see you're becoming very upset Mary,' he said, adopting a gentle tone. 'What is it you're not telling us? Why would you feel humiliated? It's quite common these days for marriages to break up. Did your husband leave you for another woman?'

Mary slumped back into her chair, tears streaming down her face.

Rachel, collecting herself, stood and went across to her. 'Can I make you a cup of tea, Mrs Wells?'

'No. I don't want any bloody tea. But thank you for offering,' she said after a pause. 'Oh, I may as well tell you, but you mustn't say anything to Sarah.'

Rachel returned to her seat and they waited while Mary reached out for a tissue from the box on the table next to her chair. After wiping her nose and face she eventually said, 'You can't tell Sarah anything. Not until I've told her at least – she knows nothing. And no one at the church knows about John's betrayal either. They all think he's dead. I would be cast out from the church if they knew. And I have so little in my life I didn't want lose that. It was John's idea to say that he'd died.'

'So your husband is not dead?' Frank asked looking surprised.

'No. Not as far as I know. Although he might well be by now. It was true that he went travelling in America and England. He might still be over there. I don't know where he is. He had another secret family you see. Once he sold the business he used to disappear and spend time with them as often as he could. He lied to me and said he was going on long weekend fishing trips and all the while he had another *family*. When he announced he was leaving me, he told me the truth – well part of it anyway. I never got the full story. He suggested I tell the church that I'd received news that he'd died in a car accident after a suitable period of time. They knew he'd gone travelling. He didn't want me to be cut off from all my friends.'

'Right. So did you hear from him once he arrived in England?'

'Yes, he sent some postcards so that it would all look real. But I don't know if that's where he really was.'

'Would you still have any of those postcards?'

Mary Wells sighed, stood, walked across the room and, after opening a drawer in the sideboard, pulled out a couple of postcards and passed them to Frank.

The first one was from a coastal town called Plymouth near Boston in Massachusetts. The second was from a place called Dedham, in Essex England. It showed a picturesque town which was on the border of two counties – Suffolk and Essex. Frank knew from his brief trip to England back in 2000 that Essex was close to London, but it wasn't an area he'd visited. Beth had been back to the UK once since they'd married, and they'd talked about taking a trip together sometime, but it wasn't high on his priority list. There never seemed to be enough time to plan for overseas trips. Perhaps when he eventually retired, they might get to make some journeys.

Frank passed the postcards to Rachel so she could make a note of the locations.

'Do you know why your husband visited these places in particular?'

'He told me he was visiting communities where they had religious groups living communally. I know he was planning to visit another one in Wales, and one in Ireland. But he didn't send any further postcards. He'd suggested that he be killed off at the one outside London.'

The hair on Frank's arms stood up at the mention of religious communal living. Could John Wells have a connection to the Mark Foundation?

'He'd always been interested in places like that,' Mary continued. 'He wanted to set up somewhere with me and the kids when they were young – way out in the bush somewhere. But I wasn't having any of it. I'm a city girl.'

'Do you know where John used to disappear to on his fishing trips?'

'No, I've no idea. When he announced he was leaving me, he didn't mention where his second family lived or where he'd been with them on those weekends or weeks he took off.'

'How long ago was it that he sold the businesses?'

Mary shrugged. 'I don't know – perhaps as long as ten years. I couldn't be absolutely sure. He didn't tell me that he'd done it immediately. He told me that he'd employed a manager to lighten his work load – John was in his early sixties by then. He never took much time off before that and worked six days a week. Never on Sunday mind you. I became suspicious about how much time he was taking off for his *fishing* holidays and that's when he told me he'd sold the shops and he was merely an employee. I was so shocked I didn't think to ask him when he'd done it. But those little holidays started about ten years ago. Whether he was seeing the *other* woman before then I really don't know.'

'And what happened to all the money he gained from the sale?'

Again, she shrugged. 'I don't know how much he sold them for. He never talked to me about money. Throughout our marriage he paid the bills and gave me an allowance each month for food, clothing and other bits. Later I also had a credit card that I could buy larger items on. I spent my time bringing up the children or involved with church work. When he left, he showed me how to take care of the household bills, then left me a lump sum and the house of course. I guess he took the rest of it with him to his new family.'

'You didn't think to seek advice from a lawyer?' Rachel asked. 'You were entitled to half of any money he had.'

'Money doesn't interest me that much young woman,' Mary Wells said turning to Rachel. 'As long as I have a roof over my head, a comfortable home and a bit of money in the bank, what more do I need? I gave some of the money he left me to the Church. I had more than enough. Sarah and Levi will get whatever's left over when I pass. Now if there's nothing else, you will have to excuse me. I have some visits to make on behalf of the church. We have some elderly housebound women who are part of our congregation. The only visitors they receive now are from us and the occasional health carers.'

'Before we go – do you think there's any chance that Lee knew where his father was living and has gone to join him?' Frank asked her.

Mary shook her head. 'I couldn't tell you. John was distraught when Levi was charged and convicted. He said that's why he had to get away. But those two were as thick as thieves so I wouldn't be surprised if they somehow remained in contact – or if Levi knew all about his father's second little family and where he might have moved to.'

'I know when Lee was released on bail pending his court case, he gave this as his formal address. Did he actually stay here?'

'Only the first night. John had Levi join him in the flat above the Mayfield store. That was the one John continued managing and where he was supposedly staying –

although no one from the church knew that. The flat had a kitchen, bathroom and a couple of bedrooms – one that Levi was able to use. There were other rooms which were used for storing small appliances. John even gave him some work there – working out the back mind you, out of the public eye. He loaded orders onto the delivery truck and unloaded stock as it arrived.'

Frank nodded. They would have to get a warrant to check out the premises.

'Would you happen to have any information related to your husband's bank accounts lying around the house?'

'No, he burnt all his paperwork before he left. And many of our photographs. I caught him throwing it all into the brick barbeque out in the yard before he left. There's nothing about him here at all. He even burnt our marriage certificate – but I've managed to obtain a new copy from the registrar. If I didn't have that and the one remaining wedding photograph, I might start to believe he was just a figment of my imagination.'

'What about your bank? If he transferred money to you it would show up in your bank account.'

'It does, but it won't do you any good. I know he was banking with the ANZ when he settled the money on me and that he closed that account. I couldn't tell you who he banks with now.'

'I'm sorry to hear all you've been through Mary. Okay, well thanks for your time then. We'll come back to you if we have any further questions.'

Mary nodded. 'Now you won't go telling Sarah anything I've told you, will you?'

'No, we'll leave that to you to do Mary.'

36

'Well, that was interesting,' Frank said as they drove off heading back to the station. 'Do you remember I mentioned that the guy who had been talking to 'bear man' from the vehicle at the Mark Foundation was an older man?' He glanced around at Rachel who nodded.

'You're wondering if it could be John Wells?' Rachel asked.

'Yes. We need to see if we can follow the money. I wanted to look into the Mark Foundation's finances while we were in Tamworth but Rawlings said no. Now I think we have greater reasons to do so. I'm sure the Chief Super down here will agree to it, so we can bypass Rawlings. I'll get a warrant to investigate Wells' finances and his tax records to see how he disposed of the money from the sale of his businesses. With so many shops he would have made a tidy sum.'

'I can't believe John Wells would want his own daughter to think he was dead. What kind of father does that?'

'From what Sarah told us she wasn't particularly close to her father.'

'Hmm. Yes, but still. Interesting that the mother lied to

everyone, including her daughter. I gained the impression that she's a bitter, unhappy woman. I suppose you can understand it. And what's that nonsense about the church cutting her off if they knew the truth? What kind of church would do that? It's not very Christian.'

'No, but I've come across it before. On one investigation I had years back – where it turned out to be suicide – the particular church – or I should say the religious group involved had cut the family off when one of the sons had dropped out. The family were ostracised and excluded from the community – I think in the hope that by putting pressure on the family they could persuade their son to return to the fold. Instead, it led to his suicide.'

'Were the family re-admitted to the community or were they ostracised further due to the suicide?'

'I don't know. Once we closed the case, I had no further contact. Changing the subject – I've just realised I haven't eaten anything since breakfast and I'm also thirsty. I didn't fancy any lunch after the post-mortem. Beth will probably kill me if I eat too much now before our evening meal but I'm going to stop in Hamilton and grab something to eat. I might be having a late night at the station anyway.'

'Sounds like a good idea. If we're going to be having a late night, I'll get something as well and phone Andy to warn him.'

Back at the station Rachel was able to grab Ryan Pullman before he left for the evening to get an update. He told her that Pollard's mobile phone showed little activity in the days before his death, so as he didn't have a land line, they surmised that he might have had a second phone that had been removed. The few calls he'd made were to family members shortly after he was released and there'd been no further contact. He'd spoken to Pollard's parents who'd been notified on Saturday of their son's death.

'They didn't seem terribly upset,' Ryan said. 'They claimed they've had little to do with him for some years. Few members of the family have seen him. One brother visited him in prison a couple of times.'

'How sad,' Rachel said. On previous investigations she'd come across families who had severed all ties with their drug addict children or siblings claiming it was impossible to have any kind of normal relationship, that they'd done all they could to help and that they had to cut them off to protect themselves and their property. She couldn't ever imagine her parents cutting her off – or her doing the same to a child of her own. But then she'd never experienced addiction in the family. The closest she got to it was an aunt (by marriage) who became addicted to playing poker machines and had run up huge debts trying to win jackpots that forever eluded her. Her uncle had banned her from all club or pub outings in an attempt to cure her and by all accounts it had worked. But Rachel had no idea what it was like to live with a drug addict or alcoholic, day in day out.

Frank had asked her to get onto immigration to see if there was any record of John Wells returning to Australia in 2006. Once Ryan had left, she placed the call hoping she'd still find someone on duty. The one good thing about Australian Customs was that they kept very efficient records. She was in luck – when her call was answered she gave the official Wells' details. The customs' woman said she'd get back to Rachel as soon as possible, but it might take a day or two. With any luck Frank might let her go home now.

Frank managed to persuade his Chief Super that he needed to obtain tax records and all financial details for John Wells. He had only agreed to this because it was possible that Lee Wells had gone to join his father or had been in touch with him. The Chief Super wouldn't agree to looking more closely at the Mark Foundation, claiming, like Rawlings, there was no justification. If a search of John Wells' records yielded any information linked to the Mark Foundation, then he would re-consider the situation. Frank felt so frustrated. The Mark Foundation remained an elusive entity that he couldn't touch, and yet his gut told him they were at the centre of everything. The missing gliders, Lee Wells, Timothy O'Leary and now possibly John Wells. He knew some links were tenuous, but surely with two potential murders they warranted some investigation. He couldn't understand why everyone was so reluctant. Was it some misguided loyalty linked to religion? Frank knew his Chief Super was a church goer. He wasn't sure if the same applied to the Chief Super in Tamworth. He knew Rawlings wasn't, but she claimed the negative request to look into the Mark Foundation came from her superior.

He wouldn't be able to put anyone on to Wells' financial records until he had the paperwork in hand and knowing the tax office, they would take their time about things. After receiving an update from Phil Rogers about the squad's efforts Frank decided he may as well go home. He'd already sent Rachel home. He wanted to place a call through to the UK but he could do that from home later. It would still be too early there to catch the person he was after.

'There's plenty of food in the oven. When you said you might be late, I did a one pot casserole. You only have to heat it up. I've done it in an enamel casserole dish so you can heat it up on the hob if you can't wait,' Beth told him when he arrived home.

Beth must have noticed the look on his face as she turned to him accusingly, 'You've already eaten something haven't you?'

'I did grab something earlier on the way back to the station,' he mumbled. 'I'm not feeling hungry right now, but no doubt I will in another hour or so. I'll have a small amount then.'

'How's everything going? Is there any news on Harry or Felix? Did you get any response to the appeal for sightings of their car?'

'No, there's no news on the boys. You've probably heard from Matt that it wasn't them at the services.' He wasn't able to tell her about anything else.

Beth nodded. 'Matt has persuaded Steve to travel back to Brisbane in another couple of days if there's no further news. They're just running up motel bills in Manilla and there's little they can do.'

'I know just how they feel,' Frank said slumping into his favourite chair in the lounge.

Harry had digested everything Dee had told him and thought long and hard about his options. If the only way to move things forward from his current predicament was to pretend that he was interested in Dee, then that's what he'd have to do. It wouldn't entirely be a pretence. She was the predominant human contact he'd had since his glider accident, and he relied heavily on her. They'd shared many embarrassingly intimate moments. But he'd long since stopped worrying about those. Dee wasn't as stunning as some of the girlfriends he'd had but she wasn't too bad looking either. He had started to feel a connection with her and really looked forward to her visits. What was it called – *The Stockholm Syndrome* or something when you fell in love with your captor? Not that she was his captor. From everything Dee had told him it sounded as though she was just as much a captive as him. What he had to decide was how far he could go. He needed to convince the audience who spied on them through the cameras directed towards his cage that he was *interested* in Dee. Should he take her into his arms and give her a kiss? No, they might think he was being too sexual and send a back-up squad in to rescue her. He'd have to show his interest at a snail's pace. From what he could gather they sounded as though they had strange religious beliefs. Maybe he could take hold of her hand to show his appreciation on her next visit. Then in the following visit he could kiss her hand. Yes, that's what he'd do. One small step at a time.

37

Tuesday

'There were two men on the doorstep looking for you while you were out,' Leoni told Wade when he returned from seeing his agent.

'What? Who were they?'

'They didn't say. I asked them why they'd be looking for you here and they just smiled. It was creepy. They said they'd call back another time. You're not in any trouble, are you?'

'It wasn't one of those policemen we spoke to, was it?'

'No and they didn't announce themselves as being from the police. Don't they normally?'

Yes, it was usually the first thing they did, Wade thought. Shit! Perhaps Detective Jacko was right. Perhaps his life was in danger and now he'd also put Leoni at risk. *They*, whoever they were, must have been watching him. But he didn't *know* anything. Well not much anyway. He'd have to re-think his situation.

Jacko smiled when he hung up the phone. His strategy of

using two plain clothed colleagues to call on the girlfriend without identifying themselves – knowing Wade was out, had worked. Wade Collins was waiting downstairs to see him. It would be interesting to see what he had to say.

Frank called Rachel into his office to give him an update on John Wells. Before they started, he filled her in on his call to Alex Reardon.

'I finally managed to get hold of the elusive Doctor Reardon,' he told her.

He could see she looked confused so he reminded her he was the pathologist who had visited the Mark Foundation after the death of Roger Wilkinson.

'What did he have to say then?'

'He assured me the death was consistent with a fall as they had explained. They visited the site where the accident happened and saw the ladder Wilkinson had used was still in place. He went on to describe the infirmary set up they had at the Foundation, praising it no end. There were a couple of in-patients at the time. A woman who had miscarried and developed an infection. And a young boy who had toxoplasmosis, an infection they believed he'd caught from touching cat faeces.'

'Lovely,' Rachel said shuddering.

'The Foundation's doctor, who was one of the founders, was there so we were lied to when they said he was away on business.'

'That's interesting. Why would they do that?'

'To keep us from questioning him I suspect. The Coroner and Pathologist's visit coincided with our search. They probably wanted the doctor to remain preoccupied with them.'

'Unless they have more than one doctor.'

'Reardon told me his name was Doctor Jacob Phillips, so I'm assuming it was the same man. Right, what have you learned about John Wells?'

The phone on Frank's desk rang before Rachel had a chance to open her mouth. 'They're putting a call through from Jacko,' he announced. 'He must have some news. I'll put it on speaker phone so you can hear.' He waited until he heard Jacko's voice then pressed the speaker button. After exchanging greetings Jacko told him Wade Collins had just paid him a visit and updated his statement.

'How did you persuade him to do that?' Frank asked.

'*I won't bother you with the details. Let's just say I employed some sneaky scare tactics,*' Jacko said.

'Okay. Shoot then. What did he have to say?'

'*In the days before his release Wells asked him to call on Nick Pollard in Newcastle before heading home to Tamworth. Pollard gave him a disposable mobile and said he'd be in touch. Apparently, Lee Wells had wanted Wade to do him a favour. Collins said he owed Wells as he'd protected him from predators who were planning to gang rape him inside. Collins said that was the only reason why he became pally with Wells and that the other prisoners were scared of Wells for some reason. He said he told Wells point blank that he wouldn't do anything illegal for him, but Wells assured Collins the favour wouldn't be anything illegal. He was instructed to rent a property with a garage – which he did. Anyway, Pollard contacted him and asked him to leave his garage door unlocked because a parcel would be delivered there. He was told he wasn't to open it or attempt to look at its contents. Within a few days the parcel would be collected. That's all he had to do.'*

'Was there a *parcel* or was it the black bag?'

'It was the black bag. Collins swears he didn't look inside it or touch it. But after we paid him a visit asking questions about Lee Wells, he panicked. He locked the garage and phoned Pollard to warn him we'd been and told him not to get in touch again or come near the place in case we were watching it.'

'So O'Leary broke into the house to collect the bag.'

'He thinks so. He doesn't know. Like he said in his previous statement, he'd had no contact with O'Leary. But the black bag was gone after the break in. As well as the personal cash he had stashed there.'

'What did he think the bag was connected to then?'

'He said he didn't know and didn't want to know. He thought Wells had done some sort of deal with locals. He didn't know Wells was planning to take off.'

'Why didn't he tell us all this before?'

'He was terrified of having his parole revoked. I pointed out that we could charge him for obstructing our investigations and withholding information and then he would be sent back to prison. So he spilled the beans and now he's asking for protection for him and Leoni. I assured him he wouldn't need it.'

'Are you sure about that?'

'Not one hundred percent, but I'd say Collins role was so low key, it wouldn't be worth their while following it up. The only thing he's been able to tell us is that Nick Pollard and Lee Wells were involved. It's quite likely O'Leary was delivering the bag to Wells.'

'Hmm. Maybe. There's nothing in Wells' record that indicates he'd become involved in a murder though.'

'Wasn't he convicted for imprisoning and injuring a young

woman?'

'Yes, but there were some extenuating circumstances which is why his sentence was so light. It's a big step to murder. You've heard about Pollard's death no doubt. We're ruling that as a suspicious death. So, we're potentially looking at two murders which could be drug related. The contents of the black bag *might* have been drugs. There's no doubt that Pollard and O'Leary are linked to Lee Wells, but whether he was responsible for the deaths is another question.'

'Okay. We haven't been able to move any further forward on the O'Leary investigation. Sydney police haven't found the glider's station waggon. There's been no further sightings of it. And we've had no luck linking a particular four-wheel drive to the crime either. It's like you said — the vehicle used is probably off road somewhere.'

Yes, Frank thought that likely. In a handy out of the way property like the Mark Foundation where they had plenty of four-wheel drive vehicles.

'Thanks for updating me Jacko. Can you send a copy of Collins' statement through to me?'

'Will do.'

Frank terminated the call and looked at Rachel. 'What do you make of that?

'Do you really believe Collins was about to be gang raped or do you think Wells set that up to draw him into his little circle?'

'Who knows? Rape of good-looking men like Collins is common in male prisons. It might have been true.'

'When Ryan and I visited Cessnock prison, the warden confirmed what Collins told Jacko — many of the other prisoners kept well away from Wells. They were frightened of him. Although nothing came up on his record, it could be because he has a violent streak.'

'Hmm. Maybe. I suspect it's more to do with superstitious fears linked to religion. But I may be wrong. If you remember he was a bit creepy when he went off on one of his religious rants. Okay what have you learned about John Wells?'

'He re-entered Australia on the eighth November two thousand and six. He hasn't travelled abroad since.'

'So we know he's back in the country somewhere. When we receive his tax records we might learn where he's located these days. I hope to have them within the next twenty-four hours.'

'Phil Rogers was telling me that the glider's station waggon was spotted out on the highway, but not anywhere in Newcastle.'

'No, it would seem whoever was driving it headed straight to Sydney. The team picked up several large four-wheel drives, but with so many families opting to drive the bloody things these days it's like looking for a needle in a haystack. The only rego plates they've managed to pick up are locally based ones and it would be stretching it to say they were very close to Pollard's flat.'

'So we've lucked out there?'

'Looks like it. I did manage to pick up a bit of news from a DCI I know in England however. I met him briefly in London when I was looking into Beth's case back in 2000. You might remember he visited Australia a couple of years back?'

'Yes, I remember you mentioning him.'

'Anyway, he's based out in Essex now. I gave him a call last night and asked him to see if he could track down the religious commune in Dedham. He was familiar with them – only because there's apparently been some boundary disputes in recent years. Anyway, he sent one of his team out there to enquire about John Wells. Wells definitely visited them in 2006 and told them he was part of a group who had set up communal living in New South Wales.'

'The Mark Foundation?'

'Unfortunately, he didn't give them a name. But he told them it was in the middle of nowhere.'

'It's got to be them.'

'I suspect so, but for all we know there may be loads of these groups around. I did hear of a group up near Coffs Harbour way.'

'But we had the sighting of Lee Wells in *Tamworth*. That can't be coincidental.'

'Mm. I suspect you're right. But proving anything seems to be our problem, and also persuading anyone to let us look more closely at them.'

'On the other hand … '

Rachel stopped mid-sentence and shook her head as though she had changed her mind.

'What were you going to say?'

'It doesn't matter.'

'No, go on'.

'Well, the deaths might be completely unrelated to the Foundation. It could be that Wells *also* owed someone a favour and Pollard and O'Leary were part of that – involving a third party, totally unconnected to the

Foundation. That black bag could well have contained drugs – but I would question why the Foundation would become involved in *drug* deals when they supposedly earn money from sales of music and their broadcasts?'

Rachel looked at Frank who was frowning. 'Sorry – I was just thinking out loud,' she said. 'I know you think the Foundation is at the root of it all.'

'No, no – it's good to share your thoughts. You're right – the deaths, the potential drugs and the Foundation don't make sense. But then when you factor in the missing gliders – how do they fit into the puzzle?'

'I've said it before. It could be that they landed on someone's property where they are growing crops for drugs.'

'Yes, we talked about that, but according to Tamworth police they routinely fly over areas searching for drug crops. Including the Foundation property. None have been spotted in the area. And we've now got the report back on the drug used in Pollard's lethal overdose. It is similar to those that were picked up during raids in Sydney where the drug squad have confiscated pure heroin before it's been mixed and put onto the market.'

'So drugs are coming *out* of Sydney?'

'Most likely, but not necessarily. They might have been transported *to* Sydney.'

'How is the heroin even getting into the country?'

'When I received the news about the heroin trace, I was also told about a big cache that was discovered hidden in the tubing of a furniture consignment that arrived in Brisbane back in early December. It could be that Brisbane has been the landing point in Australia for some time. Not every container is checked in minute detail. It's believed that the drugs were removed from the furniture and possibly transported by road from Queensland down through New South Wales. The furniture is then sold in shops with no one being any the wiser. Of course, another way drugs enter the country is through human mules but that is very risky.'

'Oh God, it's hopeless, isn't it?'

'Yes, with so many drugs coming into the country it's difficult to keep on top of it. The Feds in Brisbane, working with the drug squad up there and in Sydney, are in the process of trying to bring down the network and its distribution. If the missing black bag contained drugs from the Brisbane source – it's likely to be the last one they'll receive for a while. Which would inflate its importance and increase its value.'

'And make it very dangerous for anyone who was involved with it. Like O'Leary and Pollard.'

'Exactly. Now shall we pop over to Mayfield and look at the flat there? The warrant has come through.'

38

Wednesday

'Come on Dad, we need to get on the road. The car's all packed.' Steve was sitting on a chair in their motel room with his arms and legs crossed and a stubborn expression on his face, refusing to budge. Matt was feeling increasingly frustrated. He would prefer to arrive home during safer daylight hours. The later they left, the more that option was looking increasingly unlikely. It meant they would have to stop over en route. He didn't have a roo bar on his car and it could be dangerous driving on country highways at night when the kangaroos were out feeding. They didn't emerge until just before dusk and retreated just after dawn.

When he'd first come to Australia Matt had travelled around the country by coach and had seen first-hand the hundreds of roos zipping across the highways at night. Coaches he'd been on had flattened many and driving during the day they'd come across many road kills or damaged vehicles that hadn't managed to avoid them. When he asked a coach driver what the roos did during the day, he was told they slept. He conjured up an image of thousands of roos bedding down together, blending into the landscape.

'I've changed my mind. I don't want to go. I know Harry is still in the area somewhere.'

'I know that's what you think and I agree. But there's little we can do. The police aren't going to help us anymore. We can't get onto that property where we thought we saw the glider and we're just running up costs here, neglecting our families, my work and your business. Felix's car hasn't been sighted again. As Detective Jacko told us yesterday, it's likely it's been taken into a garage and stripped down. It won't be seen again. What good can it do to hang around here?'

'We could be here for Harry when ...'

'When what Dad? When he escapes? Or recovers from potential injuries he might have received in the crash?'

'Something like that.'

'I need to get home Dad and so do you. We could be here for *weeks* and still have no further information. We've been here nine days already. If we were going to hear something, we would have by now.'

'I can't just give up.'

'It's *not* giving up. It's accepting that our hands are frustratingly tied. Until we do hear something, there's nothing we can do. Going home is not suggesting we've given up or that we'll never see Harry or Felix again. It's accepting we're not able to help them at the moment, wherever they are.'

Steve nodded at him, but went quiet. The sulky pout, which Matt had become familiar with on this trip appeared on his father's face. The older he became, the more Steve seemed to retreat into childish behaviour. Matt hoped he didn't get like that as he aged. He felt his anger rising, so walked out to the car to calm down. There was no point in being angry. It wouldn't help the situation. He'd promised his wife Sophie that he'd send a text just before they set off. His phoned pinged and he could see a message had just come in from Sophie asking if they *were* heading back today. He was about to reply that he didn't know when Steve joined him outside.

'We'd best get on the road then,' Steve said.

Matt texted Sophie saying they were just about to leave.

Heaving a great sigh, Steve walked slowly around to the passenger's side.

As they drove off, Steve unwound his window and called out, 'We'll see you soon Harry.'

Matt hoped he was right.

Harry's strategy seemed to be working on Dee. He was looking forward to her delivering his breakfast and hoped she'd be able to spend some time sitting with him. Last night as they'd held hands and talked, she'd confirmed that Doctor Jacob was coming to check his wounds today. He was looking forward to meeting Jacob, but on their brief walk yesterday afternoon, Dee had made him promise not to talk about 'leaving'. Instead, she suggested that he ask when he might be able to be up and about more. Yesterday's walk had taken them in a different direction – away from the growing fields and buildings heading into open scrubland. It was rough and bumpy but he didn't care. Just getting out into the sunshine and fresh air felt wonderful. And Dee was opening up to him more and more. He was gathering useful information.

After breakfast Harry persuaded Dee to take him for another walk. Normally she preferred to take him out in the early evening after much of the work had stopped for the day and she was free. But he knew she was on dairy duties this week which meant a very early start and another shift in the afternoon when there would be no time for a walk. She finally agreed and they headed off. He wanted to learn more from her today and how she'd ended up at Babylon.

Once they'd stopped for a rest Harry turned to her. 'How did you and your mother come to Babylon? From what you've told me you've been here since it started.'

'My mother was working with Doctor Jacob up in the Blue Mountains. He was a practitioner in a clinic there. He ran a bible study group at the clinic that my mother attended. They fell in love and married when I was about six.'

'What about your father? Where was he?'

'He died when I was about four. I don't remember much about him. Mum told me he died in a fall when out walking in the mountains. He used to love exploring new areas and went out with hiking groups most weekends. He was a miner who spent most of his working day underground, so when he wasn't working, he liked to be outdoors. One of my few memories of him is playing in the snow outside our house.'

'Snow? It snows in the Blue Mountains?'

'Yes, only for a few days a year. Not enough to go skiing

or anything – but it was exciting for a little kid like me.'

'So how did Babylon come about? You said Doctor Jacob was one of the founders. Who were the others?'

'I'm not sure. My mother sold our house and put some of the money towards buying the land here. I know Elder Moses put quite a lot in too. At the beginning and then later. We were able to build all the extra houses with the money he gave us. Then more people were able to join us.'

'How did Elder Moses and Doctor Jacob know each other?'

Dee shrugged. 'I think through their bible studies. Elder Moses ran a Church.'

'Did you ever meet Elder Moses before you moved to Babylon?'

'Yes. He came to our house many times and I remember going to his church when I was very little. I couldn't tell you anything about it or where it was. All I remember was we had to drive a long way and I slept for much of the journey. As a little kid you don't take in all that kind of information.'

Harry nodded. 'Doctor Jacob is your stepfather but you always refer to him as "Doctor Jacob" when talking to me about him. What do you call him in private? Do you call him Dad?'

'No,' Dee said shaking her head. 'I've always called him "Father Jacob".'

'Was that by choice or did he ask you to call him that?'

'My mother told me to call him that.'

As though Jacob was a priest or something, Harry thought. It was very weird and didn't sit right with him – why would you want your stepdaughter to call you *Father*

Jacob?

'Now enough about me,' Dee said. 'Tell me more about your family.'

Frank finally received an email from the Tax Office with attachments showing John Wells records for the past twenty years. He printed them out and asked Rachel to join him.

'I thought we could go over these together,' he said splitting the paperwork up.

After doing a quick scan down to the last entries he said, 'There's no records after 2006 and his last registered address is the home he shared with Mary Wells. Damn.'

'There might be some clues in earlier records,' Rachel said hopefully. 'Oh my God – he grossed six point four million for the sale of the businesses back in ninety-seven. That's a hell of a lot.'

Frank whistled. 'Who would have thought appliances could be so lucrative.'

'There's detailed records here from Wells' accountant. Perhaps we should pay the firm a visit.'

'Yes, we definitely should. But let's go through this bit by bit first. See what more we can learn.'

39

Thursday

'John Wells owned most of the property on a Torrens title where his businesses were located,' Aleid Janssen told them. 'That's why they were so valuable. There were also a couple Strata titles and he held commercial leases for two shops on retail parks – one here in Newcastle and the other down the Central Coast. Of course, he had to pay a hefty tax bill after the sale as you will have seen.'

Frank nodded.

'He inherited a few of the shops from his father, but John Wells was an astute businessman and he increased the number of shops he owned,' Janssen continued. 'Janssen's did the Wells' family's accounts since the business was started by John's father. My father worked with John's father.'

Janssen said this with obvious pride, a beaming smile on his face.

'Did John Wells explain why he wanted to sell the businesses?'

'At the time he said he'd had enough of the responsibility

and he didn't want to go the way of his father – having a fatal heart attack before he reached retirement. He also had no one to pass them on to. He had children, as you know, but they weren't interested in the businesses.'

'Do you know where he lives now?'

'I assume with his wife Mary where he always lived. Sadly, I haven't seen him since he retired. He said he'd take care of his own tax returns. Unless ... he did talk about retiring to the country. I laughed at him when he said that. I couldn't understand why a city boy would want to move to the sticks. You said you were trying to locate his son Lee – I saw on the news that he'd disappeared. I can't imagine that John would be harbouring him from the law. Have you visited him at home?'

Frank ignored Janssen's judgement on Wells.

'John and his wife Mary are separated. He has a second family. Would you know anything about that?'

By the look of surprise on Janssen's face, he clearly didn't.

'No ... no I didn't. I can't believe that.'

Frank shrugged. He only had Mary Wells word for that bit of information. Wells might or might not have been telling his wife the truth.

'Well thank you for your time Mr. Janssen. We'll see ourselves out.'

John Wells was proving as elusive as his son and now they'd hit yet another dead end. The flat in Mayfield was being used for storage and there was no sign of anyone living there. Their enquiries at the ANZ Bank confirmed Wells no longer held accounts there. When he'd closed the account, he'd withdrawn the last of his money in cash.

A sizeable amount of cash. In the preceding years Wells had also made large cash withdrawals at regular intervals but there was no indication how he'd used the money. His tax returns shed no light on the matter either. Frank didn't have any proof linking John Wells to the Mark Foundation and therefore there was no way he was going to obtain warrants to examine their records in detail. The Foundation had started off as a charity and as such, public records were available, but they told Frank very little. Some years back they'd dropped their charitable status, so no further records were available. What he really needed to do was a thorough search of the Foundation property and a detailed examination of any records they had on the premises. He was sure they would prove enlightening.

Harry was excited. He'd been seen by the doctor the previous afternoon who'd declared that his wounds were sufficiently healed for him to start moving around with the aid of crutches. Dee was going to bring him the crutches and he could practise with them for a short time each day. With his arm still in plaster it wasn't going to be easy, but the doctor said he was to take it slowly and continue using the wheelchair for another few weeks.

After questioning him for some time, Doctor Jacob seemed to be convinced that Harry was enthusiastic about becoming part of their community. He'd managed to put on a convincing performance, realising he had no choice. Ethan had paid him another visit – this time accompanied by two other men. He made it clear in no uncertain terms that if Harry didn't do as he asked, he could be made to disappear. He'd shuddered at the thought and quickly made a decision to get Jacob on side. He wasn't sure, but he didn't think Jacob knew anything about the threats. He was convinced Ethan had his own agenda, but for the life of him, Harry couldn't work out what it was.

Tomorrow night he was going to be joining some of the others in the dining hall for a meal for the first time. If that went well, he was to be transferred to one of the shared houses where he'd have a proper bed and a bathroom. He couldn't wait.

Dee said that they would provide a covering for his plastered arm so he could have a shower. A proper shower where he could wash his hair – although Dee had told him he would only be able to do this with their home-made soap. They didn't use shampoo at the farm and apparently only washed their hair with water. Dee had told him her hair hadn't been washed with shampoo since she'd come to live at the farm. She'd allowed him to feel and smell her hair and he couldn't believe it. It seemed so clean. He hadn't washed his hair since the night he and Felix had arrived at their cabin. It seemed like a lifetime ago and, although Dee had rinsed his hair with water, it hadn't been washed. His hair hung in thick greasy clumps and his scalp felt unbearably itchy. Dee said it took about six weeks to pass through the itchy stage and then it would be fine. He wasn't convinced though. If soap was available, he'd be washing his hair with it.

40

Friday

Frank had had to pull most of his team off the investigation into Wells' disappearance and Pollard's death. They had a new murder case to investigate. Early this morning the body of a young woman had been found in an access lane that ran behind houses in Islington. A local resident had almost run over her as he'd backed his car out of his yard. The access lane was just off the Hunter Road leading into the city and was the red-light district where unlicensed sex workers attracted customers in cars. The girl had been found partially dressed, in skimpy clothes, so it was assumed that she may have been working the streets.

Rachel had wanted to take the lead on the investigation, insinuating that the male detectives wouldn't take the investigation seriously if the woman was a sex worker. In some ways she was right – he knew the attitude that prevailed among many of the men about sex workers but he'd put Phil Rogers in charge with strict instructions to treat the young woman's death like any other.

He wanted Rachel to continue combing through John

Wells financial records. They had the ANZ bank records now and he didn't trust anyone else to do a thorough job. Besides, the team looking at this new death would be working all hours over the weekend and he knew Rachel and her husband had planned to look at properties. He didn't want her to miss out on that again because he believed the couple should be settled in their new home before the baby arrived. He wouldn't dare tell Rachel his thinking though – she would consider her work more important than looking at houses and would be likely to resent him for acting like a concerned father figure. She would also think he was reluctant to make her senior investigating officer on cases due to her pregnancy. It wasn't that at all and once the couple had found a place to buy, he'd be happy to assign her to new cases.

He would pop out to see her shortly. If she hadn't finished going through Wells' records, he would suggest she take them home. She didn't need to be at the station to go through them and then she could fit the work in around her house visits.

Jacko had sent through the transcripts of his interview with Wade Collins together with information on the sim card Collins had handed in to Jacko. Jacko had checked the call details and only one number had contacted Collins which he claimed was Pollard. The number Pollard had used to call Collins did not belong to the mobile phone they'd found in Pollard's flat. It had obviously been Pollard's burner phone which someone had removed; possibly on the night he died. Records Jacko obtained from the provider showed Pollard had received and made calls with several other numbers. Jacko's enquiries into those numbers had led nowhere – they were all from burner phones which were no longer in use. The mystery numbers had last bounced off towers in Newcastle, Tamworth and Sydney.

Catching up for a further chat about it, Frank and Jacko had come to the conclusion that one of those numbers had been used by O'Leary and perhaps one by Lee Wells. Unless they were able to crack the case, they would never know for sure. In the absence of new evidence, Frank knew his superiors would shut the investigation down when other serious crimes cropped up and the Pollard and Wells cases would be shelved.

Dee was wheeling Harry towards the dining hall when a vehicle pulled up, partially blocking their way. Dee pulled the wheelchair back and found another route to skirt around the car.

Harry noticed a couple of battered looking men climbing out of the four-wheel drive. They looked like they'd been in a fight. The man called Ethan stepped out from the driver's side.

'What happened to them?' he asked Dee when they were out of earshot.

'Rueben and Samuel went to Sydney on a business trip last week. They were mugged.'

'How come Ethan's with them then?' Harry wondered if the young men had tried to escape and Ethan had been sent to find them. Maybe he was the one who had battered them.

'Ethan drove down to Sydney last night to collect them. They've been in hospital,' Dee told him.

'Right.' Harry wasn't sure if Dee was telling him the whole story. Or whether she hadn't been told everything. The wounds on the men didn't look that fresh – in the bright lights outside the building he could see bruising that had turned yellow on one man's face. That didn't happen overnight. So the mugging story might have been true.

With his thoughts distracted Harry hadn't realised they had entered a building. He suddenly found himself in a huge dining hall where everyone was standing, looking at him.

'Welcome brother,' he heard someone shouting.

'Welcome brother,' everyone else in the room chorused.

He felt his face turning bright red and just hoped he was going to be able to do this.

41

Saturday

Jacko persuaded his sister Jess to take a trip across to Lake Keepit for a picnic for the day. Baby Chloe loved car trips and he knew the journey would lull her into sleep. Jess didn't drive and on nights she couldn't settle the baby, he'd taken Chloe out in his car which worked like magic. Chloe's older brother Clayton had been the same as a baby and if the three-year-old slept it would give Jess a few hours of peace and quiet. He had the weekend off for a change but thought while he was at the lake, he could leave his card with the caravan park owners in case they heard anything about the missing gliders. He was also considering calling into the horse stud farm on the return journey. Their property butted up to the Foundation boundary and they had actually seen the gliders. Steve and Matt Meredith had told him they'd received a welcome reception from the owners.

Jacko knew Clayton would be delighted to see a real horse – he talked about them non-stop when he saw a picture of them in his little books and loved galloping around the house and backyard neighing. It was something he and Jess had done as children and wondered if all kids were fascinated by horses.

Where they had grown up, outside Windsor, there had been a real horse in the paddock next door. They weren't supposed to go near it and the horse's owner had told them to "bugger off" a few times when he'd caught them. Jacko didn't think it was because the owner was worried about their safety but because they were "bloody abbos". He'd heard the owner mumble this about them a few times. Undeterred, on many occasions they sneaked the odd apple or carrot out of the kitchen and enticed Nellie over to the boundary fence. Nellie was the name they gave the gentle, friendly horse. They didn't know her real name – they'd only ever heard the owner call her 'girl'. When Nellie gave birth to a foal, she brought her baby over to visit them and they spent hours stroking it through the fence railing.

The following year Nellie and her foal disappeared and were replaced by an enormous, highly strung and unfriendly male horse. Jacko often thought that the owner had deliberately moved Nellie and replaced her with this aggressive stallion to frighten them. It worked – they couldn't get on with *Danger* (as they'd christened him), and gave up trying to befriend him.

The Lake was crowded with holidaymakers – picnicking, fishing or boating on the lake. There was even swimming allowed at designated spots. The lake's water had been replenished with the overnight storms they'd had on and off the past week. On Thursday it had hammered down all day and Jacko had expected the ground to be wet and soggy, but the intense heat they'd had on Friday and again today had quickly dried it out. The local papers were assuring readers that the drought had lifted and saying if predicted April rains materialised the area would completely recover.

Jess wasn't a swimmer and had baulked at Jacko's suggestion that he take Clayton for a dip. He didn't understand why she was reluctant to learn to swim and, concerned that she was instilling her fears into her children, he gave her a little lecture before persuading her to let him take Clayton into the water.

'See, he's perfectly alright,' Jacko said when they returned dripping wet to their picnic spot. He looked at baby Chloe contemplating whether to suggest taking her in. At six weeks, Chloe was a chubby, smiling baby and she seemed content enough right now, stuffing a soft toy into her mouth and pressing down on it with her toothless gums. Everything she could get her hands on went into her mouth. He decided he'd leave her to it.

'How would you like to see a real horse, Clayton?'

Clayton's eyes widened in surprise. 'A real giddy-up?'

Jacko nodded. 'Yes.' Turning to Jess he mentioned the stud farm he would like to call into on their way home.

'Yes, Yes, Yes,' Clayton said nodding his head vigorously.

'Is this about work? About those missing gliders? Is that why you asked us here today?' Jess asked.

'No. I just thought if we were passing, we could drop in so Clayton could maybe see some real horses. I have no reason linked to work to go there, but I could use it as an excuse and leave them my card.'

He could see Jess was frowning and about to shake her head.

'Please mummy. Please, please, please,' Clayton begged her. He had a habit of repeating things three times, much to his mother's amusement.

'Oh alright. I wouldn't mind seeing some horses in the flesh again,' Jess said smiling at her son. 'It's been a long time since we were friends with Nellie.'

Harry could hardly contain himself. He was moving into a shared house today as promised. Last night had gone well and, despite Dee's warnings that some members might be hostile towards him over John's death, they were all very friendly and welcoming.

Dee had told him he'd been allocated a ground floor room which had widened doors to accommodate a wheel chair as he'd still need it for the next few weeks. A previous wheelchair user had once occupied the room. He noticed that Dee avoided answering his question about where the man currently was and he suspected it was because he'd passed away. Perhaps she didn't want to worry him about using a dead man's room. He wasn't bothered about that. His new bedroom had a shared wet room next door and he was looking forward to having his first shower.

Part Two

42

Babylon
May 2009

It was his wedding day. Harry couldn't believe it had come to this. He was marrying Dee today. Everything had proceeded according to their plan. If all went well, it would also be the day they left Babylon. Reflecting back over the past three months it seemed an unreal journey he had made; his life had changed so much. He wasn't sure he would ever be able to tell his mates what his daily routine was like at Babylon. His university chums and Felix would double up with laughter if they knew. He had to admit though he'd begun to understand why the life appealed to those who chose to live at Babylon. It was a simple life without the stresses and strains of trying survive out the in the real world. It wasn't because they had no responsibilities. Everyone who lived here had responsibilities. But daily life was mapped out in a simple fashion and everyone knew what their roles were. They didn't have to worry about earning money to pay the bills. Even though the community earned money from the sale of animals, their broadcasts, and music – plus a couple of books they'd published in more recent years, Babylon was almost self-sufficient. And that was as a result of everyone's hard work. They grew the majority of their own food. They generated their own power. They recycled and made use of everything possible. Although they spun wool after shearing the sheep, cotton and hemp were grown for some basic garments and there was a small tannery which made leather products, they still required additional clothing items. If anyone needed new clothing and there was nothing available in the store, they put in a request and the items would be purchased on the next trip to Tamworth or Sydney where they went for bulk items that weren't made on the farm.

Not being able to try on shoes or clothing in a shop was one point about the community that Harry didn't like. Members of the community could try items on at their central store before they put in their requests. Some were second hand; other items were new. Due to his injury Harry had been given several shifts in the 'store' once he was mobile enough to contribute to the community. It didn't have the fusty smell of charity shops like Vinnies or Salvos but he hadn't liked the idea of wearing clothes that had once belonged to other people. It was something he'd never experienced in his life – apart from once wearing one of his father's jackets when they were on holiday and the weather had turned cold.

He wondered how his father was and hoped he hadn't become too distressed by his disappearance. His father was no longer a strong man and Harry was concerned that any worry it might cause him could lead to another heart attack. He was reassured to think that Felix would have been to see his family to tell them he was alive. And if so, why hadn't they come looking for him? Or maybe they had and didn't know where he was. When Felix was dropped back into Manilla Dee seemed to think they'd told him that Harry had elected to stay at Babylon. But he couldn't imagine Felix falling for that. Perhaps Felix had no idea where Babylon was located. If they had driven him back in the dark, he would have struggled to identify the location. It seemed to be in the middle of nowhere. That was probably what the problem was. He hoped to remedy that little issue after tonight.

Once Harry had been able to move around on crutches, anytime he and Dee met they were chaperoned by Dee's mother Deborah; to ensure he made no sexual advances towards Dee, he was told. Deborah walked at a respectful distance behind them, leaving them able to talk quietly and make plans. In some ways he'd been relieved by Deborah's presence. It meant they had a witness in case Ethan or his mates accosted them. Thankfully they hadn't approached him again but he'd seen them around the property, or in the dining hall, on a regular basis.

Harry found it interesting how quickly he'd adjusted to life at Babylon. Apart from all the prayers and religious stuff, he quite liked it and would have been happy to live here in the short term. But not forever. He couldn't do that. There were too many things he missed. His family in particular. But with any luck he would see them soon. He looked at the suit of clothes that had been laid out for him for today's event. If this was a normal wedding, it wasn't what he would choose to wear, but his choices had been limited. He wasn't allowed to see Dee today and soon he was due to move what little clothing he possessed into their new house. It was a cosy two-bedroom wooden house, the last in a row of houses in the married quarter section. It stood at a right-angle to the other houses which he hoped would prove useful.

Dee had warned him that it might be a bit smelly as it was the closest house to the slurry pits and generally remained unoccupied as a result. They'd declared a willingness to accept the house and the smell because they had no intention of being there for long – and it was the only one available. The second bedroom was at the rear and they'd been warned that they shouldn't leave the window of that room open for long periods of time. The main bedroom had its window to the side and the smell wasn't quite as bad. He'd examined the house with Dee and shuddered at the sight of the long drop out of the rear window. With any luck she had managed to acquire the length of rope they needed and had hidden it amongst her belongings, otherwise it was going to prove difficult for him with his gammy right leg.

Dee had moved her personal items into the house this morning with the help of her mother. They'd been given a printed schedule of the day's procedures. Not that Harry had a watch to tell the time with. A church-type bell sounded out the half hour and full hours. Those working out on the property in the agricultural or flower garden sections could hear it. It they were out in further paddocks; the team leader always carried a pocket watch. Harry had been harvesting vegetables this morning and his back was aching due to the position he'd had to adopt when bending over. He'd been able to walk without crutches for the past month, but he found it difficult to crouch and his leg was still painful. Despite attending the clinic each day for physiotherapy exercises he walked with a limp and his running ability was rubbish. Dee suggested that they delay their departure, but tonight would be their last opportunity before Christmas.

Consumption of alcohol at Babylon was only allowed on special occasions. Such as weddings, new births, Easter and Christmas. Tonight, many of the community would be indulging themselves with glasses of wine or beer and, being unused to the alcohol, they would hopefully crash out quickly and be suffering hangovers in the morning – despite the quantity each person could drink being limited. Dee assured him that many of the wives passed their share to their husbands. During the Easter celebrations, he'd experimented by passing his two beers to his single housemates who had staggered back to their quarters and crashed out within minutes. They reminded him of his own first drunken experience. He'd swallowed the dregs of wine in glasses left by guests at one of his father's gatherings. He must have only drunk the equivalent of two full glasses but unused to alcohol at the age of thirteen, he'd passed out in a drunken heap on the veranda's couch. His father had left him there as a punishment, placing a cowboy style hat over his face. He'd woken in the early hours of the morning, his lips almost sealed with dryness, his heading pounding and his arms covered in mosquito bites.

The half hour bell sounded and Harry stood, looked around his room one last time, picked up his meagre set of clothes – most of which were ones he'd brought with him on his trip to Manilla and stuffed them into his small rucksack. Lastly, he placed his moccasins (which were skilfully made by a couple of the women in the community) at the top of his rucksack and walked in his socks to the front door. All outdoor footwear had to be left in a porch area just inside the door. After slipping his feet into the new winter boots he'd been allocated (the trainers he'd been wearing when he crashed had long ago disappeared) he opened the door and stepped out. It had rained again that morning and the gravelled area felt muddy underfoot as he made his way across to his new home, careful not to lose his footing.

In the main bedroom Harry arranged his clothes in the built-in cupboards, noticing that Dee had already placed many of her belongings on the lower shelves. He turned and looked at the newly made bed that he and Dee were expected to occupy from tonight. An attractive patchwork quilt had been placed over the sheets and blankets, which he knew that Dee and her mother had sewn; the traditional marriage quilt.

He was still coming to terms with sheets and blankets. At home he slept with a sheet in the summer and a light doona in the winter months. He'd only ever experienced sheets and blankets in the odd cabin rental on holidays. As the weather had gradually turned colder at Babylon, he'd woken each morning with them in a twisted heap, feeling freezing cold. The bedrooms at the farm had no form of heating. Growing up in Brisbane they hadn't needed heaters. They had reverse cycle air conditioning in the main living areas, but not their bedrooms. The temperature rarely dropped below 14°. This part of New South Wales was another matter and for the past few mornings it had dropped to an average of 1°. Dee had told him it could drop to minus five in the depth of winter. With any luck he wouldn't be here to experience it.

Harry was putting on his boots ready to leave the new house when he was startled by Doctor Jacob appearing at the door.

'How are you, Jeremiah? Settled in okay?'

He looked around expecting to see another man behind him before realising "Jeremiah" was his new name, given to him only last week. Prior to that he'd been known as "brother J". Apparently it was a letter that was available. The community had some weird system where, unless each new member possessed a biblical name that was available, they were allocated a letter of the alphabet by the Elders until a suitable name was given. He couldn't be Harry because, as Dee had told him at their first meeting, it wasn't a biblical name. She thought he might be given 'John' to replace the man who'd died and believed that was why the elders had chosen 'J'. But they'd chosen Jeremiah. He hadn't realised that the same principle applied to Dee's name. She'd told him that she had been called Deidre at birth, which had been shortened to 'D' when she moved into the community. Women weren't given their biblical name until they married. 'Dinah' had been kept in reserve for her and that was now *her* new name. He'd had to stifle laughter threatening to explode from him when the new names had been announced; name giving was a serious matter in the community.

'Yes, thank you,' he said in reply to Jacob's question.

He was supposed to address Jacob as "Elder Jacob" or "Doctor Jacob". Harry avoided using either term of address and did his best to speak directly to the man. Doctor Jacob seemed to have genuine affection for Dee, but there was something about him that Harry found troubling – although he couldn't pinpoint what exactly it was and thought it must be simply his strange religious beliefs. Jacob was a slim man, about 180cm tall and had what he knew women would call a handsome face, framed by thick straw blond hair. With his clear blue eyes Jacob epitomised the Nazi ideal of an Aryan male. Harry had noticed that there were very few members of the community from ethnic backgrounds. Did they have an unwritten policy about who could join? Dee told him Jacob was in his early fifties, but he looked much younger. All the women in the community thought the sun shone out of his arse. He'd sensed that Dee was wary around him, but she refused to speak a bad word against him. Harry felt uncomfortable around the man, but found him easier to converse with than Moses – a man who really gave him the creeps. He did his best to escape contact with both of them. Apart from Ethan and his cronies, the rest of the people in the community were easy to be around and had been welcoming and friendly towards him.

Men who were not elders were supposed to be addressed as "Brother" followed by their name; women were called "Sister". Although he'd noticed this was not strictly adhered to. He'd heard similar old-fashioned terms of address in films set in earlier centuries and wondered if the community looked back nostalgically at the simplicity of those days (while at the same time enjoying the comforts and technology of modern living). He thought it was all rather ridiculous, but he'd complied with the practice to become more accepted.

'Are you looking forward to the wedding this afternoon?'

He and Dee were due to be married at 5pm. An early buffet dinner would be available following the service, with music and dancing after the meal – or jigging about more like. A group of the men had formed a makeshift band for celebrations where they played fiddles, guitars, drums and flutes. The songs they played were like Irish country/folk music. He'd heard them play back in March. After the celebrations they would be allowed to retire to their house from 9pm onwards, meaning they'd have sit it out for four long hours. He knew it was going to be an agonising event. At least there wouldn't be any 'family' or 'best man' speeches, so they were saved the embarrassment of that.

'Er… yes, of course,' Harry said, nervous about why Jacob was asking him this. Was Jacob simply being friendly – or did he have suspicions? Had Deborah overheard some of the plans he and Dee had made and passed them on to Jacob? Had Dee been caught stealing the rope and confessed their plan? Was there even going to be a wedding or was Jacob now about to confront him?

Harry felt his body freeze in panic. He had an urge to run.

43

Jacob pursed his lips and leaned in close to Harry. 'Is there anything you would like to talk to me about brother Jeremiah? Only you seem a little nervous.'

Shit! Shit! Shit! He knows. His heart beating wildly, Harry forced himself to take some deep breaths. He needed to brazen this out.

'No. No I'm fine thank you,' he said, shaking his head. 'Why do you ask?'

Harry could see Jacob scrutinising his face and felt himself blushing. His last words had been a bit squeaky, his nerves showing through. He cursed himself for being such a wimp.

'Most men have their fathers to talk to before their wedding day. I wondered how you were feeling and whether you might want to chat.'

The last thing Harry wanted to do was "chat" to this man. He seemed well meaning, but with his crazy beliefs they had little in common. But perhaps he should say something to cover himself as Jacob had clearly seen his jittery behaviour.

'I *am* feeling a little nervous, but I am confident all will be well,' Harry said.

'It's only to be expected. Marriage is a big commitment. I only hope you see it as the sacred binding that the Almighty intended it to be.'

Here we go. He's going to go off on one of his rants, Harry thought. He couldn't bear the idea and needed to get away. He had the rest of the afternoon off and wanted to ensure his head was clear.

'Of course I do,' Harry said, doing his best to sound genuine. He *did* believe marriage should be a long-term commitment. He'd struggled to come to terms with his parents' divorce and vowed he'd never marry until he found the *one*. And yet here he was about to embark on a sham marriage.

Jacob cleared his throat as though there was something else he wanted to say. 'Sister Debrah and Sister Dinah have told me you have no problem with Dinah's past. Are you sure you're okay about it?'

'Yes, of course I have no problem with Dee – I mean Dinah. Now if you will excuse me, I'd like to take a breath of fresh air before showering and changing for the service.' He suspected Deborah had sent Jacob to check up on him and hoped that Jacob, with his very busy schedule, wouldn't have the time to suggest he accompanied Harry on his walk.

'Right, well if you're sure, I'd better get back to my duties,' Jacob said.

Relieved, Harry nodded and watched as Jacob walked away.

The wedding proceeded smoothly and Harry and Dee

found themselves surrounded by community members wishing them well. Neither of them could stop grinning and Harry was puzzled as to why he didn't feel as though he was putting on the performance of a lifetime. It felt natural and very real. Did Dee feel the same?

After the meal Harry was standing admiring the dancers – especially Dee, when Brother Joseph came along and handed him a glass of beer. When Joseph teased him about the tiny sips he was taking from it, Harry mumbled quietly that he wanted to make sure his wedding night went smoothly and winked at the man. Joseph jabbed him in the ribs and moved off with a raucous laugh, leaving a winded Harry clutching his side. He heard the church bells chime the hour. *Christ, another two hours to go.*

When the nine o'clock bell sounded, Dee and Harry looked at each other and smiled. Now they could finally leave. Unable to participate in the fast dances, Harry had encouraged Dee to accept offers and be whirled around the dance floor. He and Dee had opened the dancing with a slow shuffling dance that he was able to manage with his leg. He'd felt a warmth spread through his body as he'd held Dee close in his arms and was surprised at the extent of his feelings for this woman. Was she feeling something also? They'd never expressed any 'love' towards each other – although when talking to the elders about marrying, they'd convinced them they were in love. Discussions around marriage when they were alone had been done without emotion. More as an arrangement that would suit them both if they could achieve their objective.

'Shall we?' he asked Dee, standing and offering his

hand.

'Most definitely,' Dee replied smiling at him. She turned to speak to her mother and Jacob briefly before standing, placing her shawl around her shoulders and taking Harry's hand.

'Let's slip away. I told mum we wanted to leave without any fuss, so with any luck we'll manage that.'

The hall was filled with loud chatter and laughter, competing with the music. Harry hesitated.

'If we avoid a cheery farewell, do you think some of this lot will come bashing on our door later tonight? Just to wish us happiness?'

'No. Jacob will ensure they don't. It will all be over by ten. Anyway, they did all their well-wishing after the ceremony.'

Harry nodded. They certainly had. He'd received endless pats, punches, jabs, handshakes or cheek kisses. Dee had been hugged almost to death and whispered in his ear that she couldn't wait to remove her dress because after all that well-wishing she said it smelled funny. He hadn't noticed it himself, but felt himself stirring down below at her words. Thankfully they were seated at the tables by then.

Dee had worn a three-quarter sleeved, cream, lace trimmed cotton dress that Deborah had made. Not being a virgin, she wasn't allowed to wear a white dress. Not that either of them was concerned about that. Harry had been worried that she would be cold but Dee had a rust-coloured shawl she draped around herself after the service, which was discarded after embarking on a few dances.

Stepping down behind the elevated table where they'd

been placed as VIPs, they moved towards the exit. A few people noticed them, giving nods and smiles, but they made their escape into the fresh air without being intercepted and headed towards their house. They had no need of keys for the house; none of the houses had them, but thankfully there was a bolt on the inside so they could lock themselves in and wait until it was all quiet before putting their plan into action.

In the privacy of their bedroom, Dee stripped off her dress and underwear, pulling her long hair into a bunch at the back and clipping it.

'I'm going to take a shower,' she said. 'I need it after all that dancing,'

Harry stood mesmerised by her beautiful body. He could never have imagined she would look like this naked. Not with the clothes she wore around the farm.

'Would you like to join me?' Dee asked him shyly.

Harry felt like a schoolboy on his first date; tongue tied and unable to do anything but nod. He thought when Dee had talked about marriage it would be a complete sham and that there would be no consummation taking place. Had the ceremony been legal? Was Moses an ordained minister with the right to marry them?

44

In the shower, Harry and Dee were overcome with passion. It started as an intimate exercise in washing each other until Harry could contain himself no longer. Taking Dee into his arms he kissed her again and again, then began kissing other parts of her body. She moaned in ecstasy before whispering, 'take me now.'

He lifted her against the shower wall asking her to wrap her legs around him. He was aware of Dee letting out a painful grunt as he entered her, felt her body first tense, then relax as he thrust. It was over all too soon for him and he struggled to retain his hold on her as he shuddered to a halt.

'We'd better be careful with the water,' Dee said a moment later, common sense returning.

'Oh right,' Harry said. He eased out of her, lowered her down to the shower floor and they quickly finished washing. He couldn't look Dee in the eye. He felt so embarrassed and worried. Worried that this little episode would interfere with their plans.

'Are you alright?' Dee asked him. Harry noticed that she refrained from using his new name when they were alone.

Like his strategy with the Doctor, she didn't address him by name. He wondered if that would change when they left Babylon.

'Yes, yes fine,' he said. 'I just wasn't expecting that.'

'Me neither. But when we were dancing tonight, I found myself really wanting to make love with you.'

So she had also felt it.

'Are *you* alright?' he asked her. 'I mean ...'

'Stop worrying. Yes, it hurt a little at first – but then it was fine. You're the first man I have ever made love with. My mother told me it was a pleasurable experience, but I didn't really believe it until just now. My memories of the rape were ... but I don't want to think about that now. I'm getting cold. Why don't we jump into bed for a while where we can be warm? We can't do anything for a few hours anyway.'

Dee snuggled up to her husband under the covers. *Her husband.* The words thrilled her even though she knew it was only a temporary situation. That they would only be together for as long as it took them to be free of Babylon. And believing he was her true husband shed the shackles of guilt she would have felt if they were having sex outside marriage. Even though it was a temporary arrangement he had promised her that he would make sure she had somewhere to stay and would remain in contact with her. She didn't know what her future was going to look like, but she was looking forward it. Maybe she could do a proper nursing course and once she was qualified, travel overseas. That idea appealed to her. In the meantime, she would enjoy her time with her *husband.* When she'd told her mother she didn't want to have babies straight away, she'd given Dee a small sponge, explaining that she could use it as a form of contraception. She'd inserted it when she'd been dressing for the wedding. Even with all that dancing it had remained in place. She had to remember to remove it before they left tonight.

She could feel *his* hands beginning to stroke her body, making her feel all aroused again. At least she thought that was what was happening. She felt *wet* down there. The only other times she'd felt like this was when she'd been riding a horse around the property some years ago. At first, she'd been worried that she'd peed herself – although she had felt exhilarated, not frightened. Confused about it, she'd discussed it with her mother, who said she couldn't ride again, saying it was wrong that Dee felt like *that*. Which left her more confused. It hadn't seemed wrong to her.

'But you ride all the time,' she'd said to her mother.

'That's different. I'm a woman. You're only a girl and it will lead you into trouble,' was her reply.

At the time Dee hadn't understood. But now she thinks she does. Her mother was trying to protect her. Not punish her.

It was four years since she'd been on a horse, but tonight, if all went well, she'd be riding again. Taking the ride of her life.

She turned to kiss him and within minutes he was inside her again. This time there was no pain and she lifted her lower body to meet him, soon losing all thoughts; allowing the feeling of pleasure to take over.

They dozed off afterwards until Dee woke with a jolt on hearing the eleven pm chimes.

She nudged him whispering that they ought to take another quick shower and prepare for their journey.

'Did you get the rope?' Harry asked Dee as they were dressing later.

'Yes, it's in my bag. I was terrified Mum was going to look in there at one point while she was helping me pack. I managed to distract her and avoid it. When we arrived over here, she offered to help me unpack, but I said I'd do it later. It was touch and go; I can tell you.'

He watched as Dee rummaged in her cloth bag and pulled out a length of nylon rope. She said it would soon be missed. They didn't have much stock of it in the store and it was always returned after it had fulfilled its purpose, to be reused. She hadn't taken it until this morning to avoid its absence becoming noted too soon and sparking off a search. Dee would have immediately been questioned as it would have been known she was in the store this morning, returning other items.

When they'd viewed the house before accepting it, they'd decided that if they could obtain a length of rope, it could be tied to the wooden bed frame in the back room and they could use it to lower themselves from the window. The ground sloped down from the back windows and the houses had been purposely built in that location to make is easy for bathroom waste to be drained away to the human slurry pit. The bathrooms were at the back of all the other houses whereas theirs, built at a right angle to the others, had a bedroom *and* bathroom at the rear. It was a good 5 metre drop down to the ground. Too far for Harry to jump with his gammy leg without risk of further injury.

'Once we've packed all the essentials, we can test it,' Harry said.

They'd agreed that they'd make their escape at midnight when, in principle, everyone should be long retired to their quarters and hopefully asleep. The good thing about their house being the last one in the line and at a different angle was that the rear bedroom protruded further out the back, way beyond the other houses. If anyone in the other houses was awake and looking out of a rear window they wouldn't be seen.

The man called Ethan was making his way down to check on some livestock. An animal had been attacking sheep in the middle of the night on and off for months. Some of the men thought it must be a dingo, but he knew dingoes weren't commonly found in this area. No, he thought it was more likely to be a mongrel dog which had been abandoned and gone wild. Armed with a rifle fitted with a silencer, so that the other animals weren't disturbed (or the residents) he was hoping to catch the bastard mongrel tonight.

He heard a noise echoing over the paddocks and turning he saw a faint light in the window of one of the houses. He stopped and peered back into the darkness trying to get his bearings. It was the end house. The newlyweds. As he'd knocked back a couple of beers tonight, he'd scrutinised the couple. He hadn't believed for a minute that the young glider was keen to marry that girl Dinah. Brother J, hadn't fooled him. He thought it more likely that the pressure he'd put on the glider had convinced him he needed to show a willingness to remain at Babylon and make no further demands. Marrying Dinah would at least mean the fool could have regular roots, which was more than he was getting these days. He'd had his eye on the slut himself, but he knew Jacob wouldn't approve.

The glider's mate had soon learned the hard way not to make threats to *him*. Now it looked like Brother J was attempting to do a moonlight flit. He laughed at the very idea. *No one* got out of Babylon without it being agreed. He'd have to put a stop to it and expose the bastard. Perhaps his weapon might accidentally go off in the process. The Elders wouldn't like it but maybe he could get around that. Claim he thought it was the animal who'd been attacking the livestock. *He* was the one who really ruled the place. The Elders and Brothers were easy to manipulate, fool or intimidate – including his two regular *helpers*. The new Brother who'd appeared with his wife and child a few months back was proving a bit tricky though – the one he called 'the stupid bastard'. Too smart for his own good. He'd had the cheek to challenge him about Rueben and Samuel's unfortunate experiences in Sydney. Like Ethan, he'd been inside. With Ethan's regular trips to Tamworth or Sydney, he'd clocked what the stupid bastard had done and learned that he had links to the contacts they'd used recently. The bastard's presence could jeopardise everything before Ethan was ready to take off. Just one more run then he'd be sitting pretty. He wasn't going to let anything get in his way.

Ethan sighed. He just hoped that stupid girl, who had fallen for the glider's lies was not going to give him any trouble or he'd have to deal with her too. The fact that she was Jacob's stepdaughter could prove problematic.

Harry lowered himself and waited for Dee to follow. The moon was bright tonight and he decided not to turn on his torch. Her head had disappeared from the window. *What was she doing?* She finally reappeared and climbed through the window twisting herself around in readiness. She paused on the window ledge, and gripping the rope, with one hand, lowered the sash window with the other. Halfway down the rope went slack and she dropped to the ground, almost knocking him over. He managed to retain his balance and grab her before she tumbled off the narrow strip of earth behind their house. He could see that the rope had followed her.

'What on earth were you doing?' he whispered. 'What happened with the rope?'

'I thought it might be useful for us to have for climbing the fence,' Dee said, winding the rope up and stuffing it in her bag. 'I loosened it, thinking it might hold my lighter weight and then we could pull it free once I was down.'

'You could have gone tumbling over the edge and ended up in the slurry pit.'

'I knew it would be alright. Even if I had gone over here, I would have been able to climb back up. It's behind the dairy that will be dangerous. We'll have to walk in a single file. You go on ahead, I'll grab the shovel.'

Harry shook his head in exasperation. From what he'd seen of the fence it would be tricky to climb. They'd agreed they would look at digging out a gap underneath it. With all the rain they'd had lately, the earth would be fairly soft.

He was making his way along the edge of the slurry pit when a voice he recognised startled him.

'And just where do you think you're going?'

It was Ethan. One of the men he studiously avoided after his two threatening encounters with him. He'd sensed then that the man was dangerous and here he was pointing some sort of shotgun at him. Ethan had a torch attached to a band around his head, but Harry couldn't make out the details of his face. He froze, worried about Dee. Where was she? There was no sign of her.

'I … I was just getting some fresh air,' Harry said.

'Yeah, sure. Pull the other one. You're just like your mate. He thought he was a clever bastard, but he soon learned.'

'What do you mean?'

'Your mate. The other idiot who crashed with you. We showered him with hospitality and what did he do? He threatened us, that's what.'

'Threatened you how?'

'He thought he was gunna set the cops onto us, but he soon learned.'

Oh shit. They'd hurt Felix. He *knew* it. That's why no one had come to his rescue. Felix had probably been held prisoner all this time in another part of the property. Was he even alive?

'Where *is* Felix?'

'Well, that's a tricky question,' Ethan said, with a sarcastic tone in his voice. 'I *think* he was scattered on one of the flower beds or … I don't know – maybe he's—'

'You mean Felix is *dead*?'

'Sure is mate. He didn't survive the last bashing I gave him. Don't worry I won't put you through that – it caused too many complications. I think a bullet through the brain might be best for you. You won't feel a thing – it'll be real quick.'

Harry stared open-mouthed at the man. He was talking as though killing another human being was nothing. And he'd said Felix might be *scattered?* Did he mean Felix's *ashes?* They'd burnt him? My god these people were worse than he thought. And Dee, did she know about this? Had she led him into a trap?

Ethan raised the shotgun. With nothing to defend himself except his small rucksack Harry didn't think he stood a chance of escaping death this time.

45

Harry was considering throwing his rucksack at Ethan when he glimpsed the shovel swing through the air hitting Ethan on the side of the head. Ethan dropped his weapon, his legs crumpled and before Harry could grab hold of him, he went toppling off the narrow ledge they were on and disappeared. He heard a splash and a gurgling sound. Switching on his torch Harry shone it down into the slurry pit. A solitary elbow was there for a second before it disappeared beneath the murky surface. Harry shuddered.

'It's too late to save him,' Dee whispered as she walked up to him. He could see she was shaking. 'I had to do it, otherwise he would have killed you. I heard what he said about your friend.'

'Did you know about Felix?' he hissed at her. Had this woman lied to him from the very beginning?

'I was suspicious. But Ethan lied and said the other man in the barn was John. He warned me to keep away. They were watching me all the time, monitoring me on the cameras. I didn't *dare* look. I checked John's body when they put him in the fridge and he *did* have damage to his face like you'd noticed, so I thought maybe Ethan had told me the truth.'

'Did Jacob know?'

'No, I'm sure he wouldn't have known. He was away part of the time. He would *never* agree to someone being killed. Anyway, we shouldn't be wasting time talking about this *now*. We can go over everything tomorrow. We need to go.'

'What about Ethan?'

'We can't do anything for him now. We can report his death as soon as we're out.'

Dee bent down and picked up what Harry could now see was a short-barrelled shotgun with a silencer attached.

'What are you *doing*?' he whispered.

'We need to take this with us. It's evidence – otherwise someone might make it disappear. It could come in handy anyway. But I am going to empty the barrels. We don't want to have any accidents.'

Harry watched as Dee deftly emptied the weapon. She'd clearly handled them before. He was struggling to digest everything he'd heard and what had just happened. He couldn't move. It could have been him instead of Ethen disappearing under the murky liquid.

'Come on Harry, let's go and get Starlet,' she whispered holding out the shovel for him to take.

'You just called me Harry,' he said surprised.

'Well, it's your name, isn't it?' He could just make out a broad grin spreading across her face.

At the side of the barn, now having passed the worst of the muddy areas, they changed into their moccasins and looped their boots with their long laces around their necks. Two young stable boys slept in quarters above the horses and Dee had stressed to Harry that they needed to be very quiet. There was a concrete floor in the stables and she was worried their boots would prove too noisy.

Dee greeted her friend Starlet in soft whispers. Although no longer allowed to ride her, she visited Starlet almost every day with a little treat. Starlet trusted her. Fixing a blanket over Starlet's back and a bridle and reins around her head, Dee walked Starlet out to the stable entrance where Harry was keeping a lookout. She cringed as Starlet's shoes clopped over the floor, praying the stable boys would not hear anything. They planned to walk Starlet to the first bench where they could mount her without difficulties. Tonight, they'd be riding bareback – something which she had never done. But attempting to saddle her up was too risky.

'The coast is clear,' Harry whispered as she reached the barn entrance.

Harry. She hadn't dared think of his real name all the time she'd been nursing him and, knowing he'd be given a new name, she'd deleted it from her mind, otherwise she might slip up in front of others. But tonight, once they were in the privacy of their home, she'd been practising the name in her head. It did suit him. Far more than Jeremiah ever would.

The problem they had now was skirting other outbuildings where the dogs slept. The last thing they needed was a chorus of dogs barking. They would soon attract unwelcome attention. There was no other option than to go through the wheat fields. She hated the idea of potentially causing damage to the precious crops, but they had little choice. Benches or anything else they could use to mount Starlet were not placed in convenient locations. However, as they set off, she recalled seeing a couple of the tractors abandoned at the end of the fields early this afternoon. If they were still there, they could use them instead. She crossed her fingers.

The tractors were there and she encouraged Harry to climb up onto the platform and mount Starlet while she held her, all the time whispering reassurance to both of them. Once he was settled, she passed Harry the shotgun and could just make out his eyes widening in alarm.

'It's alright, it's not loaded,' she said. 'Take it. Then I'll pass you the shovel. A few seconds later he was clutching both awkwardly. It was a good thing she'd emptied the barrels. Harry admitted he had never been on a horse before and was nervous. She doubted he'd ever held a weapon either, judging by the look on his face.

Dee's mother had taken her shooting many a time when she was younger, saying it was always good to know how to use a weapon out in the bush. It was some time since she'd handled one though.

She mounted Starlet in front of Harry and told him to place one arm around her. Before setting off, she tied a scarf around her head and moved Starlet off at a slow trot. Riding Starlet to the boundary fence would make their journey so much easier. Harry would have struggled to walk the distance with his leg and he was going to need all his strength once they made it onto the horse breeder's property. They would still have a long way to go before they reached the homestead.

Dee had been to the stud farm once with Jacob and her mother when they'd bought Starlet. She was fifteen at the time and seriously depressed, having never really recovered from her rape two years prior – or from the attitude of many of the other community members. The horse purchase was a desperate attempt to shake her out of her depression. And it had worked. For a whole year she experienced the delights of looking after Starlet and riding her most days once her chores and schoolwork were complete. Until her mother put a stop to it. Now Starlet carried other young members of the community on her back and Dee had to be content with visits.

They'd driven to the stud farm that day, going out through the back gates and seemed to travel for miles before they reached the place. The homestead was located on the far boundary of Babylon, so she knew they had a lot of ground to cover before they arrived there.

Dee had told Harry that the boundary fence they were crossing was one of the few that wasn't electrified. Meaning it was safe to use. When they arrived at the fence – after what seemed like hours, he knew he was going to be sore and stiff once he dismounted. He'd managed to doze off for a few microseconds which could have proved disastrous if he'd dropped everything. He found the ride excruciatingly uncomfortable – with Dee's bag digging into his side he was sitting awkwardly; one hand wrapped around Dee, the other clutching the shovel and shotgun. Several times he'd been tempted to ask her to stop because he couldn't take any more.

It was still dark, but shining the torch onto the fence he could see it was a good ten feet high with barbed wire looped across the top. The ground looked and felt rock hard, despite the recent rain.

'I think we should climb the fence,' Dee said. 'If we place my jacket over the wire, we should be able to climb over without any problems. The gaps in the wire fence are quite wide and we should be able to get a toe hold in those for climbing. I don't think there's any point in using the shovel.'

Harry was relieved at the idea of that. He could discard it. Dee destroyed that notion with her next statement. 'But we need to bring the shovel with us anyway to hand in to the police. I did use it as a weapon after all.'

He'd forgotten about that.

'We can tie the shotgun and shovel together using the rope and pull them up once one of us is up on the top of the fence. I think you should go first,' she said. 'I need to stay with Starlet until the last minute.'

Wriggling her bag off her shoulders, Dee dug out the rope and asked him to pass her the shotgun and shovel. It should be him doing all this, but he didn't seem to have any energy. How he was going to make it across the fence and then trudge all the way to the farmhouse, he wasn't sure. Dee must think he was a useless idiot.

She'd already taken off her jacket and passed it to him. 'Tie this around your neck. When you reach the top, spread it out over the barbed wire.'

Once he'd done that, she instructed him to lean across, grab the fence and slide himself off the horse. Easier said than done. Grunting and groaning while Dee clung to the fence with one arm and kept the horse steady with the other, he finally managed to free himself and start to climb.

'Wait!' she called out to him and threw him the end of the rope. Using one hand he manged to loop it around his waist and resumed his climb. Dee's idea of the jacket worked well and being extra careful he slid his legs across the top in a scissor-like action. Once on the other side he pulled on the rope and slowly lifted the two items up and over the fence and then lowered them down to the ground.

'Now you,' he told Dee. He didn't want to climb down until Dee was safely over the fence. It would probably take both of them to free her jacket anyway. Although stiff, he thought with a few stretches he might be okay. Throughout their journey there had been a gentle breeze which Dee had said helped her to remain alert and awake. The wind had now picked up pace and had served to startle him into wakefulness. He was beginning to feel a surge of renewed energy. He was sure it was the idea of freedom beckoning.

As Dee was murmuring goodbye to her horse he looked up and spotted what looked like headlights of a vehicle in the far distance. They were coming from the direction of the Babylon buildings.

Shit! They'd already discovered they were missing.

'Look Dee. Someone's coming. You'd better hurry up,' Harry said, attempting not to show panic in his voice.

46

Dee looked around and spotted the vehicle lights. It had to be one of the four-wheel drives.

'I doubt they'll be looking for us. Not yet anyway. That'll probably be Isaac and Daniel looking for Ethan.'

But Harry was right, she needed to get a wriggle on. It would only take about another ten minutes for the vehicle to reach their location. She didn't think whoever was driving would head straight over their way – they would be heading for one of the sheep paddocks. She'd heard that there'd been problems with sheep being attacked and was sure that was where Ethen had been planning to go tonight before his little diversion. There were no sheep in this part of the property – but she still had to get moving.

She turned Starlet around so that she was facing the home stables. She removed Starlet's bridle and shoved it into her bag. Sliding off the horse she also whipped the blanket off and wrapped it around her shoulders. It would be better for Starlet to be found without any equipment on her. Once she had a grip on the fence, she smacked Starlet on her bottom and told her to go home. Not moving, Starlet turned her head to take a look at Dee. She smacked her again. 'Home Starlet,' she said. Starlet didn't need telling again and Dee watched, tears in her eyes as the horse cantered off back towards the stables.

With any luck they would think someone had left her stall open and she'd wandered out.

After she'd climbed across the fence the two of them set to work freeing Dee's jacket. It was a harder task than she imagined and it kept snagging on the wire. All the time she kept a watchful eye on the vehicle they'd seen in the distance. She knew Ethen would have had radio contact with his mates. Had he reported that he was going to investigate her and Harry? Were they now looking for the two of them?

The newly-wed couple were not expected to work today. They had been provided with food to make their own breakfast and lunch in their house, so it wouldn't be until they were due to join the others in the dining hall for the evening meal that they would be missed. Unless …

'Look. They've turned the jeep around. They're heading this way Dee. Shit! We need to just leave the jacket,' Harry cried.

'No. If they see the jacket then they will know someone has climbed the fence. Come on Harry keep working at it.'

A few frantic seconds later they freed the jacket and clambered down, picking up the blanket, shotgun and spade before moving off. While on the move Dee wrapped the two items in the blanket and tied the rope around them while Harry clutched the jacket.

'They're going to see us unless we can make it across to those bushes,' Harry said. He was moving as fast as he could, but Dee sensed the pain it was causing him by his rugged breathing.

They made it to the clump of bushes just as the four-wheel swung round and turned to drive beside the fence to the very spot they'd been minutes before. They crouched down and waited as the vehicle stopped.

One of the men jumped out and called Ethen's name. Dee recognised Daniel's voice echoing across the still darkness. Without her jacket she began shivering and her teeth clattered. She was sure it was also partly due to fear. If those men spotted them their lives could be in danger.

Harry must have noticed her shivering and placed her jacket around her shoulders. It didn't stop her shaking.

When Daniel received no response from his calls, he climbed back into the vehicle and it drove off. Harry went to stand, but she cautioned him.

'Wait,' she said. She wanted to make sure the vehicle didn't do a U-turn and drive back the way it had come. Once she saw the tail lights disappear, she heaved a sigh of relief. 'Okay, they've gone. We can get moving now.'

They could see the sky beginning to lighten in the distance by the time Dee and Harry knocked on the homestead door. She recognised the sleepy looking man who opened it, a jacket over his winter pyjamas.

'Good morning, I don't know if you remember me. My name is Dee and my family bought Starlet off you some years ago.'

'And my name is Harry Meredith,' Harry said cutting in. 'My paraglider crashed on the property next door some months ago. Could you call the police for us? We have some serious crimes to report.'

The man's eyes bulged in surprise. 'Well stone me …,' he said. 'You'd better come in. Sally!'

He ushered them into a vestibule area and told them to follow him through to the large kitchen where Dee immediately felt the warmth radiating from a solid fuel stove. She headed towards it and held her hands above it hoping it would help to stop the shaking.

A woman with ruffled brown hair appeared, clad in a fleecy dressing down. The man spoke to her in a low voice and she turned with surprised eyes and looked at the two unexpected guests.

'I'll make you a hot drink,' she said, taking the kettle from the range and placing it over a hob. She grabbed mugs from a cupboard and asked them what they wanted to drink.

'Tea for me,' Dee said.

'Coffee for me thanks,' Harry said.

'While the kettle is coming to the boil, I'll just get dressed,' the woman said, rushing out of the kitchen.

'A detective from Tamworth left me his card a few months back. He was involved in the search for you,' the man said turning to Harry. 'Your father and brother Matt also called in to see us.'

'My father and Matt came here?'

Harry was pleased to hear that. They hadn't given up on him then. The man explained what had happened and how he had taken his visitors over to the boundary fence. When his wife returned to the kitchen calling her husband Matt, Harry was confused.

'I'm another Matt,' he explained. 'Matt Flinders.

Nothing to do with the explorer,' he added. 'This is my wife, Sally.'

It took Harry a moment to absorb the explorer comment. Back in primary school they'd learnt about a Matthew Flinders who'd explored parts of Australia during the early settlement days. There was an island named after him off the north coast somewhere.

He nodded at the Flinders couple.

'I'll just go and phone that Detective and then get dressed.'

'Would you like some breakfast?' Sally asked them. 'I can do you some bacon, eggs and toast.'

Harry's mouth salivated at the idea of bacon. It had seemed like forever since he'd tasted it.

'That would be wonderful, thank you'.

'Just an egg and some toast for me thank you,' Dee said.

Dee had finally stopped shaking and had moved to sit on a stool at the kitchen island. Her hands were clutching the hot mug of tea Sally had just made her.

Sally lit the gas under a pan and a few seconds later he could hear the bacon sizzling. The smell of it was heavenly.

Matt Flinders returned to the kitchen with a worried look on his face.

'Detective Jacko has asked if I could drive you over to Tamworth and stressed that we are not to make contact with anyone at this point. I told him we'd set off straight away. He's worried that people from Babylon might come here looking for you. He thinks we should both go with them Sally.'

'I'm in the middle of cooking breakfast. Can't we leave after eating?'

'I don't think we should. Perhaps you should make it to eat in the car. As toasted sandwiches? I know I could do with one.'

'Righto. I'll make a flask of tea as well.'

Ten minutes later they were bundled into the Flinders' four-wheel drive. The sun was not fully up and, as they approached the entrance gates, Matt Flinders announced that he could see the lights of a vehicle fast approaching, coming from the direction of Babylon.

'You two had better duck down and hide – just in case. Throw those blankets over you. I'm sorry but they'll smell of the dogs a bit.'

Harry had just been about to open his greaseproof paper wrapped toasted bacon and egg sandwich. Now his stomach churned at the thought that Babylon thugs were searching for them. Unclipping their seat belts Harry and Dee flung themselves down out of sight.

Sally turned and helped to hastily cover them up. Matt Flinders had been right. The rugs did smell of dogs. He wasn't allergic to dog hairs but the blankets made him want to sneeze. Harry held his nose and his breath. And waited.

47

'False alarm,' Matt Flinders said. 'I recognise the car – it's another farmer who lives beyond Babylon. 'You can sit back in your seats again.'

They clipped themselves in again as Matt turned right, heading towards Manilla.

Harry's stomach settled and he thought he might be able to brave eating his sandwich. Dee was already tucking into hers and he could see Sally and Matt were doing the same in the front.

'I'll pour us all a small cup of tea in a moment,' Sally said, her mouth full of food.

Rachel woke cursing the ring of her mobile phone. Who on earth could be calling at this hour? She could see through the slit in the curtains that light was beginning to creep across the sky. It was dawn. Andy stirred beside her and mumbled. 'Answer the bloody thing Rach, for God's sake.'

Reaching out for the phone she saw it was Frank Bailey and pressed to accept the call.

'Good morning,' she said thinking it couldn't really be a good morning if Frank was waking her this early.

She listened with incredulity to what he had to say before edging out of bed. 'Okay see you in fifteen then.'

Turning to Andy, she told him she had to head off to Tamworth and that Frank would be picking her up soon. She packed a bag with a couple of days' worth of clothes, unsure whether they would be staying over. At seven months pregnant, she couldn't move too fast these days. Her baby bump was quite large now and although Frank had allowed her to participate in some serious investigations over the past few months, he was very cautious about how much he would let her do, explaining he didn't want to place her in any potentially dangerous situations. He must have thought any action they'd be taking in Tamworth would be safe. He'd mumbled something about the glider being held in Babylon all this time and that they would finally get their search warrant for the place.

'Jacko called me about thirty minutes ago to say the glider and a young woman from Babylon had turned up on the doorstep of the neighbouring horse stud farm,' Frank explained once they were on the road. 'The couple from the stud farm are driving Harry Meredith and the young woman, whose name is Dee, to Tamworth to meet Jacko. They said they had a number of *serious* crimes to report.'

'No word on the second glider?'

'Not as far as I know. Presumably all will be revealed when we arrive.'

'Did you tell Beth about her step-son?'

'Yes. I left her to phone her son Matt with the news and gave her Jacko's number for contact. Jacko stressed that news of Harry Meredith's escape needs to be kept very quiet until we know the full story. He doesn't want Steve Meredith or any members of his family making contact with the press, otherwise it could jeopardise any investigations we are making.'

'But Steve Meredith will want to see his son as soon as possible I imagine.'

'Yes, I'm sure he will,' Frank said sighing. 'Although I'm not sure if he will be up to the journey. He had a mild stroke shortly after returning to Brisbane and he is still struggling with balance and movement. The stroke didn't affect his brain, but left him with impaired use of his left arm and leg – but he's been receiving a lot of physio and things are improving for him. His son Matt persuaded him to sell the business and Meredith is living off the invested income now. Although I believe his wife still works.'

'At least he didn't die. He'll get to see his son again.'

'Yes, there is that at least.'

'Does Rawlings know we're coming?'

'Jacko said he'd called her immediately after hearing from Flinders, the stud farm owner. She told Jacko to contact us and invite us up, knowing how much I wanted to search the property.'

'That was good of her then.'

'I suspect her motive was more to placate me if does turn out that Lee Wells has been there all this time – and serious crimes *have* been committed.'

'Sounds like there was a kidnapping for starters. The glider being held against his will.'

'Hmm. Probably.'

'Has there been any mention of Wells?'

'Not as far as I know, but with any luck this will be our opportunity to find out. Changing the subject, how are you settling into your new house?'

'Oh, you know, it's still a bit chaotic with boxes everywhere. We've only been in a few days.'

'You must be relieved to have made the move before the baby's born though.'

'I'll say. The house is much more child friendly. With my bump, I was struggling with the stairs at our rental – but now with everything on one level it's much easier. Norm seems to be much happier.'

'Norm?'

'Norm is the nickname Andy and I have given the bump.'

'Right,' Frank said nodding. He'd forgotten that Rachel and Andy knew they were expecting a boy. 'You must be looking forward to the birth.'

'Oh, I wouldn't go as far as to say that.'

Jacko was buzzed to say his visitors had arrived. He recognised the Flinders from his visit to their stud farm with his nephew back in February. He shook hands with Flinders and turned to the younger man.

'G'day, you must be Harry Meredith. I'm Detective Constable Jacko,' he said holding out his hand. 'I met your father and brother shortly after you went missing. Have you been in touch with them since you arrived at the Flinders' house?'

'No ... um Mr Flinders told me you said not to make contact with anyone.'

'Good. Your family are being informed this morning,

but I'm afraid you won't be able to speak to them until we take your statement.'

Jacko turned to the young woman. 'And what is your name?' he asked her.

'Dee,' she said.

'What's your surname Dee?'

'Um, Phillips … I think.'

He thought that was a strange thing to say. Why wasn't she sure of her name?

'Any relation to Doctor Jacob Phillips?'

'Yes, he's my stepfather. I *think* my name was legally changed to Phillips when my mother married him. It was what they put on my school books at Babylon anyway, although I'd had another name before we moved there. I was quite young at the time.'

He nodded. That explained her confusion. He'd pick up her full details when they interviewed her. He wondered what her story was and why this young woman had helped Harry Meredith to escape.

'If you'd all like to follow me upstairs,' he said waving an arm towards the staircase.

'You need us to stay then?' Flinders asked him. 'Only we thought we might head back.'

'We will need to take a brief statement from you about this morning's events. Do you need to go back? Would any of your employees be there?'

Jacko had been introduced to a young man who worked for the couple when he'd visited them and he'd spotted another young man out on the property.

'I have two stable hands due in. I've sent them a message saying I will see them later.'

'Have you told them where you are?'

'No, I followed your advice and said nothing. We have dogs though and they will need feeding.'

'Can you ask the stable hands to feed them today? Is there anywhere you could stay in Tamworth overnight?' Jacko was concerned about the couple returning home in case Babylon residents came calling. It was clear Harry had been there all this time and he wasn't sure what the young man was going to reveal.

'My sister lives in Tamworth,' Sally Flinders said. 'Do you really think it would be dangerous for us to return home?'

'I don't know,' Jacko sighed. 'I'm just suggesting it as a precautionary measure. Would you be able to stay with your sister?'

'I expect so. I'll give her a ring shortly. She does shift work at the hospital and is likely to be at work right now. I know she was rostered on the early shift this week.'

Jacko nodded and led them up the stairs. He wanted to separate the young woman called Dee from Harry Meredith for their interviews. Ideally, he would prefer to interview them with DCI Frank Bailey. But he wouldn't be arriving at the station for another few hours yet. He decided he'd interview Harry Meredith first and hold out on Dee Phillips. Her statement was likely to include information Chief Bailey would want to know. He'd get a couple of uniforms to take a statement from the Flinders couple.

He showed them into a lounge area and asked one of the civilian staff to offer refreshments while he organised everything.

48

'So, just to be clear, you *were* being held at Babylon against your will?' Jacko asked Harry for clarification. The young man had blurted out his story out but it was muddled and confusing. He couldn't tell if the man *had* been held against his will or not. Seems he'd settled in there and had even gone through a 'marriage' ceremony to the woman he called Dee the previous day. And yet he claimed he was not there willingly. It didn't sound right to him.

'Well, yes and no,' Harry said. 'It's more complex than that. I told you the man called Ethan came to see me while I was being kept in the cage in the barn. He told me that if I wanted to get better – and I was very vulnerable at the time – I should stop asking to make contact with my family and pretend to be happy about being there. He told me the doctor thought God had sent me to them or some such rubbish. Dee told me something similar. Ethan frightened me – so when I finally got to see the doctor, I thanked him for treating me and said it sounded like they had a wonderful set up at Babylon.'

'You think the doctor had no idea about the threats made by this Ethan?'

'I have no idea whether the doctor knew what was going on or not. His ideas just seemed quite bonkers to me. I *did* ask him about the injured man in the other cage. He seemed confused for a moment and then said it must have been John. The one who'd had the fatal fall. The Doctor was away when the accident happened. Whoever it was in the other cage – and I believe it was Felix, not John, had been removed by then. Then Ethan paid me another visit. Dee had taken me for a walk in a wheelchair and had just pushed me back into the barn. Ethan told her to leave. He was with two other men this time, who I later learned were called Daniel and Isaac. They all have these biblical names you see.'

'And what did they have to say?'

'Ethan gave me another warning.'

'What *exactly* did he say?'

'He told me that he could make me disappear with the snap of his fingers, which he did. Snapped his fingers I mean. And he told me to keep the doctor sweet. The other two kept quiet but I still found them quite intimidating.'

Jacko could just picture it. A young man, incapacitated by his injuries, confronted by three bullies. He'd experienced similar intimidation when he was in high school. He'd been hobbling around on crutches after tearing the ligaments in his left foot at a footie match the week before when the bullies surrounded him in a local park. The crutches proved to be a useful weapon when one of them tried to attack him.

'What do you think he meant by that?' Jacko asked Harry.

'Ethan didn't elaborate, but I worked hard then at

establishing a good relationship with Dee, culminating in our so-called 'marriage' yesterday.'

'Ah yes, Dee. The Doctor's stepdaughter. So do you think she had any inkling as to what was going on? Was she aware of what happened to your friend Felix?'

'We haven't really had a lot of time to talk about it with all that's happened. I did ask her after she killed Ethan. I say killed – I'm certain she just intended to knock him out with the spade to prevent him from shooting me, but he lost his balance and fell into the slurry pit as I told you. Anyway, I asked her if she knew about Felix and she said she'd had suspicions, but when she looked at John's dead body, she saw he had injuries to his face and thought Ethan must have been telling the truth. You'll have to ask her.'

Jacko nodded. 'We will be asking her, don't worry. Now, can you take us through what happened with Ethan last night again?'

Frank and Rachel made the journey to Tamworth in record time. The roads had been clear leaving Newcastle and apart from a small snag at Singleton, where Frank had used the blue flashing police light to get through, they'd not encountered any further hold-ups.

He knew he'd startled Rachel a couple of times with his speed, but it was important that they gathered as much information as possible this morning and surprised the community at Babylon with a search later this afternoon if possible.

Jacko had phoned them to give an update after interviewing Harry Meredith. With two deaths already on record, they had more than sufficient information for a warrant. He'd started his interview with Dee Phillips to verify information Harry had given in his statement, but Jacko was waiting for him to arrive before completing the interview with her.

After signing in, Jacko led him to an interview room where the young woman was being watched over by a uniformed constable. Armed with a file containing photographs of Lee and John Wells, he was hoping that the young woman would recognise them. He'd left Rachel to chase up the search warrant with Rawlings.

'For the record, Detective Chief Inspector Frank Bailey from Newcastle Police Area Command has entered the room,' Jacko said. 'Also present is Detective Constable Jacko, Deidre Phillips and duty lawyer Carmen Rodriguez.'

'Good morning Dee,' Frank said. 'I am going to show you some photographs and would like you to tell me if you recognise the men in them.'

He pulled out a photograph of John Wells placing it on the table.

'Do you know this man, Dee?'

She nodded. 'That is Elder Moses.'

'Elder Moses? You know him by the name of Elder Moses?'

'Yes. Why are you asking about Elder Moses?'

'And how long have you known Elder Moses?'

'Since I was little. When we lived in the Blue Mountains, he used to visit us with his wife and little daughter. He and Jacob started Babylon together.'

'How long ago was this?'

'I was almost seven at the time.'

Frank looked at her waiting for further clarification. Jacko leaned over and told him Dee Phillips was 20 years old now which surprised him. She looked much younger. Thirteen years ago tallied with what he'd learned about the Foundation being set up at Babylon. So the *wife* and young daughter who had been with John Wells must have been his second family.

'Do you know the name of Moses's wife and daughter?'

'Of course I do. His wife's name is Leah and his daughter's name is Rachel.'

'And they've lived with you at Babylon since you moved there?'

'No. Not at first. They only joined us permanently a few years ago. They used to come and go before that. It was due to Elder Moses that we were able to build all the new houses at Babylon some years back.'

Frank nodded. That would account for where much of John Wells' money had gone. And he knew that Wells legal wife had not moved with him, so he must have moved with his other 'family' to Babylon.

'And what about this man?' Frank asked, pulling out a photo of Lee Wells.

'That's Brother Levi,' Dee said, smiling and nodding. 'He's Elder Moses's son from a previous marriage. He only joined us a few months ago. Although he visited us quite a bit in the past.'

'When he joined you, did he have a woman and young child with him?'

'Yes, his wife and daughter.'

'And what are they called?'

'His wife's name is Martha and his daughter is called

Rebecca.'

Frank's instincts had been right all along. Wells had been hiding at Babylon all these months. Not for much longer.

'Thank you, Dee. You have been very helpful.'

'Why are you asking about Elder Moses and Brother Levi? They haven't done anything wrong? It's Ethan, Isaac and Daniel who are the bad eggs there. Mainly Ethan. I think the other two are a bit afraid of him. Well, Ethan *used* to be a bad egg I should say, until I accidentally killed him. He would have shot Harry if I hadn't hit him though.'

'Yes, we know Dee,' Jacko said. 'However, a man has died and until it's fully investigated, I'm afraid we are going to have to keep you in custody.'

'You mean I can't leave with my husband?'

'From what I understand you were married under the names of Jeremiah and Dinah. As they are not your real names the marriage will not be valid.'

'Oh. Well it doesn't matter anyway. I think Harry only agreed to marry me so that we could escape.'

'Out of interest Dee, why did *you* want to escape?' Frank asked.

'I told Detective Jacko about being raped when I was thirteen. I was a bit of an outcast after that. While I love my parents and most of the people at Babylon, life there for me was very limited. I've hardly experienced life outside Babylon. I want to see some of the world.'

Frank nodded. 'Well, I guess you might have the opportunity to do that very soon,' he said. *Unless you are locked up for manslaughter*, he thought.

49

Before they joined the convoy of vehicles heading to Babylon, Frank popped in to see Detective Superintendent Sue Rawlings.

'Deidre Phillips has just identified Lee Wells. He's been at Babylon all this time.'

'Well now you have that solid evidence, you can look for him while you're there. As senior ranking detective, I'm happy for you to lead the search. Are you okay with that?'

'Yes, fine thanks.'

'Good luck with it all then. I doubt you'll find anything there that will surprise me though. I've seen plenty in my time.'

Frank nodded. 'The search might take more than one day. It's a big place. Forensics will have to go over everything. And the body of the man called Ethan will have to be recovered.'

'You or Jacko need to phone me later with an update then.'

Frank, Jacko and Rachel together with a convoy of vehicles

carrying forensic technicians and uniformed police officers arrived at the Babylon gates shortly before 3pm announcing they had warrants to search the whole of the property.

Doctor Jacob Phillips, accompanied by several men drove to the gates to meet them. Frank introduced himself, Jacko and Rachel and presented the search warrants to Phillips. After scrutinising the paperwork Phillips instructed his men to open the gates.

'I'm puzzled Inspector Bailey. Can you explain why you have warrants to search Babylon?' Phillips asked.

'This morning we received reports of various serious crimes committed on your property. We are here to investigate the truth of those reports,' Frank said. 'I would ask that no-one leaves the property as shall be interviewing everybody here.'

'Serious crimes? What are you talking about?'

Frank looked at Jacko. Doctor Phillips appeared to have no idea what he was talking about. Either that or he was a very good actor. He looked confused and had an innocent air about him.

'If you don't mind, we'd rather speak to you in more private surroundings,' Frank said, looking at the two men standing nearby. They looked like dogs guarding their master, ready to pounce if they sensed danger. They could be concealing weapons. He wondered if the two were the men called Daniel and Isaac. Not that he believed those were their real names. He'd seen both of them on his last visit. Missing this time was the bear like character who seemed to be the leader. Could he have been the one called Ethan?

'Is this something to do with Ethan?' the doctor asked. 'He disappeared last night while trying to find out who or what is attacking our sheep. Daniel and Isaac,' he said gesturing to the two men beside him, 'went out searching for him late last night and again this morning. Others are still searching for him. Did someone break onto our property and harm him?'

'I'm afraid I can't say any more right now. As I said, I would rather we spoke in—'

'Alright,' the doctor said, holding up his hands as though surrendering. 'I can take you to the infirmary. I have an office there. Then there is the dining hall and communal lounge. Your people could set up there and we will bring you refreshments.'

Phillips turned and asked one of the men to radio through to the kitchen to prepare some drinks and snacks.

'It is kind of you to be so hospitable. In the meantime, I need you to point out the dairy to us. That's one of the first places we will be wanting to look at. Our forensic technicians will be heading straight there.'

The doctor looked even more bewildered now.

Turning back to Jacko and Rachel, Frank spoke quietly. 'Those two men are Ethan's cronies. When we arrive at the main buildings, I want them detained and separated. Rachel, you come with me to talk to the doctor.'

'Your stepdaughter Deidre Phillips confessed to the killing of a member of your community last night. We believe there have been other killings on the property and that you are harbouring criminals,' Frank said, once they were settled in Phillips's office.

'What? No, no no … you are mistaken. My stepdaughter Dinah married her sweetheart last night. Jeremiah. He only joined us a few months ago. They're in their house right now. I could prove it to you,' Phillips said preparing to stand.

Frank held up his right arm. 'That won't be necessary Doctor Phillips. I can assure you we have Deidre in custody at Tamworth Police Station.'

'Tamworth Police Station? In custody? How on earth … she didn't do something to Jeremiah did she? I thought she was over all that business. I thought they seemed genuinely in love.'

'When you say "over all that business" I assume you're referring to the rape she experienced as a young adolescent? A *crime* you didn't report?'

The doctor looked at them blankly for a second, then his eyes took on a startled appearance. Frank suspected he was beginning to believe they did have Deirdre at Tamworth otherwise they couldn't have known about the rape. Not wishing to discuss the rape at this point he continued.

'Deidre has told us that she hit the man you call Ethan over the head with a shovel last night to prevent him from shooting Harry Meredith – the man you call Jeremiah. Ethan fell into the slurry pit behind the dairy and died. They were unable to do anything to save him. Her version of events was backed up independently by Harry Meredith.'

Frank could see realisation dawning on the doctor's face.

'Shortly before she hit him, Ethan had confessed to

the killing of the other paraglider who crashed onto your property. A young man by the name of Felix McMurray.'

'No, that isn't right. Unlike Jeremiah, that young man had few injuries from their crash. He spent a couple of days with us before some of the brothers dropped him back into Manilla to collect his car and personal items. He gave the brothers his friend's things to bring back here.'

'Which *brothers* are you referring to?' Frank asked. He knew the doctor was using the term of address in use at Babylon, rather than talking about literal brothers. Although until they identified everyone at Babylon, they wouldn't know if any of the community members were related.

'Ethan and Isaac ...,' the doctor trailed off, realising he had possibly just confirmed Ethan's involvement in Felix's death.

'I believe you have an incinerator here at Babylon? Would you be so good as to show us where it is? We'd also like to see the flower beds. Our forensic technicians will be wanting to examine both. We will then have further questions for you and John Wells, aka Elder Moses.'

The doctor's face turned a deathly shade of white. He looked as though he was going to be sick.

'We've arrested the men called Daniel and Isaac. They're in the waggon waiting to go back to Tamworth to be interviewed under caution,' Jacko told Frank. 'They're claiming they are *real* brothers. One of them is actually called Daniel, the other's birth name is Ross. Surname Clarke. We have their driving licences and have checked them out. They're legit. Ross has done time for dealing drugs.'

'Could they be tied to O'Leary's death or a drug smuggling ring?'

'I have my suspicions. But we won't know until we examine all the vehicles here and see what they say back at the station. The techs have found fragments of bones in the garden beds which they believe could be human. They also found more human bones and various teeth underneath the incinerator grate which they believe come from more than one person. If Felix McMurray was incinerated, he wasn't the only one. I can't believe deaths happened here without other community members knowing.'

Frank shrugged. 'I'm inclined to think, from what you picked up from Deidre Phillips and from the few conversations Rachel's had with members, that Ethan basically ruled the roost here and has done for some years. With back up from the men known as Daniel and Isaac. They were responsible for security among other things. They were the ones who left the property regularly to collect supplies. They had means and opportunity to be getting up to all sorts. Seems some of the members felt a little intimidated by Ethan in particular.'

'Hm.'

'Are you planning to go back and take charge of the interviews?' Frank asked Jacko.

'I thought I might. What about you and DI Sharp?'

'They've kindly offered us Harry and Deidre's marital house for the night. There are two bedrooms. The techs climbed in the back window after taking prints and unbolted the front door. Deidre's mother Deborah, has offered to make the beds up for us with clean sheets. The poor woman is devastated to hear about her daughter being held in custody. That and the fact that she absconded without mentioning how unhappy she was here – or the plans she made with Harry. Rachel is with her now.'

'Have you spoken to John Wells or found Lee Wells yet?'

'Yes, we have Lee Wells isolated. I would like him to be taken back to Tamworth with you and be held in custody there. I've yet to question him. If we get through everything here by tomorrow, I'd like to interview him then. I've spoken to John Wells aka Elder Moses. He claims he had no idea that his son hadn't been formally released.'

'Didn't you say he had attended Well's trial? If he did, he must have known that he received four years, and that when he appeared here, he would have possibly been on parole. Meaning he'd have to check in with his parole officer.'

'I put all that to him. He said he left the country before sentence was handed down. We checked and he did. He claims he thought Lee had completed his full sentence and that's what Lee told him.'

'Do you believe him?'

'No, not for a minute. Despite being a 'minister',' Frank said using inverted commas in the air, 'I think he's lying. But I doubt we'll be able to prove it or charge him with anything.'

'What about financial irregularities?'

'Don't think we could get anything on him there either. He donated quite large chunks of money to the Foundation and they declared it in their books – putting it down to an anonymous donor as he didn't wish to be named. To be honest I'm not that interested in him. It's the trail of deaths that's more concerning. O'Leary's, Pollard's and the young glider. We need to establish whether members of the foundation were involved. And now from what you've told me, we need to know who else went into the oven.'

Frank shuddered, a cold shiver running down his spine. The news that human teeth had been found under the incinerator conjured up images of the Nazis burning the bodies of those they'd murdered during the holocaust.

'I know,' Jacko said. 'Chilling, isn't it? I'm heading back to Tamworth now. I know the mobile signal here is rubbish so I'll email you when I have an update. Keep checking your mail. I'm sure Doctor Phillips won't mind you using his computer for that. How is the good doctor anyway?'

'He's in shock. Genuine shock I believe. I don't think he had any idea about the glider's death. And, like his wife, he's devastated that Deidre in particular, and Harry, will no longer be part of the community. He keeps calling them Dinah and Jeremiah. We left him praying.'

50

Frank watched as the bulky body of a man was raised from the slurry pit. Covered in a dark green slime, it bore little resemblance to the man he'd encountered at Babylon some months back. But the shape was right. He'd ascertained that Ethan's real name was Einar Johanson, descended from Icelandic immigrants to Australia. That fitted. He had the look of a Viking. Johanson had done time back in the mid-90s for being part of a drug distribution gang. Both Johanson and one of the Clarke brothers had links to drugs in the past. Could they have had some new project on the go? Been part of a new distribution network? The three of them were the regular members who left the property to purchase supplies or deliver livestock. They had the means and opportunity. It would be interesting to see what Jacko learned from the brothers and what Lee Wells had to say. How did he fit into it all?

'Ethan had a thing goin' with drugs. Isaac and I were persuaded by Ethan to turn a blind eye to what he was doin' for a small payoff. I dunno what he made from it all, but I don't imagine it was a small sum. We learned that Ethan had kept in touch with some old friends who were gang members and they'd made a deal with him as Babylon wasn't all that far from their distribution route. We didn't have a choice – you didn't *ever* say no to Ethan,' Daniel Clarke said.

Jacko suspected Clarke was attempting to deflect blame from himself and his brother. Clarke had been willing to conduct the interview without the presence of a lawyer. Jacko had read him his rights though.

'How long has this been going on?'

'Almost two years now.'

'Explain how it worked then.'

'I dunno the full details. Ethan was shiftin' drugs that came through Tamworth from Brisbane, when it all fell apart. We used to pick up cattle feed from a store in Tamworth and I think that was his collection point as he would tie in a run to Sydney soon after. He didn't discuss the finer details with us – I guess he thought the less we knew the better. I dunno what happened but he told us back in December that things would be changin'. We still collect our cattle feed from the same store but from what I gathered, the drug supply was no longer comin' through there. Ethan told me a big load was confiscated at the Brisbane Docks in December. Some of the shipment had managed to get through in a different container, but was bein' held up there in a safe house in Brisbane until new arrangements were in place.'

'How did you communicate with your Brisbane suppliers?' Jacko asked.

'*I* didn't communicate with anyone. I never had any contact with the gang involved. Only Ethan did. He was in contact with them by mobile phone of course.'

'I thought it was very difficult to pick up a signal at Babylon?'

'It is. But Ethan's cabin is up on the hill. He persuaded Doctor Jacob that he needed his cabin up there so he could keep an eye on everythin' goin' on around the property. He had an amazin' vista up there and a few times I saw him walk up the hill behind his house and use what looked like a phone. None of *us* had a phone'

'Okay. Tell me how this last small shipment was dealt with then.'

'Ethan was told that it was bein' delivered to some private home, that Timothy O'Leary would collect it, meet up with us and hand it over.'

'You knew O'Leary, is that correct?'

'Yeah. He spent time at Babylon when he was younger. A useless dickhead he was. He and Ethan had lots of clashes.'

Jacko didn't want to be side-tracked by questioning who had inflicted the punishment on O'Leary during his stay at Babylon. He wanted to know what happened the night they collected the drugs.

'Tell me what happened when you met up with O'Leary that night.'

'I was sittin' in one of the four wheels when O'Leary pulled into the disused garage where Ethan had organised the meet. He hadn't spoken to O'Leary directly. Ethan got out of his vehicle and approached him. From what I could see, O'Leary went ape-shit when he saw Ethan. O'Leary and Ethan had some history from when O'Leary had been at Babylon. I guess he had no idea anyone from

Babylon was involved. Ethan later told me O'Leary's instructions had come through one of his old prison mates in Newcastle.'

'Someone called Pollard?'

'I never knew his name. He lived in some stinkin shitty little flat in Newcastle.'

Jacko nodded. It sounded like the Clarke brothers and Ethan were the ones who had called on Pollard and left him a little present.

'How did the paraglider's car come to be involved in hitting O'Leary?'

Clarke looked up at him open-mouthed. 'How did you …?'

'Forensics,' he said without elaborating.

'The glider's waggon had been left at a contact's garage in Tamworth. We planned to drive it down to Sydney ourselves but then all these complications with the drugs arose and Isaac wasn't available so Ethan said more hands were needed. He asked a couple of the brothers at Babylon to drive it to Sydney. He told them the car had broken down when the glider was leavin' Tamworth. He convinced them that the glider had travelled on to Sydney by coach and that he was waitin' for the car and that we'd promised him we would deliver it when we next headed that way.'

'I'm going to need the names of your *brothers* who drove the car.'

'They are innocent parties in all this. They were just followin' Ethan's orders.'

'That's what all the Nazis said, the ones who were in charge of the camps when they were picked up at the end of the Second World War. That they were just following orders.'

Clarke blinked at Jacko, a blank look on his face. He either didn't know much about the WW2 concentration camps or hadn't made the connection with what he was implying.

'So, back to O'Leary. How did they come to hit him?'

'O'Leary jumped back on his bike without givin' Ethan the drugs. He drove out of the disused petrol station in a panic and took off, right into the path of the waggon. Although they were slowin' to pull into the garage, they weren't able to stop in time and couldn't avoid hittin' him.'

'What happened next?'

'O'Leary wasn't dead at this point, just dazed and obviously had *some* injuries. Ethan told the brothers to carry on – that he'd get help for O'Leary. They weren't happy but eventually drove off. Ethan climbed back into his four-wheel drive and drove over O'Leary when the waggon had disappeared. He then collected the bag, which presumably contained the drugs and shoved it into his vehicle.'

'Are you sure O'Leary was still alive after he was hit by the Elantra?'

'Yeah. I'm sure. He was tryin' to sit up before Ethan ran over him. I think he was just a bit confused.'

'After you'd killed O'Leary where did you go next?'

'*I* didn't kill O'Leary. It was Ethan. I was sittin' in the second four-wheel in shock.'

'Okay. Where did you go next?'

'Ethan told me to drive to Sydney. He went to Newcastle. He said he'd been contacted by a member of the Sydney gang who asked him to divert there to finalise some deal with the contact there. Pay him off or somethin'.'

'This was Pollard?'

'I dunno. I never saw him and Ethan never mentioned his name. But he told me that the Newcastle contact had been inside with one of the gang members.'

'Are you sure it was someone from the Sydney gang who contacted Ethan? It wasn't someone from inside Babylon he was communicating with?'

Jacko was thinking of Lee Wells. He scrutinised Clarke's face to see his reaction to his question.

'No,' Clarke said, screwing his face up in puzzlement. 'No one else at Babylon was involved. How could they be? It was all Ethan.'

'So, you called in to see Pollard at his flat?'

'No. *I* didn't. I told you I drove on to Sydney in our second vehicle and met up with Ethan there.'

Jacko's strategy of confusing Clarke hadn't worked. He was sticking to his story.

'How did you know that Pollard lived in a "stinking shitty little flat" then? Those were the words you used to describe Pollard's place.'

'When we were havin' a beer in Sydney the next day, Ethan told me what the man's flat was like. He was disgusted by it. As I said I dunno if the man's name was Pollard. It could have been someone else. If you've picked up Pollard and he was the man Ethan visited then he could confirm who came to see him.'

'The problem is that Pollard died the same night.'

Jacko watched as Clarke's eyes widened in surprise. 'He was murdered?'

Clarke seemed genuinely surprised. So if Ethan was the one who called on Pollard, and it seemed highly likely, then Clarke was unaware of the manner of his death. He'd automatically assumed Pollard had been murdered.

'I'm afraid I can't go into the details,' Jacko said. 'I was hoping that you could fill me in.'

'I dunno *anything* about this man's murder. Really. I'm not a violent man. I'll defend myself if someone challenges me to a fight, but I never seek it. And I've never *murdered* anyone.'

It was very convenient to blame everything on a dead man Jacko thought. It was a shame that news of Ethan's death had reached the ears of the Clarke Brothers while they'd been held at Babylon. Members of the community had brought them drinks and must have conveyed the news about Ethan. He wondered if Clarke would be singing so freely if they thought the man was still alive.

'What happened when you arrived in Sydney?'

'We met up with the brothers who had driven the waggon in Sydney the followin' mornin' and Ethan told them O'Leary had died. That they'd killed him. They wanted to go to the police there and then, but with a little physical persuasion they changed their mind. There's a lane runs down the back of the hotel and Ethan lured them there saying he had one of our cars parked there.'

'They were given a bashing?'

'Yeah. Not by me though.'

'How was this all explained back at Babylon? Where were they supposed to be?'

'In Sydney with us, pickin' up a large order of medical supplies. Doctor Jacob buys them in bulk. We needed two vehicles for the collection. Ethan was drivin' one vehicle, I was drivin' the other. Our two other brothers were supposed to be relief drivers. Ethan spun them a story back at Babylon that we'd swapped cars. Our brothers in one and me and him in another. Under further threats from Ethan they were told to say they'd been mugged in Sydney. Ethan actually took them to hospital for treatment while I drove the first supplies back to Babylon after grabbin' some sleep in our hotel. The brothers were admitted to hospital and didn't return to Babylon until the following week. Ethan drove back down to collect them.'

'Hm. All that will need to be corroborated. There's one thing that puzzles me. If your brothers were driving the glider's car to Sydney, how come they were heading back on the Manilla Road? Why weren't they driving straight to Sydney from Tamworth?'

'Ethan asked them to meet him at the old garage – to make the final plans. He had been waitin' to hear where they had to drop the waggon in Sydney. One of the Sydney gang was arranging it all. When they hit O'Leary, Ethan told them to drive on to the Sydney hotel and park the car nearby. He still hadn't heard back from his contact.'

'Right. Another question. Why did the brothers use the glider's card to pay for the petrol en route to Sydney? How do you explain that?' Jacko asked him.

'Ethan gave them the glider's card when we met up with them after the collision and they said that they didn't think there was enough petrol to get to Sydney. They didn't have much money on them. Ethan told them the glider had left *one* of his cards with them to pay for any necessary repairs or petrol. They didn't need to know the glider's pin number to use it for payments under a certain amount. Just to do that tap thing against a reader. I don't know what it's called. We don't use cards like that.'

Clarke had an answer for everything. He hadn't hesitated before answering, so either he was telling the truth or it had been well rehearsed. He hadn't yet asked Clarke about the glider's death. He'd save that for his brother. It was Ross Clarke who had last been seen with the glider.

'And Ross – your brother? Where was he in all this?'

'He wasn't on that trip with us. One of his kiddies had been unwell and he didn't want to leave his family.'

'Is that true or are you just covering for him?'

'No, it's true. You can check the infirmary records at Babylon. And ask Ross yourself.'

'Oh, I intend to.'

51

Ross Clarke backed up his brother's story about the drug operation, painting Ethan as the instigator who managed everything and confirmed it had been up and running for almost two years. They were paid money to turn a blind eye to everything. Clarke swore he hadn't been on the last trip and that he had remained at Babylon as his brother said. Before starting his interview with Ross Clarke, Jacko had sent an email to Frank Bailey to confirm whether *Brother Isaac*, as Ross Clarke was known as, had been at Babylon on the dates in question. He was still waiting to hear back.

'Tell me how the glider died,' Jacko said to Clarke. From what Harry Meredith had told him, Jacko suspected *both* the Clarke brothers must have been involved. It wouldn't have been possible for Ethan to manage that one by himself.

'I can't remember his name, but the stupid drongo started makin' threats to Ethan while we were on our way to Manilla. Ethan and I were drivin' him there that night. Everyone at Babylon had been very welcomin' to him and we were treatin' his mate – who did have quite

337

a few injuries. We set off and halfway there he demanded the return of his mobile phone. It had been taken off him after the accident. Ethan asked him why he wanted his phone and the drongo made the mistake of tellin' Ethan he wanted his phone to call the cops.'

According to Dee Phillips's statement, she claimed to have seen Felix McMurray leaving Babylon with Ethan and Isaac. Several of the community had waved them off.

'Why would he want to call the police?'

'He didn't like it that his mate wasn't bein' moved to a hospital. He accused us of holdin' his mate against his will and was angry that he was bein' kept in a barn. He'd gone to see him and saw for himself the injuries he had – although he hadn't been able to talk to him as his mate was unconscious. Just before we left the glider had heard Jacob say somethin' about his mate bein' "sent by God". He thought Jacob was plannin' to use his mate as a *sacrifice* or somethin' equally stupid. He kept goin' *on and on* about it.'

'And so what happened?'

'Ethan stopped the car, dragged him out and gave him a bashin'. I tried to stop him, but when Ethan loses it, nothin' or no one could stop him. The glider was so badly injured I said we'd have to take him to hospital. But Ethan wasn't having that. He said we had to take him back to Babylon and that we couldn't let him go otherwise we'd have the police swoopin' down on us. Ethan packs a pretty heavy punch – I can vouch for that. I've been on the receivin' end of a few of them. He kept hittin' the glider over and over. He was in a pretty bad way. Ethen wrapped him in a blanket we had in the four-wheel, put him in the boot and we drove on to the place they'd been stayin', collected their things and their car and took it to Tamworth. The kid had all the keys on him. Back at Babylon, Ethan put him in one of the cages. By the next mornin' the bloke was dead.'

'How did you explain the glider's presence in the barn? Harry Meredith, who was in another cage, was being nursed by Deidre Phillips.'

Ross Clarke took a moment to take in what Jacko had said.

'You mean Dee? Dee who was nursin' the other one?'

'Yes,' Jacko said nodding.

'Ethan told her it was John in the other cage. One of our community members called John had had a fatal fall that day which proved very convenient for Ethan. He told Dee to stay away from him, that there was nothin' we could do. Our doctor, Jacob, had flown to Sydney the pevious day. Daniel had driven him to the airport in Tamworth. So we had no one to treat him properly anyway. She didn't know that John was already dead and I think Dee was afraid of Ethan. Quite a few of the women were. Not just the women mind you. Daniel and I, plus some of the other men were shit scared of him too.'

'I suppose you're going to tell me that Ethan coerced you into doing everything you did with him?'

'He *did* coerce us as you say. And neither Daniel, nor I would ever kill anyone or use violence like Ethan. Turnin' a blind eye to Ethan's drug runnin' was a different matter.'

'You were convicted for dealing drugs in the past. So you have a history of being involved with drugs.'

Clarke snorted. 'That was just a bit of marijuana. I only sold enough to cover my own use. All that was behind me anyway. Daniel and I weren't involved in dealin' or distributin' the drugs. I never saw or touched any of Ethan's shipments. All we had to do was close our eyes and ears to some of the things Ethan did on trips we made on behalf of Babylon. We never saw much anyway. When one of us went to Sydney with him, he'd drop Daniel or me at the hotel and head off and meet up with his mates. We never met them. Daniel and I saw it as a way of makin' enough money to move out of Babylon and start afresh one day. Not that we *ever* received any money. Ethan hung onto it – for *insurance* he said. He said if we ever wanted to leave Babylon, he'd give it to us. I wasn't convinced he'd ever give us the money; we had no choice other but to trust him. He claimed it would be difficult for us to hide any money in our houses. Daniel and I have wives and children. Ethan lived alone. His wife died some years back and they never had kids.'

Jacko nodded. 'So, you planned to leave Babylon? You don't like living there?'

Clarke shrugged. 'It's okay. You get used to it. But my kids are growin' and my wife and I talked about being able to offer them more than a permanent life at Babylon. My wife, Esther, holds with all their religious views – as does Elizabeth, Daniel's wife. But Daniel and I, we're sceptics.'

'Why did you move to Babylon then?

Clarke shrugged. 'When I came out of prison, Daniel had already married Elizabeth. She introduced me to her sister Esther. I thought she was so beautiful and cute after being locked up with a bunch of ugly bastards for a time. We hit it off and married before we moved to Babylon. I had had trouble pickin' up work, you see. Many employers are reluctant to offer ex-cons a job. When Elizabeth and Esther heard about Babylon through Elder Moses, we all thought it seemed like a good idea to move there.'

'Now you're not so sure?'

'Well it's okay for us adults. But it's limitin' for children. They might want to go to university one day. Kids from Babylon are encouraged to stay, not go out into the wider world.'

Jacko could understand that. They needed young blood to keep the community ticking over. It's not a life he would ever choose, but he could understand why some did.

'And we all wanted to get away from Ethan.' Clarke added. 'We had hoped that once he'd made a stash of money he'd take off. But it didn't look like he was in a rush to be goin' anywhere. I think he liked all the power he had at Babylon.'

'Hmm. You must realise that charges will be brought against you,' Jacko said.

'Yes. But I played no part in *anyone's* death. That was all Ethan.'

This was why the Clarke brothers were keen to confess to their peripheral involvement in Ethan's drug side-line. They didn't want to have murder added to their charges.

'You *were* aware that people were killed by Ethan though and both you and your brother concealed those crimes.'

'Under threats from Ethan. I'm tellin' you if he was still alive, I wouldn't be tellin' you *anythin'*. It would have placed the lives of my family in danger. When I objected to what Ethan did to the glider and threatened to go the Elders with what he'd done, he reminded me that my daughter was a sweet pretty little thing and that he wouldn't like to see anythin' happen to her. He was *threatenin'* me with her life. Ethan frightened the life out of Esther with one of his little antics. I know he made similar threats to Daniel about his boys before Daniel returned from Sydney because he'd witnessed Ethan killin' O'Leary.'

'Nevertheless, it's likely that you will be charged with being an accessory to murder. It holds the same penalty as a murder charge. You might have legitimate mitigating circumstances you can argue. Your lawyer, when one is appointed, could advise you on that.'

'I shoulda had a lawyer like you offered for this interview then, shouldn't I?'

'We did offer you one, explained your rights and cautioned you.'

'Yeah, but I didn't know I was gunna be charged with murder. What about Daniel?'

'I'm afraid I can't discuss Daniel with you.'

'Right well I'm not gunna say another word then.'

'Come on Ross. There's only a few more things to cover. The more you help us, the better it will be for you. I can make a note on the files that you co-operated fully. It could help you get a lighter sentence.'

Clarke looked at Jacko with suspicion. Jacko thought the Clarke brothers had been naïve to think that all they might be charged with was turning a blind eye to the drug shipments. And thinking they might get off without a sentence for that also.

'Okay, he said after a while. I may as well now then. What do you wanna know?'

'How did Ethan dispose of Felix McMurray's body?'

'That was his name?'

'Yes. Ethan told Harry Meredith, the glider who survived and remained at Babylon, that he spread Felix's remains over the garden. What do you know about that?'

Clarke shook his head. 'I wasn't sure, but I suspected Ethan had incinerated the bloke. He was in charge of the job rotas and I noticed he put himself on incinerator duty around the time the body disappeared from the barn. I thought he'd either done that or buried the body out on the property somewhere.'

'So you didn't see Ethan put the body into the incinerator?'

'No. And he didn't say anythin' to me about it.'

Jacko wasn't sure he believed Clarke. He'd have to see what his brother had to say.

'And who else has Ethan put into the incinerator?'

'What? I dunno what you mean.'

'Teeth belonging to more than one person were found in the incinerator scrapings. That means other bodies were burnt.'

Clarke looked shocked. Jacko thought it was genuine.

'I know *nuthin*' about that,' Clarke said shaking his head. 'As far as I know everyone who dies at Babylon is buried in the cemetery. They're never cremated.'

'What about the young fella who raped Dee all those years ago? What happened to him?'

'Ethan took … Ah I see what you mean. Ethan was supposed to drop him back into Sydney. I know he gave him a bit of a beatin' before they supposedly left. Ethan did head off to Sydney that day – there was other business he had to deal with while he was there. I didn't see him leave. He often left late at night to arrive in Sydney in the mornin' when businesses were openin'. You think Benjamin was murdered and went into the incinerator?'

'I'm asking you.'

'I've no idea. Esther had just had our daughter and I was spendin' a lot of time with her. I dunno exactly what Ethan did or didn't get up to in those days. Daniel wasn't workin' with him back then. I was assigned to him for security, but I had little to do with him outside our hours of work. It was years before he became involved in the drugs.'

'Who would have been on security duty the night Ethan left with Benjamin?'

'It could have been Mark. He worked a lot with Ethan in those days. Unfortunately, Mark died shortly after … hey you don't think Ethan killed him as well, do you?'

'How did Mark die?'

'His horse reared. He fell off and hit his head, dyin' instantly.'

'Who was with him when he died?'

'I dunno. You'd have to ask Doctor Jacob. He might know as he had to deal with Mark's body. If anyone dies, he has to determine cause of death and issue a death certificate. Then he has to call the coroner and the Shire pathologist. They usually come and check everythin'.'

Jacko nodded. He knew that was the process. He'd have to email DCI Bailey and get him to check those details out with the doctor. If it was the young man known as Benjamin who went into the incinerator, they would have a hard time proving it. DI Sharp had spent some time trying to trace the kid without success. Benjamin might not have even been his real name. They'd have to trawl through records of missing persons to see if they could find a match. With any luck they might be able to pick up some DNA from some of the teeth they found.

52

Frank asked Rachel to join him in Ethan's cabin following the techs' search.

'We found this large cache of money, a mobile phone and a couple of different sim cards behind one of the wall panels,' one of the techs said. 'We've estimated that there's about six hundred thousand dollars in this stack and about another ten thousand in the second one.'

Frank whistled. Ethan's share of the drug running operation must have been lucrative. Jacko had emailed him a summary of the Clarke brothers' confessions, where they both stated that they had never actually received any money from Ethan. After discovering that the doctor had a landline in his clinic, which he claimed he only used for outgoing official calls, Frank used it to phone Jacko for a more detailed update. Following that call he'd set Rachel the task of examining the records.

'That smaller pile must be the Clarke brothers' promised share,' Frank said.

'Are we going to search their houses as well?' Rachel asked him.

'We'll have to. But I suspect they told Jacko the truth. It

looks like Ethan hung on to all the money.'

'Hopefully we'll get something off the mobile phone and the sim cards.'

'Hmm. We'll be passing any information on to our drug squad colleagues in Sydney once we've checked them out. We'll need to do that pretty quickly or all the numbers will become obsolete – if they aren't already. Once the press gets wind of Harry's Meredith's escape from Babylon, and Ethan's death, his fellow gang members in Sydney will soon realise they're open to exposure.'

'By the way, they're serving food in about twenty minutes. It's later than normal due to our little visit and tonight's film has been cancelled.'

'Tonight's film?'

'Yes, they have film sessions for the adults a few nights a week. They also have family films and children's film sessions on the weekend. None of the residents have TVs, so this is one of their few forms of entertainment.'

'I'm surprised to hear that. I expect the films are vetted and carefully selected.'

'Deborah told me that they have a film group who purchase old classic films, pick up cheaply priced films that have been around a while and look at new ones that are available to buy on DVD. They're all ordered by mail and sent to their post office box. They do the same with books. You should see their library. It's impressive. Of course, they have a large selection of religious books, but they also have non-fiction books across a wide range of subjects and fiction across all genres. As people moved to Babylon, they donate many of their books and they're added to each year.'

'You do surprise me. It's a more liberal lifestyle than I thought it would be.'

'Yes. Ditto. I said we'd join the Phillips for the meal in their private quarters. Elder Moses, ie John Wells, is going to make an announcement about Ethan's death to the community at the meal and tell everyone that some members of the community are helping the police with their investigations. The Phillips don't feel up to dining in the hall and asked if we would join them. I hope you don't mind.'

'No, that's fine. I have further questions for the good doctor anyway. But I'll wait until after we've eaten to ask those.'

'So what made you think that Harry Meredith, the young glider you called Jeremiah, was sent by God?' Frank asked the doctor. He was curious as to the doctor's reasoning.

'I had a dream about him. Several dreams in fact – before he arrived.'

'The gliders didn't exactly *arrive*. They crashed.'

'Led by God though,' the doctor said with a serene smile on his face.

Frank wasn't sure he actually wanted to hear any more. Over the years he'd found that once people developed a belief about something, it was difficult to persuade them it was anything other than the truth.

'In my dreams he had exactly the same face and I saw him falling in love with and marrying Dinah. Deborah and I trained Dinah as a nurse so I thought it was imperative that she nursed the young man who was to become her future husband.'

'Yes, Jacob told me about his dreams at the time and told me not to worry as Dee, I mean, Dinah, would soon be happily married,' Deborah Phillips added.

'Did you mention any of this to Dee?'

'Only that he had been sent to us by God,' Jacob said. 'We didn't tell her he would become her future husband. We had to let the couple fall in love and let nature take its course.'

Frank smiled at them. He was sure it was nature taking its course. By all accounts the couple had been attracted to each other, whether it was love was another matter.

'Why did you treat the glider in the barn? Why not in your infirmary?'

'One of our members was in the infirmary with a fever which took me some time to diagnose. I couldn't take the chance of the pilot developing complications on top of his other injuries. It could have placed his life in danger.'

'Okay. So why did you not admit that the glider had crashed here. Why hide the fact?'

'We didn't hide it. I thought the other glider reported what had happened and contacted Jeremiah's family. We just didn't want reporters or the police all over the place.'

Phillips' reply didn't tally with what had actually happened but Frank decided to leave it for the moment.

'Right. Okay I need to raise another matter with you. It's concerning the death of a man called Mark. By all accounts he was thrown by a horse and killed instantly by the fall.'

'That's right. A very sad accident. The horse, normally a gentle soul, reared up and threw him. Ethan said he'd spotted a snake slithering away and so we believe it was the snake that caused the horse to rear.'

'Ethan was with Mark when he died?'

'Yes. They'd been checking the boundary fence in a part of the property where vehicles can't go. Ethan thought he'd seen some breeches in the fence the previous week and they were investigating it.'

'Were there any breeches?'

'Do you know, I can't remember. I don't know if they actually managed to check it. If there was, I assume Ethan would have dealt with it. We were all so shocked with Mark's death.'

'And you definitely believe Mark died from a fall?'

'Yes, Ethan brought back the rock which Mark had fallen onto when he brought Mark's body in. It was covered in blood and coincided with the injury to Mark's skull.'

'So you didn't see Mark's body in situ?

'No, but I believe others did who weren't working too far away. Ethan radioed it in.'

'Could the rock have been used to hit Mark and then his body placed against it on the ground to make it look like he fell?'

'Why are you … you're not suggesting Mark's death was anything other than an accident are you?'

'I *am* querying it. DI Sharp has been looking at your daily records. All very immaculately kept. Mark was on duty with Ethan the night a young man called Benjamin was due to be driven back to Sydney.'

'Yes that's right. Benjamin had … he'd done something terrible. We were expelling him.'

'We know what Benjamin did and that's not what I want to discuss here. We don't believe that Benjamin made it back to Sydney. We believe that Ethan killed him and incinerated his body.'

The doctor's face turned deathly white.

'Why would you even suggest that?'

'You know we have been examining your incinerator? Well, we found teeth that clearly belong to more than one individual. We believe some belonged to the second pilot who crashed on Babylon land. The other teeth might well belong to the young man known as Benjamin from all we've learned. Your man Mark was on duty with Ethan the night they were supposed to leave. He might have seen Ethan doing something that he didn't wish to go along with. He might have even participated in the murder of Benjamin himself. He might have threatened to tell—'

'No, this can't be true,' Phillips said shaking his head. 'Why would you say such terrible things?'

'I'm telling you what we found in your incinerator Doctor Phillips. We know the pilot was murdered by Ethan. We have a witness statement to corroborate that. Ethan himself told Harry – or Jeremiah if you like, that he'd spread Felix McMurray's ashes on the garden bed. We have a witness stating that Ethan beat the boy called Benjamin the night he was due to drive him back to Sydney. We know that Mark was on duty that night.'

'Mark wouldn't hurt a fly. He … he just wouldn't.'

'But you believe Ethan might?'

'Ethan was … Ethan was a tricky character. A reformed criminal, but I think jail had made him hard. Without his beloved wife he seemed to become harder.'

'Out of interest how did Ethan's wife die?'

'Cancer. Lois had had skin cancer many years before, then developed a secondary ovarian cancer – the silent killer. By the time it was diagnosed in hospital it was too late to do anything for her. She'd kept quiet about the discomfort she was in. We just had to make her comfortable in her last weeks and support her with painkillers.'

'Who administered those painkillers?'

'I did, most of the time. Towards the end I connected her to an automatic morphine drip.'

'Could Ethan have hastened her death?'

'I don't think … maybe. I left supplies for him to refill her drip that last night. I didn't notice anything untoward. And Ethan seemed heartbroken.'

'You did notice a change in him after Lois's death,' Deborah Phillips said.

'Yes, and I often wondered what went on in his mind. But he was a committed worker and more than earned his place here. He seemed reliable, trustworthy and very capable. I wouldn't like to think he'd do something as terrible as murder anyone, but I suspect he would have been capable of it. I know he hit a couple of the men he worked with a few times.'

'Do you mean Daniel and Isaac?'

'Yes. After one such episode Isaac approached me and begged me to take him off duties with Ethan. He said they couldn't get along. I spoke to Ethan and he said it was just boy's stuff and he'd sort it.'

'Mm.' Perhaps the Clarke brothers *had* been coerced by Ethan as they claimed. Rachel had arranged to interview the Clarke wives after they had put their children to bed. It would be interesting to hear what they said.

'Picking up on Mark's death again – could Ethan have bludgeoned him to death with the rock?'

'It's possible but … oh dear, I can't bear to think that *any* murders have taken place here. And Moses and I will be blamed if it is true. Me especially. We've worked so hard to build up our little community of like-minded people. What will become of us?' Phillips asked, tears sliding down his cheeks.

'We will get through this my love,' Deborah Phillip said, taking hold of his hand. 'We will get through this.'

53

Rachel and Frank met up for a coffee later in the newlywed's house to discuss what she had gleaned from Daniel and Ross Clarke's wives.

'Both women claim that their husbands hated working with Ethan; they were frightened of him.' Rachel said.

'That tallies with the Clarke brothers' accounts. Did you get the impression that the women knew what Ethan was up to? Did they know about the drugs?'

'Daniel and Ross/Isaac told them that Ethan had some sort of deal going on the side that was nothing to do with his duties here and that earned him money. Daniel had hinted that it was linked to cattle feed and told them Ethan had made threats towards them about keeping quiet. Both wives were accosted by Ethan a couple of times when they were playing with their children. Elizabeth – Daniel's wife – that's her real name by the way – although Daniel calls her Beth – said Ethan pretended to be friendly and nice towards the kids. He often picked them up and swung them around – but she said that he often had a vicious glint in his eyes. He once swung one of Daniel's boys out over the slurry pit pretending he was going to throw him in. She knew that if her son went into the slurry pit, he wouldn't survive. They'd had accidents with calves in the past.'

'Ironic that Ethan should die in that precise way,' Frank said.

'Karma more like. Daniel and Elizabeth were terrified he was going to hurt one of the boys. Apart from the slurry pit episode, which did scare them, the kids thought Ethan was just kidding around and didn't seem too affected by it. Esther told a similar story related to her daughter. Ethan disappeared with her one day for about an hour and when he returned her, she'd had a fall and scraped her knee. Ethan claimed she'd tripped but they didn't believe him and the daughter wouldn't say a word she was so distressed. Daniel was convinced Ethan was showing them how easily he could get to the kids if he wanted to and that these were warnings. It made them all decide they wanted to leave Babylon. They said they know it sounds terrible, but both of them are glad that he's dead. They said Ethan's wife Lois would be turning in her grave if she knew what he'd become.'

'She's only been dead a few years by all accounts, so she must have had some idea what he was like when he was alive. If he murdered Benjamin and Mark, it would have been during their marriage.'

'Mm. Some women have the knack of taming wild men. Perhaps she was one of them or maybe he didn't reveal his true colours around her.'

'Well, we'll never know. Saying that I am absolutely shattered, so I'm off to bed,' Frank said standing. 'We have another early rise tomorrow. Goodnight Rachel. I hope you sleep well.'

'Night … Frank. You too.'

Rachel sat in the quiet of the kitchen after Frank had gone, thinking about her conversations with the two women earlier that night.

Elizabeth, Daniel's wife was a tall, full bodied and shapely woman with chunky features. A chunky nose and voluminous lips that many women paid a fortune to mimic cosmetically. She wore her long, thick chestnut brown hair tied back in a plait. Rachel thought Elizabeth epitomised the image she had in her head of what a healthy farmer's wife would look like. She wasn't pretty but she had a natural beauty. Esther, on the other hand was almost the opposite in shape, size and appearance. Apart from the chestnut brown hair and amber eyes, the sisters had little in common. Esther was petite and slim. Her facial features were delicate looking and perfectly formed. When Esther had opened the door to her, she was wearing her long hair pinned up and covered by an old-fashioned looking cotton cap. Rachel was immediately struck by the woman's long, slender, elegant neck, bringing to mind an old film she and Andy had seen last month about Anne Boleyn. One of the wives Henry VIII beheaded. At her execution scene in the film Anne had her hair covered in a similar white cap and reference was made to her slender neck.

A few minutes after greeting her, Esther had removed the hair covering, and unpinned her long wavy hair, explaining that she had been cooking that night and wore the cap to avoid her hair absorbing the smell of food. When wrapping up their conversation Rachel had asked Esther whether she and Elizabeth were full sisters. Esther had assured her that they were, explaining that Elizabeth took after their father, and she took after their mother and that sadly both parents had died in a car crash.

A kick and a wriggle from her baby brought Rachel back to the present. 'Now Norm, I hope you're going to be quiet tonight. I need a decent sleep,' she said talking out loud to her bump.

The following morning Frank left Rachel at Babylon to interview Reuben and Samuel, the young men who had hit Timothy O'Leary and driven the Elantra station waggon on to Sydney. She was also going to speak to Martha, Lee Wells' young woman. Forensics and some of the uniforms had worked around the clock and were packing up. They'd matched tyre prints from the Timothy O'Leary murder with one of the four-wheel drives. A vehicle which Ethan drove regularly.

Leaving Rachel his car, Frank hitched a ride to Tamworth with the first techs to leave. He was due to be interviewing Lee Wells this morning.

'So Lee, can you explain why you decided to skip the formalities of being released on bail and hide out in Babylon?'

'I was worried about Martha and Rebecca. I thought their lives were in danger. Little did I know that one of the ones who could have been a danger to them was also at Babylon.'

'Are you referring to Ethan?'

'Yes.'

'So why did you think Martha and Rebecca's lives were

in danger?'

'Before Nick and Wade were released in December one of the real hard gang inmates approached me in Cessnock. He said there'd been a problem with their supply line being disrupted and he needed back-up systems in place in case any more problems arose. He wanted me to persuade my *mates* as he called them, to become involved.'

'And how did that concern you or Martha?'

'I'd heard about Rebecca's birth through my sister. But neither she, nor I knew where Martha was living. The inmate who approached me showed me photos of her so *his* gang knew where Martha and Rebecca lived. They said if I didn't want anything to happen to my girls, I needed to help them out. They asked me to set up a drop spot in both Tamworth and Newcastle. I was told to persuade Nick and Wade to help with it. Nick was no problem, but Wade proved difficult. He didn't want to know. So to avoid them attacking him to forcing him to cooperate, I came up with an idea where he didn't have to have any face-to-face contact with anyone.'

'The unlocked garage.'

'Yes. Nick had to hire a lock-up and be the contact person for others. He had to co-ordinate things. Some of the stuff was heading to Newcastle. Some to Sydney. I don't know what the ins and outs were. He was more than willing to go along with everything as he planned to start building up his own little supply and distribution network in Newcastle.'

'Wouldn't that have clashed with the gangs' set-up?'

'I don't know. Probably. I warned him to be careful, but he was an arrogant bugger. Has he got himself into trouble then?'

'Nick Pollard is dead.'

'They killed him?'

'As good as. And Timothy O'Leary.'

'Oh shit. So, Nick brought Tim into his plans then. They always were thick with each other inside. How were they killed?'

'I'm not at liberty to discuss that Lee – as you well know. So how did you find out where Martha lived?'

'I put Nick onto it. After seeing the photos, I had an idea where she was. One of the women who came to the drop-in centre I used to work in lived in the same block. I recognised the building in the photos. We had a bus at the drop-in that used to take people home. I often accompanied them. Anyway, Nick found her, waited outside and spoke to her one day to warn her that I would be coming out soon and that I would be in touch. He gave her a mobile phone and said I'd phone her when I was free. She doesn't know that I skipped out and we're married now so her parents can't force her to return.'

Frank nodded. He expected as much. He didn't think John Wells would allow his son to live at Babylon in sin – although the hypocrite had been shacking up with his second wife for years before they married and moved to Babylon. When he'd interviewed John Wells, he'd produced evidence of his divorce from Mary and marriage to his current wife Leah. He claimed that Mary was completely in denial about the whole thing, that they had been separated for some time before he began divorce proceedings. For her sake he'd pretended to the wider community that they were still together and attended church with her on Sundays until he left the area.

'How did you make contact with Nick Pollard while you were still in Cessnock?'

'He contacted me through a friendly inmate who had a mobile phone that had been smuggled in some time before.'

Frank knew mobiles were a perpetual problem in prisons and suspected it was only going to get worse.

'So he organised some Rohypnol that he smuggled into your sister's garden? Is that correct?'

'Yeah. There was no other way I could do it. My saintly sister and her husband wouldn't have helped me.'

'How did you make your way to Tamworth?'

'A contact of Nick's drove us up. Don't ask me his name as he didn't give it.'

'And how did you make contact with Babylon to let them know you were coming?'

'I'd already written to my father. A friend of a friend smuggled the letter out. I knew the date I was going out on day release so I told him I was being released and would soon join him with Martha and Rebecca. I gave him a time, date and rendezvous point so they could pick me up.'

'So he didn't know you were an escapee? Surely, he must have seen the news bulletins?'

Wells shook his head. 'No, they're not particularly interested in the news up at Babylon. They don't have TVs or radios. Ethan found out from his trips into Tamworth and threatened to tell my father and Jacob when I challenged him about Rueben and Samuels's injuries. I don't think he said anything though and from what I hear he won't be able to threaten anyone ever again.'

'That's right. But of course, your father and Jacob know all about you now. Your father asked me if he could come and see you before you were sent back to prison. Are you okay with that?'

'Yes, of course. I want to know that my family will be able to stay there and be safe.'

'When you go back inside Lee, you do realise that you will probably have to complete your full term.'

'As long as Martha and Rebecca are safe, I'm okay with that. Couldn't I plead that I was in fear of their lives? You know, mitigating circumstances?'

'You could. And it would help your case if you were to pass on the name of the man who approached you inside.'

'You know I can't do that Detective Bailey. I wouldn't live to see any of my family again.'

54

Rachel, Frank and Jacko met later the same afternoon to share the outcomes of their different enquiries.

'Daniel and Ross Clarke have had lawyers appointed and been formally charged. Jacob Phillips is paying for their defence. If they're lucky they might get off with a short sentence,' Jacko said. 'Testimony from the wives about Ethan threatening their children will definitely help.' Rachel had already passed on all the information that she'd gathered the night before.

'Wells is being returned to Cessnock prison on Monday,' Frank said. 'Detective Superintendent Rawlings has agreed for him to be held here over the weekend so his family can come and visit him. Apart from outstanding questions on the statements Rachel took this morning, she doesn't plan to bring charges against anyone else at Babylon.'

'She's putting Reuben and Samuel's case to the prosecution service,' Rachel said. 'With their statements and Daniel Clarke's statement, plus hospital records being acquired from Prince Alfred's, they might not have any charges brought against them. They were unable to give me any details of where the Elantra ended up. Ethan told them to leave it around the corner from the hotel and he dealt with it apparently.'

'What's happening with Deidre Phillips?' Frank asked Jacko.

'She's being released on bail. Deborah and Jacob Phillips came to see her this morning and they had a tearful re-union. Although she's not returning to Babylon with them. She wants to remain in Tamworth until her next hearing. Harry Meredith has elected to remain with her. He spoke to his family at length yesterday afternoon and told them not to drive down again after hearing about his father's stroke. He said he'll try to pick up some temporary work in Tamworth to tide them over. Although I think the father is putting up some money so the couple can find a place to live and to buy a car for use down here.'

'They're staying together then?' Rachel asked.

'For now, anyway.'

'What do you think Dee? Do you like the place?'

'It's okay,' Dee said shrugging. '

'At least it's partly furnished so we don't have to rush out and buy a load of stuff.'

The flat was the third they'd viewed that afternoon and as far as Harry was concerned it was the best one of the bunch. The agent had popped outside for a ciggie so that they could make their decision in private.

'Are you sure you want to do this Harry? You don't have to. Jacob said he'd give me some money if I needed it to keep me going. Don't you think you ought to be getting home to your family?'

'I've spoken to them as I told you. They understand why I want to stay here with you.'

'You don't owe me anything.'

'That's not true. I owe you my life. And besides I want to stay with you.'

'You do know our marriage isn't real seeing we didn't use our real names?'

'Yes, Detective Jacko told me.'

'As much as I care for you Harry, I want to have some experiences alone out in the wider world. I told you I'd like to train to be a nurse. Jacob told me that he could confirm the training I've had at Babylon so I might not have to complete a full course. I might get credits towards a nursing degree.'

'There's a great university up in Brisbane where you could do it. I could be around to support you – if you need it. I realise we were thrown together in unusual circumstances Dee, but I'd really like to stay with you for now and to see you settled in to whatever you want to pursue. The future is an unknown quantity for both of us.'

'That's what is so exciting about it all, don't you think? For *both* of us. With your father selling the business, you no longer have to cover for him. You could use your Surveyor's qualifications and go anywhere you want.'

'I guess. But not just yet. Look if you feel uncomfortable about sharing a bed with me, then there's always the second bedroom,' he said, hoping she would say they wouldn't need it. He'd asked to view two-bedroom flats in case things became awkward between them.

'Oh I don't feel uncomfortable about that Harry. I might find it strange to share my bed with someone night after night, and if sleep becomes a problem, I can always nip into the second bedroom afterwards.'

'Afterwards?'

'Yeah, after we've made mad passionate love, you silly galah. I think we should take it – if you're sure,' Dee said, walking right up to him.

'I'm very sure,' Harry said leaning in to give her a kiss.

55

Newcastle
July 2009

Rachel lay in the hospital bed, her new-born son cradled in her arms. She heard the door open and looked up to see Frank Bailey and Ayesha Patel coming into the room, laden with bags and flowers.

They both leaned over to give her a kiss and examine the baby – Frank seemingly not the least bit embarrassed. She felt *her* face flush red.

'There's a couple of things from the team for the baby in there,' Ayesha said.

'The flowers are also from the team,' Frank added.

'Thank you,' Rachel said. It seemed very weird being visited by her boss and colleague while she was in a *bed*.

'What have you and Andy decided to call the little one? Tell me it's not going to be Norman,' Ayesha said.

Rachel laughed. 'No, Cameron. After Andy's grandfather. We had several possible names lined up and we've decided he looks like a Cameron. Cameron Andrew Sharp. The Andrew after Andy of course.'

Rachel been off work for the past five weeks, preparing for the birth and madly decorating and furnishing the baby's room in their new house. She missed work though and found herself wandering around the house some days feeling lost. With the baby's arrival she knew she'd soon have her hands full and every second of her day taken up. So far baby Cameron had been a dream. He'd taken to breast feeding without any problems and slept peacefully between feeds. She knew that wouldn't last though and she would be counting the days until she could return to work. A whole year seemed like an impossibly long time.

'I've had non-stop baby talk from friends and family for the past twenty-four hours. It's doing my head in. I wouldn't mind a change of subject. Tell me all about the new cases you're working on,' Rachel said smiling at her two surprised visitors.

Acknowledgements

As usual I'd like to thank Judy and Laura. They are always my first readers and point out areas that I need to amend.

Also, Thanks to members of the Netherton Writing Group who were subjected to various chapters for comments and feedback.

Thanks to Liat, my typesetter, for her prompt and professional service.

About the Author

L.E. Luttrell was born in Sydney, Australia and spent the first 21 years of her life there before moving to the UK. After working in publishing (in the UK) for a few years she went on to study and trained as a teacher. From the 90s she spent many years working in secondary education, although she's also had numerous other part time jobs. A frustrated architect/builder, L.E. Luttrell has spent much of her adult life moving house and wielding various tools while renovating properties.
L.E. Luttrell lives in Merseyside England, but also spends time travelling between there, Wales (UK) and Australia.

Follow on:

www.leluttrell.com

: L.E. Luttrell – Author

www.ingramcontent.com/pod-product-compliance
Lightning Source LLC
Chambersburg PA
CBHW010255100726
47904CB00011B/2612